**Wicked Words 6**
*A Black Lace short-story collection*

D1638684

Look out for the nine other *Wicked Words* collections.

# Wicked Words 6
A Black Lace short-story collection
## Edited by Kerri Sharp

**BLACK**LACE

Black Lace books contain sexual fantasies.
In real life, always practise safe sex.

This edition published in 2004 by
Black Lace
Thames Wharf Studios
Rainville Road
London W6 9HA

First published in 2002 by Black Lace

Design by Smith & Gilmour, London
Printed and bound by Mackays of Chatham PLC

ISBN 0 352 33690 0

## Contents

# Introduction

I am delighted these wonderful Black Lace erotic short story collections are getting a new lease of life, and in such fabulous, eye-catching new pop-art covers. The series has been hugely successful, and sales of *Wicked Words* anthologies have proven how popular the short story format is in this genre.

*Wicked Words 6* kicks off with the fantastic *You Spoil Me*, one of the most subtly crafted pieces of vicarious perversity I've read in the genre. There is, as ever, a wonderful outpouring of experimental, joyful and downright filthy stories on offer in this volume. Special mention goes to *Peaches*, for its heart-warming loveliness and pagan sentiments; to *Just a Job*, for its full-on, horny, girl-on-girl antics; to *Under Wraps*, for its fetishistic detail of underwear, and last, but not least, to the unusually cool *Liar Liar*. This is 1950s Americana with an evocative, provocative bad girl central character. Great Fun. In this eclectic mix, there will be something to suit everyone's tastes.

The fun doesn't stop with these reprints. There is much more to come from the series next year. As from February 2005, we will be publishing themed collections – which will be a fun way of diversifying the list. The first books will be *Sex in the Office* and *Sex on Holiday*, and after that we will be having *Sex on the Sportsfield* and *Sex in Uniform*. I can't wait! In the meantime, the first six *Wicked Words* volumes are available now, as of this month – October 2004 – to be followed by *Wicked*

*Words 7 and 8* in November. If you never got the chance to buy all the books when they were first published, you can now complete your collection and be the envy of your friends! Look out for the colourful covers – guaranteed to stand out from everything else on the erotica shelves in bookshops.

## Do you want to submit a short story to Wicked Words?

By the time these reprints hit the shelves, it will be too late to contribute stories to the first two themed collections, but the closing date for submissions to *Sex on the Sportsfield* is end Jan 05 and, for *Sex in Uniform*, end April 05. The guidelines are available on our website at www.blacklace-books.co.uk. Keep checking for news. Please note we can only accept stories that are of publishable standard in terms of grammar, punctuation, narrative structure and presentation. We do not want to receive true confessions or stories that are about 'some people having sex' and little else. The buzzwords are surprises, solid characterisation and an awareness of what makes great erotica. All stories need to be between 4000 and 6000 words and laid out to house style: double-spaced, printed on one side of A4 and in a point size no smaller than 12. We do not accept submissions by email. We cannot reply to all short story submissions as we receive too many to make this possible. Competition-style rules apply: you will hear back from us *only* if your story has been successful. And please remember to read the guidelines. If you cannot find them online, send a large SAE to:

Black Lace Guidelines
Virgin Books
Thames Wharf Studios
Rainville Road
London W6 9HA

One first-class stamp is sufficient. If you are sending a request from the US, please note that only UK postage stamps 'work' when mailing from the UK.

# You Spoil Me Mathilde Madden

It's early evening, already starting to get dark, and you are on your way back from buying tobacco from the corner shop at the end of our street. Coming out of the shop and heading back down the road, you're not looking where you're going, rolling a cigarette, and nor is he. You bump into him and send him sprawling, head first, into the wall.

'Sorry,' you say, looking up, and, as he wipes his messy hair out of his face, you see who it is.

It's him, the beautiful young man from over the road. The one I have a little crush on. The one I've been going on about. Neither of us knows his name, so we refer to him using the number of his house: we call him Number Eight. And it's Number Eight you've just collided with.

And it's such a coincidence, because only last night I'd persuaded you that Number Eight should be the star of one of your particularly dirty stories. Your beautiful stories: the whispered filth that you breathe into my ear in the dark. It's one of my favourite things about you, darling, the way you bring my fantasies to life in every way you can, even when all I want is the words. The way you happily talk about whoever I want and in whatever scenario I want. You're never jealous. Why would you be? You know that some little cutie I spy in the street or on television could never be any real competition. Of course not! You're the one, and you know it.

After a little probing last night, checking out what I was in the mood for, you had invented a fantasy for me.

Your story featured me as an evil seductress and kidnapper, one of my favourite roles. I had pulled up in my car next to Number Eight as he walked home. You had described in exquisite detail his dark fuzzy hair, thin little student body, cute squashy nose and dark heavy brows. He had been wearing tight, faded denim, tight on his arse, one of the first things that had attracted me to the beautiful Number Eight.

Under the pretext of asking him for directions I had persuaded him into my car and whisked him away to a deserted and mysterious cabin in the woods.

Oh, that I had such a den in real life!

In your version of my fantasy I was ruthless, far more ruthless than I could ever be in reality. Perhaps, I'd wondered, this was a little of your own fantasy too. I had noticed how as I had got crueller in the tale, you had become harder, pushing yourself against me in the dark as you breathlessly recounted the endless torments I had inflicted on poor abused Number Eight.

For over a week I'd kept him prisoner in that cabin, blindfolded and helpless, tormented by a tight gag. You'd thrown it all in, from bondage (chains, collars and handcuffs) to torture and humiliation (beatings and starvation, and at one point I'd hosed him down with cold water, just to make him even more uncomfortable). As you'd described me laughing as Number Eight squirmed in his chains trying to escape the dousing, and how his begging for mercy was muffled by the cruel gag, I was fighting to hold off my orgasm, desperate to hear the end of the story. Finally, of course, he'd capitulated and agreed to become my sex slave, kneeling naked before me, bowing his head and vowing eternal devotion. I love a happy ending. As your tale had reached its climax, so had I, panting and crying out in the dark next to you as you pulled me tightly into your arms.

I'd recovered and found you were squirming, rubbing yourself against my body, demonstrating that you had enjoyed the fantasy, too, but were left hanging. And I'd reached over and found your hard cock with my hands. You had come, too, within a few moments of my well-practised manipulations and I had rolled over to sleep, exhausted, leaving you to feel under the bed for your tissues and clean up before following me to dreamland.

And now, with the memory of last night still fresh in your mind, you feel a little ashamed to be looking the poor victim right in the face less than 24 hours later.

'Er,' mutters Number Eight. He seems a little bit confused, bashful, even. He raises a hand to the back of his head and rubs it.

'Did you hit your head?' you say. 'Let me have a look.'

Reaching up, you brush his hair aside and feel the spot he was nursing on the back of his head. It seems fine, not even a bump. You smile and your eyes meet his.

It's the first time either you or I have seen Number Eight at close quarters. Up until now he's only ever been a glimpsed figure hurrying in and out of the tatty shared house across the road, where he lives with a group of what we assume to be fellow students. Now, as you look at Number Eight, you realise a couple of things.

First, I'd always said I thought that Number Eight was about nineteen, maybe twenty, but close up you can see he's a little bit older than that, more like twenty-five.

Secondly, and rather more significantly, you realise something else about him. I'd always assumed Number Eight was straight, but looking at him now, so close to, in those too-tight jeans and with that devastating little pouty mouth, and looking at the way he is looking at you, you're not so sure.

And, if that look in his eyes is what you think it is, who could blame Number Eight for being attracted to you? You are, as I am always telling you, a fantastically attractive man. In fact one of things I first noticed about Number Eight was the fact he looked rather like a younger version of you. Truth be told, it was that above all that attracted me to him. My type is so clear-cut: I've always been attracted to men who look the way you do. You share his dark brows and thin elegant frame, although your nose is bigger and sharper and your similarly dark hair is close-cropped, the way I like it, not shaggy and overlong like his. In fact, as the two of you stand there, facing each other in the darkening street, your hand cradling the back of Number Eight's head, you could almost be brothers.

So perhaps it is noble fraternal concern for your surrogate brother that drives you to invite him back to our flat for a while, so you can observe him and ensure he has suffered no serious damage. Perhaps.

'I live just across the street,' you say, pointing to our front door.

'I know,' Number Eight whispers rather shyly. 'I've seen you around.'

Interesting.

In the flat you make some tea and small talk and then lead Number Eight into your small study to sit down.

It's a bit of a mess as usual and you have to move a pile of papers and books off the battered sofa so he can sit down. You sit at your desk, balancing your cup of tea on top of a pile of books about film and filmmaking, swivelling the chair so you are facing him.

Now, with a plan forming in your mind, you look at Number Eight. He is not particularly attractive as far as you're concerned (I guess you're no narcissist), but you know how I feel about him and you know what I would like you to do. Yes, making my fantasies come to life has always been your speciality. And, as well as in verbal form, you've often taken things a step further and role-played for me. You can be a wonderful actor with the right motivation and an appreciative audience, playing everything from a slutty street-walking rent boy to a nervous *ingénue*.

I'm so lucky to have you, I know that. I never thought I'd find a man who understood me so well, who indulged me so completely and found pleasure in the things I did – who found pleasure in my pleasure. When I told you how much I fancied a certain television presenter, or some bloke in my office, or, of course, the young man who lived at number eight, you revelled in the knowledge, turning it to your advantage. You loved to encourage me to tell you exactly what I'd like to do with my latest object of desire, giving you plenty of material to draw on when, late at night, you'd recount the stories back to me, delighting in my obvious arousal.

You never blanched when the fantasies I shared featured you, either. Frequently you were the kidnap victim, the object of my dominating desires.

Together we'd always experimented. I loved to tie you up and watch you struggle for me. I bought leather straps to bind you comfortably and safely for hours. One day you had come home with a short black crop and that was when I discovered how much you loved pain. A true masochist! The pain got you hard and I loved to see that. Our toy collection had grown from there.

Tying you up will always remain one of my greatest pleasures. I love to see men helpless and struggling, especially when their helplessness turns them on. When they're hard and moaning with frustrated desire. There's something beautiful about the way a submissive man is more enslaved by his own sexuality than by my control. And there is no doubt that you are a submissive, my darling. Pleasing me takes precedence over everything.

Truly nothing shocked you when it came to my darkest secrets. So I hadn't thought twice when I'd told you how much it excited me to think of two men together, taking each other roughly, making nasty love, bondage, beating, everything I enjoyed but darker and nastier because it was between men. And I'd told you how I liked to think of you as one of those men. Sometimes the top, sometimes the bottom.

I would tell you how I'd like to hire one of the studs who advertise in the back of gay free sheets. Pick out one of those adverts that consisted of nothing more than a name, a number and a photo of a torso – and an erection. Rent a stud and watch him take you. You'd be tied down, gagged and blindfolded with no idea, no escape, but knowing I was watching. You'd enjoy submitting to this strange man whose face you'd never see.

I'd tell you these things and you'd just smile and ask for more details, revelling in being party to the darkest parts of my sexuality.

I suppose you've probably wondered if I'd ever really go through with it. Of course I'd ask for your consent. Of course you'd give it.

Often, too, of course, I would fantasise about you and my latest crush together. You knew this. And so here you are and it falls into place. You're in your study in an empty flat, with exactly such a crush object, Number Eight, who's clearly pretty keen on you. Of course you hit upon a plan to make one of your stories, not the one from last night but another favourite of mine, come true. In the most intense way you can. You're priority is to please me, so you can hardly do anything else. You spoil me, darling, you really do.

So, after chatting for a while about your job and his, the area, the other people in the street, the poor range of stock in the corner shop, you drain your cup and move from your armchair on to the sofa next to him, smiling softly as he gives you a questioning look. A moment or two after that you place your hand softly on his leg, just above the knee. He stops what he's saying and looks up at you when you do this, then glances down, biting his lip shyly for a moment before trying to continue his sentence. After a few words, though, he falters and tails off, staring at your hand on his leg.

To break the silence you say something, asking him lightly about the others who live in his house, and he, relieved by the distraction, starts to tell you something about his eccentric landlady and her three overindulged cats.

All the while your hand still rests on his leg. In your mind you are carefully planning your next move, meaning that when he pauses you haven't been listening. So, instead of replying to his question, you pretend to check where he hit his head again, and, as you reach up and stroke his hair, he responds with a sigh of unmistakable desire, and that's all the sanction you need.

This is the moment when you decide to go for it. You take hold of a handful of his hair to keep his head still, lean forward and kiss him very slowly. You are quite shocked when he struggles a little, pulling his mouth away and whispering, 'No', but then gasping with pleasure as you yank at his hair to pull his mouth back to yours. You slide your other hand up his leg and grasp his crotch. Through his jeans you can feel he is slightly hard and you force your tongue roughly into his mouth.

He gets harder. But, despite his obvious enjoyment, he is still squirming around as if he's putting up a fight. You pull away from his mouth and look at him, confused.

'Make me,' he says very gently. 'Force me, please. I need it this way.' He shivers a little, clearly turned on by asking for what he wants.

You smile. Even better.

Grabbing his whole jaw in one hand, with the other still tangled in his hair, you pull his mouth back on to your own, roughly. He struggles and murmurs, 'Please, don't.' But he doesn't try to fight you at all.

You pin him right where you want him, pushing him back against the sofa. Then you swing one leg over his lap and straddle him. Crashing your mouth against his, you kiss him so hard he can barely breathe. You relish the taste of him.

As you force your tongue in deep, your own cock begins to stir as you grind it against his own desperate erection.

Sitting back a little, but keeping one hand firmly in his hair and sliding the other between his legs to grip his cock, you look at him. You can tell he is turned on, although trying to stay in control. His lips are slightly parted and he is breathing hard. His cheeks are flushed red and you can feel his cock growing harder all the time under your fingers.

'You dirty little bitch,' you hiss at him, making him flinch and squirm. 'You want it, don't you?'

'I . . .'

You tighten your fingers painfully in his hair and, raising your hand from his crotch, slap him hard round the face. 'Don't you?' you snap.

He lowers his head submissively and looks up shyly at you. 'Yes,' he says, very softly, 'yes I do. Use me, please. Please, sir.'

You smile and feel your own cock growing harder at his submissive posturing. It's quite strange, you wonder to yourself: you really didn't expect to enjoy this so much.

After a short moment you let go of him and snarl softly, 'Strip, now, and make me want to give it to you.'

You slide off Number Eight's lap and he stands, turning to face you, only a few feet away in the tiny room. He keeps his head lowered in deference, but holds eye contact with you all the time.

Slowly, carefully, and rather seductively, he pulls his loose-fitting top over his head. His chest is thin and pale, with a little dark hair on it, and his smallish nipples are bright pink and tightly erect. He looks vulnerable and scared standing there topless, and it turns you on. You can't help but start to tease your own cock through your trousers, getting it hard, getting it ready. Ready for him.

The boy pauses, his hands on the waistband of his jeans. He is staring at you as you rub your cock and seems to be frozen. You wait a moment or two. He still doesn't move.

'Come on,' you say, keeping your voice low, but still sounding threatening. 'Get them off, slut!'

'Please,' he says, 'please, don't make me do it myself. I can't.'

'Do I have to come and tear them off you myself?'

The boy doesn't answer, but he still doesn't move, except to tremble slightly. He looks so scared and it's so beautiful. You are sure he's done this before. He knows just how to play little boy lost. It's a role you've played for me so many times and he, like you, has got it down beautifully. He even knows just how to tilt his head and look shyly through his hair at you, just to look all the more vulnerable and helpless. The only thing that gives him away is the unmistakable bulge of his straining cock. You realise how much this boy needs to be put in bondage and punished. You realise how much you want to do it.

'OK,' you say, suddenly softer, 'come here.'

The boy walks towards you and you urge him closer and closer until he is standing between your knees.

'Put your hands on your head,' you say, and he does so, instantly appearing more vulnerable once his hands are out of the way.

Reaching out and placing your hands on his hips, you can feel now that he is still shaking slightly. He really is amazing, you muse to yourself. I really do know how to pick them.

Slowly, savouring the moment, you slide your hands along his waistband to the fly of his jeans and undo the button and then the zip. Holding your breath, you slide the unfastened trousers and then his underpants down to the floor.

Still with his hands on his head, Number Eight glances down at his own, now very erect, cock. He's so turned on that the head is adorned with little flecks of glistening wetness. He flashes you a shy grin before lowering his head again in submission. Reaching out, you grasp his cock and stroke it firmly from top to bottom. Then you scoop up a little of his wetness in you fingers you bring it to his lips. Pushing your fingers into his mouth, you force him to taste himself. He closes his eyes and sucks eagerly on your fingers, almost as if he were sucking a little cock, cleaning off every last trace.

Withdrawing suddenly, you fix him with a stern look. 'Get on your knees, you bitch.'

He suppresses a little moan and lowers himself down on to his knees between your legs. His face is now a little lower than yours and you touch his cheek, smiling.

'Turn around,' you whisper.

The naked Number Eight shuffles around on his knees until he has his back to you, and then you use your hands on both his shoulders to push him down on to the floor. His arse is right in front of you now. It's pale and rounded, flawless. You remember how much I love your arse, how I love to touch and caress it, and you reach out. He moans as you begin to stroke him, gently at first and then more and more roughly. You slowly run your fingers up and down, occasionally giving him a twisting little pinch or a light slap. You run a finger along the crevice and find the little warm bud of his arsehole. Still with just one finger, you start to tease that soft little mouth until it opens up greedily and you push inside him.

You can hear him panting hard. You slide your free hand between his legs and find his cock, which you stroke lightly, while you continue fucking him with one finger.

You continue this teasing until both of you are very hard. You'd love to fuck him right now, but it's too soon – there's so much you want to do to him before you come. He gasps and whimpers when you let go of his cock and pull out of him.

'Get over that table,' you say, in a low, matter-of-fact tone.

He looks at you with a timid expression for a moment, but obeys quickly, spreading himself face down across the low coffee table and reaching down to hold on to the legs.

Most of my bondage toys are kept in the bedroom, but not all of them. Luckily for you, because you'd hate to have to leave the room now to get equipment, there is a small bag of spare ropes and less favourite toys stashed out of the way on one of your study shelves. You stand up and pull the bag down from the shelf. A quick inspection of its contents reveals some rope, a small paddle shaped like a table-tennis bat, condoms and lubricant, and a pair of rather nasty silver nipple clamps. To begin with, you pull out four lengths of rope.

He catches his breath as you begin to tie his wrists in place. Once you are satisfied that they are secure, you move round and tie his knees to the other two legs, fixing him in place kneeling on the floor. To your delight, he squirms a little in his bondage, testing the restraints, but you know your business and he's held fast.

He seems to enjoy his new predicament. Along with his struggling, he is grinding his hips, pushing his cock into the table. Well, you'll soon put a stop to that.

You pull your belt from its loops. He hears the sound and quivers. Doubling up the belt, you draw it through your fingers and pause, making him wait.

The first time you hit him gently, checking your aim, but soon you build up some force and begin to lash his arse, hard, panting as you see bright marks come up. He squeals and makes to try to move away, but the ropes keep him in place. As the beating goes on and he struggles and yells, you find yourself wishing there'd been a gag in that bag.

You continue the lashing until you are desperate to come and he is yelling in earnest on each stroke. He starts to beg for mercy through his screams of pain.

'Please, please, sir, no more, please.'

That piece of begging turns you on more than anything. You have to have him right now. Kneeling behind him, you slide on a condom and push a finger into him again. He's even more open and ready than before. Clearly he has enjoyed his bondage and beating. You remove your finger briefly and squeeze some lubricant into him, replacing the finger to work it inside him. He knows what's coming and begins to writhe eagerly, bucking against your hand. When you replace your finger with your hard cock he moans out loud.

'Oh, yes, master, please! Fuck me, please!' You glide in and out, already close to climax from watching the arse you are now taking turn pink under your belt. Spurred on by his begging, you come quickly, thrusting hard and deep into him.

You slump back on to the sofa, exhausted. He turns his head to look at you, still tied in position, now covered in red lash marks and splashes of your come. You smile at him and spend a long moment enjoying the view. You are aware, though, of Number Eight's own frustrated arousal and after a brief respite you stand up and free him from his bonds. He stays where he is, waiting for permission to move, as you settle back down.

'Come here,' you whisper.

The naked young man stands up and makes his way over to the sofa. Again he stands between your legs, head down submissively. His cock is bright red and desperately hard. You pull him on to your lap and cradle him in your arms. 'We'd better sort this out, hadn't we?' you purr in his ear. You grasp his cock and slowly begin to move your hand up and down, starting with soft teasing strokes and then building up a firm rhythm that has him wriggling and gasping.

'Please, sir,' he gasps desperately. 'Please may I have permission to come, sir?'

'Wait for it, bitch!' you hiss, and in response he moans. A sound both of frustration and desire.

You continue teasing him, keeping him right on the brink of orgasm, while he squirms and writhes.

Eventually you say, 'OK, slut, come, now.'

He comes, that very instant, into your hands, thanking you breathlessly.

When he opens his eyes you hold your fingers up to his mouth for him to lick clean.

Later, after he has shyly thanked you and left, you check the camera. By the time I arrive home you are in bed, fast asleep. I am disappointed until I see the Post-it note on the video recorder, which says 'PLAY'.

You really do know how to spoil me.

# Peaches Anna Clare

If a person watched carefully enough they might have noticed that Alex always smiled when presented with a peach. It was an almost Pavlovian response: pass the man a peach after supper, or offer one from the fruit dish, and the smile would be there without fail. I'd tried it with various fruits, but only peaches seemed to elicit the response.

He'd sunk his teeth into an apple with matter-of-fact abandon, emasculated a banana with a savage bite that would have given a Freudian a field day, and cursed the impenetrable nature of orange peel in a perfectly normal fashion.

Watch him with a peach, and it would be an entirely different performance. The Mona Lisa smile made its inevitable appearance. If you caught him completely off guard you might catch him out with his lips very close to the fuzzy skin of the fruit, breath lightly beading the tiny hairs, as though he were trying to inhale the smell of it.

Eventually, I had to ask.

We were in his rooms that night, drinking (of all things) peach schnapps, when I asked him. We drank such a lot of crap in those days – cheap cider that had never so much as seen an apple, repellent bottled beers – whatever wasn't too hard on the wallet. The schnapps was sticky and burned on the way down, but alcohol is a recreational drug and gets used as such when you're young.

'Oh ... it's kind of a Proust thing ...' he said, when I asked him.

'Proust?' Proust and peaches? I gave him a warning look, like we were not heading for a trip to pretentious-student-burblings-land tonight, no matter how pissed we were. No way, peaches. Ain't never gonna happen.

He picked up on it and curled up cross-legged on the other end of his bed. 'Yeah. Like madeleines – you know, *Recherche de la Temps Perdu*.'

'That's the only bit of Proust anyone remembers, and you know it,' I accused.

'Yeah yeah ... we pick out the pseudo-brainy stuff and the rest kind of gets *perdu* along the way ...'

'So ... madeleines? Peaches?'

'You know how a taste or smell can send you sort of barrelling back into the past?'

'Picked up the pseudo-brainy stuff, yeah.'

'Well, it's like that with me and peaches.' He leaned back, head against the wall, mouth sticky with schnapps, a smug smile all over his face.

'Must have been a happy memory.'

'Oh, it was ...'

It was the peach smile, I swear. It lit him up from the inside. You can't spark a person's curiosity like that and hold back. So I told him to tell me.

'Kiss me and I'll tell.'

So I kissed him – a sort of sticky, burned-peaches kiss, the taste of fake fruit synthetically sweet over the burn of the alcohol. He didn't tell, so I kissed him again, hoping to get a secret out of him, but men tend to be freer with sex than secrets, so it took a lot more to get him to tell me his story. Not the kiss-and-tell type after all.

He was right about the Proust thing, though. Seven years later and I can't taste peach schnapps without

being catapulted back in time to my night with Alex –
the babyish softness of his skin, the astonishing tensile
strength in muscles that didn't seem to have any business flexing under such girlish skin. He was so perfectly
smooth all over. Even his cock felt smooth and sleek
inside me, and I can still remember every silky stroke of
it, punctuated by the hard butts of bony boyish hips and
the prickle of his small tangle of pubic hair.

After the first round, we huddled together on his
narrow plywood-and-foam student bed, trying to drive
away the ugly reality of a Hall of Residence loft room
with incense and lighted candles, and succeeded for a
short time, while we were lying spooned up in the bed,
feeling sated and depraved, sharing a joint.

'So tell me . . .' I had to prompt him again.

He laughed. 'Oh yeah, that. I was seduced.'

'What's that got to do with peaches?'

A whole lot, as it happened. I can't remember the
conversation now, so I'll tell Alex's story to the best of
my memory. He was seduced by his next-door neighbour,
a woman he swore was a witch. Sweet seventeen –
innocent as you can be at that age in a small seaside
town where there's very little to do other than grope
under the pier at night. That was our hero – Alex.

He lived at the time in a Victorian semi-detached on
the corner of the street. I know because he pointed it out
in a photo on the bedroom wall – one of those little bits
of home you cling to when you're away from the security
of your family for the first time. I could imagine myself
in the photo, in the house – a rather beautiful whimsy
of a place with a glass porch and an upstairs room with
a five-sided bay window that looked almost like an
observatory.

'She moved in there.' He pointed out the bay window
to me. 'Lene. That's where she lived. She moved in one

summer with her cat – Pyewacket, he was called. Weird fucking thing.'

He told me about the day she moved in, his harassed, divorced, eternally busy mother determined that she'd be a good neighbour and give the new arrival a hot meal on her first day in a new town. Lene ate with Alex and his mother that night. Her name was Lene Lane – a child's storybook sort of a name, and she had this fey quality that went with it.

Alex described her in sensual terms – floating dark curls, a snubby, witchy, mischievous face over rounded breasts that were barely covered by a cheesecloth blouse. He'd been trying not to stare at her tits all through dinner, he said, but it's impossible not to look at nipples exposed through clothing like that. The outline of them was clear under the thin cloth and he could tell his mother disapproved and thought she ought to put a bra on, but he was too busy trying to grab furtive glances to care about her opinion. You could see the shadows beneath her breasts, the upturned jut of her nipples, the hang and shift of them when she folded her arms or reached for more bread or salad.

Her boobs had a symmetry that her eyes lacked – one eye brown, the other blue. He later noticed that the cat was odd-eyed, too – one amber eye, one blue, peering balefully from the patch of white fur that surrounded the blue eye. He was named after a minor demon, she said, because since he had been a kitten he had behaved like an animated hairball coughed up by Satan himself.

She talked about angels and demons a lot – late at night in that observatory of a living room of hers, which she'd hung with throws patterned with mandalas and filled with burning incense and candles. She sounded to me like the quintessential hippie chick, all daisies in her hair and black eyeliner, avowing she was a witch and

reading tarot cards to finance her hash and cider crav-
ings. I'd disliked the spectre of Lene at first, being a dumb
nineteen-year-old working very hard at being cynical
and jaded. I was rebelling against the warmth and toler-
ance that my own hippie parents had taught me by
sneering at everything. Sex in those days was a transac-
tion, a necessity, and oh so very sad.

You grow out of these things, fortunately. You learn
to believe in angels and demons and witches once more,
and get back to the wisdom you had as a child, in the
days before your own pose of faux intellectualism cut off
your imagination. I think she was probably like that –
Lene Lane. Innocent as a child, pure as an angel, lecher-
ous as a demon.

She was sloppy, Alex said – so lazy he never figured
out whether it was because she had mountains of cash
tucked away or was on the social-security fiddle like so
many others. He'd call round in the afternoons and she'd
come to the door wrapped in a throw-over, some glittery
Indian thing, then trail back to what she was doing
before – lounging in bed reading and eating chocolates.

He'd sit on the end of her bed until she coaxed him to
join her on the pillows and share her chocolates and read
over her naked shoulder about palmistry, her exotic
drapery hoisted over her tits with uncharacteristic modesty. She told him he had a long life line, a deep heart
line and a fame line – a rare gift – and let him kiss the
smooth skin of her neck behind the frothy dark sweep of
her hair, as casually accepting of caresses as her nasty
little familiar, Pyewacket.

'What's a fame line?' he asked her.

'Here . . .' She held his hand out, tracing a little line
that ran from the base of what would one day be his
wedding-ring finger and connected with the curve of the
heart line that ran between his middle and index fingers.

'It ends on the Mount of Mercury at the base of your little finger here ... means you'll be famous by virtue of your natural eloquence one day.'

I could picture Alex – a wide-eyed, dark-eyed boy, raised in all the nice conventions of suburbia, before he grew the bleached blond dreadlocks he wore when I knew him, buying this hook, line and sinker. Spellbound. He loved the smell of incense, candlewax, the allure of a world of such gorgeous laziness, where you could lie in bed until four in the afternoon eating chocolates if you wanted to. I could see him snuggling closer in the bed, taking such pleasure in the touch of her fingers on the pads of his palm.

'Mount of Mercury? There?'

Their fingers would have touched on the pad of flesh at the base of his little finger, a game of tiny touches, the smallest of brushes of skin; then, with daring, she would press her thumb into the thickest pad at the base of his thumb, leaving the crescent-moon print of her nail in the flesh.

'That's the Mount of Venus. It means that you have a sensual nature.'

He was so excited he could have screamed out loud. Her thumbnail had left a mark in his skin, in the middle of the mount, which she'd squeezed and pressed and caressed as though she were trying to feel the very sensuality it described according to her crumpled books on palmistry, which lay scattered all over her bed. She took hold of his wrist and kissed the mark her nail had made, then laughed and teased him by pushing another cappuccino truffle into his mouth when he tried to move in for an inexpert kiss.

Her presence was constant, even when he was away from her in his sullen, teenage sanctuary of a bedroom. There would always be a whiff of incense in the hall, the tinkle of hot, sweet New Orleans jazz from her open kitchen window downstairs, and sometimes she'd be heard singing along in a cracked, husky but melodious voice. Old songs – 'These Foolish Things', 'A Fine Romance', 'Summertime'. He'd see the crescent moon swinging above the peach tree in the back garden and look for the faded mark of her fingernail in the pad of his palm, sometimes impressing it anew with his own thumbnail so he knew it was there whenever he got himself off to the memory of her nail pressing the crescent moon into his flesh.

The most awkward moments, he told me, were when he was with his mother, Ruth, watching her sniff with disapproval around Lene's ramshackle kitchen, noting things to pick on later – the cat's presence on the kitchen table, the stew sitting in a pan on the stove and not hygienically stashed away in a Tupperware container.

'I think that peach tree is dying,' Ruth remarked, peering out of the kitchen window. I met Ruth once at the end of term, a pinched, nervous-looking woman with fair hair and narrow lips. Alex, she told me bitterly, took after his father, which I figured was a bad thing in Ruth's eyes.

Lene looked out at the peach tree, tired, withered, a depressed-looking specimen if ever there was one. She took a big, unladylike gulp of hot tea and nudged Alex's foot under the table. 'Nah – I don't think it's dying. It's just lacking something.'

'Needs root space?' Ruth speculated. 'Maybe if you were to dig up that forsythia bush next to it – provided you didn't cut into the roots of the tree of course.'

Alex sketched the next scene in a handful of phrases and I relished the images – Lene, sloppy, scruffy, wet-lipped, odd-eyed little witch, swinging her bare foot and talking in hot, erotic metaphors while Ruth sipped her tea with tight lips and Alex sat there with an erection up to his navel and a permablush on his hairless cheeks.

'The gardener can't have done his job right when he planted that tree,' Lene said, swatting the cat on the arse and perching on the chair he'd forcibly vacated. Her elbows, dimpled and pale like something painted by Romney, rested on scarred, old wood, her white hands, those naughty, pinching nails painted glittery blue, supporting her chin. She licked her lips a lot when she talked, I'm told, and I can see her sitting impishly poised over the table, breasts squeezed like ripe fruit in one of her untidy, indecent shirts, her mouth wet and wicked as she spoke.

'The thing when you're planting something – you see, you gotta realise what, or rather *who*, you're putting it into.'

Alex nearly choked on his Brooke Bond at the double entendre, thinking of all the times he'd thought long and hard about putting it into a certain *who*.

Lene carried on unabashed. 'You see, you gotta treat Mother Nature like a lover, 'cause she's a cold old bitch really. She hates it when she gets woken up in the spring after doing her Ice Queen thing all winter. Flirts a bit, shows you her spring greens, but won't give you too many signs of enjoyment during the summer. She lies back and takes it, lazy, like she can't be arsed, sort of drowsy, you know? Autumn, that's when she comes, fruit, flesh, fowl, fish – all ripe and ready, kind of exploding out of her as she gives up the act and admits that she *loves* it.'

While she spoke she swung her foot under the table, bare toes nuzzling the top of Alex's Doc Martens, making him gulp and gasp and flush crimson with lust. Ruth smiled politely and said that that was certainly an interesting way of looking at it.

'The person who planted that tree had no juice in them,' Lene said, dreamily. 'They were all dried up. No potency. No passion. It shows.'

Soon after that, Ruth went away one weekend, to a duty family funeral, and Alex hoped he might be able to make a move on the object of his desire. His mother had given him the usual parental injunctions: telephone numbers to call, don't you dare have any wild parties – that sort of thing. There wasn't much chance of wild parties. Alex had isolated most of his peers over the summer, the company of fellow teens seeming some-what vanilla next to the spicy, intoxicating Lene Lane. The girls he'd groped before – immaculate as per the instructions of fashion magazines for which they were surely too young – seemed sanitised, all nicely encased in glitter and PVC, neat strips of perfectly shaved pubic hair and eyebrows plucked to nothing.

Not like Lene, who'd sometimes rush to the corner shop to get milk for her cat dressed in nothing but a raincoat and heels, whose disregard for electrolysis and the pursuit of well-scrubbed perfection meant that she had this nice fuzzy quality to her smooth cheeks, like peach fuzz.

'I mean, it was like she was a real woman, you know? She reeked of sex the whole time. Didn't shave, preen or pluck every hair out of her body – kinda sexy, the *nerve* she had to be all woman like that.'

I was warming to the image Alex was painting as he told me this story. She sounded like a free-spirited, cheer-ful slut with whole load of healthy contempt for every-thing that mothers told you was nice behaviour.

'So what happened?' I asked, hoping we were finally getting to the seduction part of the tale.

He was never sure who'd seduced whom, he said. She was so innocent in all her overblown sexuality that it

was impossible to imagine her doing anything as manipulative as seduction, but personally I reckon it was Alex's
ego talking there. He wanted to imagine that he'd
seduced the witch next door – a seventeen-year-old Don
Juan. Not bloody likely, in my humble opinion.

'She called me.'

'A siren song, huh?'

'No. On the *phone*.'

'Oh.'

She rang him up and asked what he was up to that
evening, since she had a bottle of Southern Comfort and
nice chunk of Moroccan and was a girl who liked to
share. Any invitation like that is honey to the bee to
any seventeen-year-old in their right mind – alcohol,
drugs and the chance to lose his cherry. You bet. He'd
be on her kitchen doorstep faster than you could say
testosterone.

They got shit-faced – stoned and pissed beyond even
the worst sins that Ruth could imagine. Lene peeled
peaches and dropped chunks of their skinned flesh into
glasses of Southern Comfort, where they infused the
liquor with the taste of bittersweet fruit. She rolled joints
and they lolled around on her scatter-cushion-infested
floor, cackling and flirting and fishing the booze-sodden
peach slices out of their drinks to assuage their
munchies.

'Wouldn't it be great if we could get the peach tree to
wake up?' Alex remarked. 'Then we could lie under it
and get smashed and let the fruit just drop off the tree
and into our mouths.'

'Make ourselves sick on 'em.' Her voice was hot and
dreamy, as it had been when she was equating garden-
ing with fucking Mother Earth to bright, blooming
orgasm in the dusty, spice-scented surroundings of her
kitchen.

'I have an idea.'

'You do?'

'Yuh-huh. Needs both of us, though.' She rolled over on the cushions and one of her breasts almost spilled out of her top. Emboldened and tanked, Alex looked, letting her know he was staring.

She took his hand and the movement of her arm made the cloth slip further, and one pale-rose nipple was exposed. His eyes were nearly popping out of his head, his dick so hard he thought it might burst, but Lene was lingering over the pad of his thumb again, pressing the crescent back into his flesh.

'There – Venus, the crescent moon, me, and you. Especially you.'

Her thumb rubbed across his palm and her mouth came down on his wrist, her tongue flickering over the pulse point like a wet snake. She kissed the crescent mark she'd left there like before, holding his hand like a prize in her palm, her weird eyes wicked, her hair floating like dark smoke over her shoulders and bared breast.

'So young, so full of juice. Potent. Powerful. I *must* show you.'

'Yes. Show me. Please.'

As you can imagine, our young hero didn't take much persuading. He was standing barefoot under the peach tree in Lene's garden in the middle of a summer night, horny, infatuated, and eager to be relieved of his virginity one way or the other. Lene, in the dark, was transformed – by booze, hash or something older – into a dancing sprite, a maenad tangled in the ivy, slipping out of her clothes. Her breasts and buttocks were like round white moons, her pubic hair a dark, untended tangle between her rounded white thighs.

He laughed awkwardly and too loudly as he took his own clothes off.

'So this is what you think this tree needs?' he asked, giggling out of nervous excitement as they wrapped their arms around one another, chilled despite the humidity of the summer night.

'Totally. Needs some potency. A little youth. A little passion. The right moon.'

He followed her gaze upwards. It was the new moon, swinging like a sickle in the sky – the moon you weren't supposed to look at through glass lest it bring you bad luck.

'Is this witchcraft?'

'Course it is. The oldest sort. Now let's get to it. This poor tree's desperate.'

Her mouth tasted of peaches, hash and Southern Comfort, her tongue rough and broad, licking slow, smooth swirls around his own. He moaned into the kiss, even more desperate than the tree, and nearly exploded with his own surprise and pleasure when she knelt down and took him in her mouth under the tree. He didn't take long, being seventeen and all that, and she emphatically spat his come into the roots of the tree.

She stood and rested her hand on his head, playfully pushing him down. 'Down you go.'

Oh. *Oh.*

He had no idea how to do this, but she'd taught him well, clearly. He demonstrated his skill to me, sinking down with a sparkle in his eyes as he looked up at me from between my legs. I was grateful to Lene Lane that night when we were nineteen, because she'd taught the boy the meaning of oral fixation and made a man of him. I was already wet from hearing his hot little story and I could feel the moisture leaking out on to the tops of my thighs, pubic hair all sticky, bristly and musky from last time.

He licked the wet dabs off my inner thighs and

opened me up with one smooth lick, and I felt like a peach, like a fruit he was holding open with his tongue and thumbs to devour the sweet flesh inside. I was thinking of a peach while he ate – the image of a crescent-shaped slice taken out of the side of the fruit, exposing the wrinkled, red-brown core, the flesh in grad-uating sunset shades radiating outwards from the creased heart of it towards the silken, furred skin at the edges. Mother Nature at her teasing, naughtiest best. He found the core, the wrinkled centre, and licked it smooth, pushing it up between his thumbs so he could iron out the creases all the better.

I think he restored my faith in magic, in the flesh, that night. I owe Alex a debt – and Lene, for teaching him so well. The way he pushed his fingers inside – as if he were trying to dig out the pit, coring me with his finger as he found the circle of my arse and pushed inside. Never have I felt so completely penetrated as I did with his fingers and mouth, hands filling both holes, tongue working relentlessly over my clit with small spirals, then deep, hard licks that made me howl out loud – not giving a shit about what that cloying confec-tion of a student nurse who slept in the next room thought.

I never found out the end of his story, either. We didn't talk much for the remainder of the night and for one reason or another we never did it again. He dropped his medical degree shortly after – said the smell of formaldehyde and the pathology classes gave him the horrors – and the next thing I knew he'd gone home to Falmouth, dropping out entirely to get a 'real job', as he put it, pissed off with dissection, academia and Proust.

It was seven years before I saw him again. I met up with him at a breast-cancer charity function. He was working as a journalist for a national newspaper, making a hack like me simultaneously green with envy and congratulating him vigorously. Hating him for making it, and loving him for proving that it could be done.

'You're still living in Falmouth?' I asked.

'Yeah. Same house, actually. Mum's place.'

'How is she?'

'Oh . . . uh . . . she died. Five years ago. Breast cancer.'

'*Shit!* Oh, God. I'm sorry.'

'No, no. Not your fault after all. Turned my wife kind of evangelical, though. She knocks herself out for these charity dos.'

'You got married!'

'Yup!' He grinned and held up his left hand, a band of white gold around the third finger, the Apollo finger, just above the fame line. 'She's here somewhere.'

I tried to imagine what kind of woman he'd marry since he'd cut off all that matted blond hair and ditched the skateboard gear he'd habitually worn when he was a down-at-heel med. student.

'Oh, there she is! Hey! Peaches!'

Peaches? Holy fuck! I thought. Trophy-wife kind of name or what? Then I found myself looking into a pair of bright, unmatched eyes. One blue, one brown.

'Lene, this is Anna. We were at King's together. Anna, Lene.'

'Hi.' She gave me a quick smile and grabbed Alex's arse. 'Nice to meet you.'

'Lene's a chef,' Alex announced, proudly.

'Wow. That's quite an art.'

'Nah . . .' She shook her head – a big Jimi Hendrix explosion of dark hair. 'It's a doddle. It's just *food*.'

'Perhaps you'd like to explain the concept of that to the caterers,' Alex said, menacing her with a piece of withered broccoli quiche. She laughed.

'Yeah, OK. So it's not that easy. The food here's *shit*. You shoulda seen those tragic-looking peaches on the so-called tarte tatin. Poor things were on the *brink*, I swear. Not like the ones we get off the tree at home ...'

Alex winked at me and I knew the end of the story at last. It *had* worked, after all.

# Just a Job Alison Tyler

I've been doing voiceovers for four years now. Mostly advertisements. Aspirin. Antacids. Automobiles. Producers choose me because I sound young and peppy. Can't help that. It's just the way I talk. Although I am never hired to play angry, tired or sad, I'm also rarely chosen for anything truly interesting. I don't sound like someone who would break barriers. Last weekend, that changed, and all it took was a single phone call from Eliza. She's the booking agent at the studio that hires me the most. This may have something to do with the fact that she's also my best friend.

'Hey, Sadie,' Eliza said, 'I've got a job for you.'

'Great,' I told her. I needed a job.

'It's an odd sort of assignment,' Eliza continued slowly. 'Have you heard of the Pleasure Zone?' She pushed on without waiting for my response. 'They're a new outfit in Berkeley. They produce . . .' she paused, 'you know –'

'I don't.'

'Sapphic sex stuff,' she explained, 'lesbian erotic audio.'

'Why would they choose me?' I didn't want to talk myself out of a pay cheque, but I couldn't imagine my cheerful vocals fitting in with an X-rated script. Yes, I have an energetic voice, but I'd be far more believable playing a cheerleader than a porn star.

'They want the girl next door, not a phone-sex operator.' She seemed embarrassed for asking. 'Will you do it, Sadie? I mean, it's really just a job.'

I answered 'yes' without hesitation. Who was I to turn down a paying gig?

'There's a little more to the taping,' Eliza continued, now that she knew I was interested. 'You'll be working with another actress.'

'Someone I know?'

'Jenna Logan.'

'Oh,' I said, but it must have sounded like 'oooh', because Eliza laughed on the other end of the line.

'Calm yourself,' she told me.

Jenna Logan and I had passed each other in the studio several times. She works for the big companies, and whether she's talking about chocolate bars or the latest sale at Betty's Beauty Box, her voice wraps you up and soothes you. Besides that, Jenna is a knockout. I don't mean a Barbie type – those bunnies do nothing for me. She is the epitome of San Francisco chic with close-cropped black hair and large blue eyes. Sleek-looking and fine-boned, the girl's got lungs on her like you wouldn't believe. I've often wondered what those lungs could produce in circumstances outside of a studio. Meaning, basically, is the girl a screamer? You assume, once you hear her talk, that she's gotta be. I've always wanted to test that theory in person.

'When do I get the script?' I asked, trying to sound professional and not horny as hell, which I was. I could already envision myself and Jenna in a clinch, her dress up over her hips, her panties around her ankles, my tongue tracing invisible letters over her clit. Round O's that would make her moan. Lush I's up and down between her juicy pussy lips. I'd press extra carefully with my tongue against her snatch so that she could try to guess the words I spelled out. Dirty words. Filthy phrases. Obscene and exciting.

'They don't want you to read it ahead of time,' Eliza

said, bringing me back to our conversation. 'They want you to sound real, not rehearsed.'

'Are they afraid I won't do it if I see the script?'

'It's fine,' she assured me. 'Soft porn and sexy. The gig's tomorrow night. Double pay, because it's night work.'

Great, I thought again. I will make my rent. And, that fantasy voice urged me, maybe something more ...

The next evening, I arrived at the studio with time to spare. Eliza greeted me warmly, handed me a package and turned around to disappear into her office. The script was in a brown paper envelope, which made me smile. 'Jenna's not here yet,' Eliza called over her shoulder. 'You can skim your lines to get a feel for the story.'

Brushing my blonde fringe out of my eyes, I sat in one of the deep burgundy leather chairs in the lobby and pulled the pages the envelope. The script was called 'Talk Dirty to Me', and a pencilled note let me know that I was going to be Marisa. I started from the top, perusing the first page quickly, then reading through again more slowly. All of a sudden, I thought that I was going to have a problem. Not because the content was offensive, but because the piece was turning me on. Would that show in my voice? Was it supposed to? I crossed my legs tightly and read on.

**Marisa:** So you like to play a little bit rough?
**Danielle:** Sometimes. I mean, handcuffs are cool. Paddles. Blindfolds. Vinyl dresses that get all slippery when they're wet. (Pause, light giggle). So maybe not rough as much as kinky.

I stopped reading. I couldn't imagine Jenna giggling. But I could picture her giving the statement a little husky laugh. Dark and smoky. That thought made me cross my legs even tighter. I glanced back at the script.

**Marisa:** I like the way you say that word. *Kinky*.

**Danielle:** What else would you like me to say?

**Marisa:** Try me. Talk dirty to me. Tell me what you think I'd like to hear.

**Danielle:** I'll tell you what I've done, instead, and what I'd like to do.

**Marisa:** OK. So start by telling me about your best time ever.

**Danielle:** That's easy. Spanking my ex-girlfriend until she creamed. Putting her over my knee and punishing her sweet, haughty ass with a hand-crafted wooden paddle while my fingers grazed her clit from beneath. The sound of the paddle hitting her bare bottom was musical. The noises she made, those soft steady moans, turned me on to the extreme.

**Marisa:** You made her cry?

**Danielle:** I made her come. (A pause for effect.) You like being spanked, too, don't you, naughty girl?

**Marisa:** (slight stammer) Yes –

**Danielle:** Well, I'd love to make that happen. I'd start by dressing you up in a little red-and-black plaid schoolgirl's skirt, white ankle socks, shiny black patent-leather shoes. Lay you out over my firm lap and lift that pleated skirt in the back. Discover that, oh my, you're not wearing any panties underneath. Such a bad girl, aren't you? Who would ever have guessed –

At this moment, the door to the office opened, and I sat up suddenly and covered the script. The person entering didn't even look at me, headed straight down the hallway as if he knew exactly where he was going. I felt myself flush, but that didn't keep me from reading more. What I really liked about my part was that, so far, I was simply urging Jenna on while she did all the talking. The tough stuff.

> **Danielle:** I'm going to give you ten with the paddle, just to warm you up. And I want you to behave for me. To be still, and take it. But I might make it difficult for you to stay quiet. That would be the fun part. Maybe I'd put clips on your nipples, make you moan and squirm.

The thought of nipple clamps immediately got to me. I've always had very sensitive breasts. Just brushing against them sets me off sometimes. I consider jogging to be foreplay. My nipples rubbing against my tight red sports bra creates the most delicious friction. Already, my round little nips were standing out at attention, and I crossed my arms over my chest to hide them, about to return to the script, when Jenna Logan walked in.

'Thank fucking God,' she sighed, relieved. 'It's you.' I guess Eliza hadn't told her that I was the co-star, and from her expression I could tell that she thought the thing couldn't be too hardcore if they'd requested me as her partner.

'Pretty wild,' I said, indicating the script.

She came to stand at the side of the sofa, looking down at the pages, which moved in my slightly trembling hand. I could smell her perfume, a light scent that reminded me of candlelight and rumpled sheets. Eliza walked in then and motioned for us to follow her down the hallway to the last studio. 'They're ready, kids. Want anything to drink before you go in?'

'Tea with honey,' Jenna requested, as I murmured, 'Whiskey, neat.' She nudged me, obviously thinking I was kidding, and her hand on my elbow sent a spark through me. I let her pass ahead of me down the hallway, following a few steps behind and watching the way her lean body moved beneath her short black dress. Eliza, walking next to Jenna, looked over her shoulder, giving me a questioning glance, but I held up a finger, indicating that I needed a minute to pull myself together.

Just a job, I thought. A job that meant I could pay my rent this month. It meant that I wouldn't have to work nine to five somewhere filing papers nobody cared about and wearing a suit that I didn't own. What it mostly meant was that I took a deep breath and started walking.

Studios are comforting environments. Entering one makes me feel as if I'm walking into a friend's apartment. I like the floor-to-ceiling window that looks into the control room and the headset hanging off the script stand. This studio was set up for a two-voice read, with hard-backed chairs separated by a slim divider. Jenna and I wouldn't be able to see each other during the read. Not unless one of us stood and peeked in on the other.

In the control room, Baxter waved at us through the window. Just as Jenna had visibly relaxed upon spying me in the lobby, I sighed happily when I saw him. He's my favourite technician. When he tells me to reread a line, he always gives it to me himself, first. Baxter knows that it can be difficult to repeat the same thing again and again. You can actually forget the meaning of the words when you say them too many times – although, I didn't think that would be a problem this evening. I'd flipped to page three of the script and saw words like 'licking' and 'pussy' and 'clit'. Saw phrases like 'inserting a butt plug' and 'tongue-fucking'. Those words weren't going to lose their meanings for me. Not when Jenna Logan was saying them.

'You ladies have pseudonyms picked out?' Baxter asked us over the speaker.

Jenna grinned at me before slipping on the headset and settling herself at the microphone. 'I was thinking of Jen X,' she said, and she gave a soft, husky laugh that was identical to the one I'd imagined while reading the script in the lobby.

'And you, Sadie?' Baxter asked, winking at me through the glass.

I hurried to my position, ducking behind the partition so that Jen wouldn't see my cheeks turn red as I said the name I'd chosen. 'Ms M,' I whispered. It wasn't original, but my last name starts with M, and I hadn't thought of anything better.

'You sure you don't want to go for "Sexy Sadie"?' Baxter suggested. But he accepted my pseudonym, and then he had us say our names a few times to get good readings of our voices. The tone. Volume. All of the little things that you never think about when you're at home, headset plugged into your stereo, getting off on the erotic sounds of an X-rated audio. Finally, we were set, and Jenna I started from the top.

The scene began with us in bed together, having already fucked once, lazing about and sharing fantasies. We pressed on past the pages I'd read in the lobby, and were well into a key scenario featuring sex toys, lubricant and wet, warm, willing women. I enunciated the best as I could in the situation, but I discovered that each dirty word I said made my pussy clench and release, spasming with yearning. Mortified, I found myself taking deeper breaths, placing my hand at the hollow of my throat, trying to calm down. Baxter didn't seem aware of my difficulties. When we finished the first section, he complimented us.

'Especially, you, Sadie,' he said. 'You really got into the flavour of the piece in the end there.'

He didn't know how right he was. My silk panties

were dripping in the centre, entirely too confining over my cunt and ass. I was desperate to excuse myself for the ladies' room, to personally take care of the need that had arisen and was screaming within me. Release. I wanted it more than I can say, but not, apparently, more than Jenna did. When Baxter told us to take a breather, and then excused himself to go outside for a Marlboro break, Jenna leaned over the barrier and kissed me hard. Really kissed me. Her mouth pressed into mine, full lips parting so that our tongues met for a moment and I felt a shocking jolt of pleasure. Soft wet heat enveloped me, and I was just about to reach forward, to cradle my stunning co-star's face, when she broke the connection.

'I've wanted to do that for a long, long time,' Jenna said, blue eyes glowing.

I couldn't think of a way to answer her. The only words in my head were from the script we'd just read: *Talk dirty to me.*

When I said them out loud, Jenna smiled deviously. 'I'll do better than that,' she promised, motioning for me to follow her out of the recording room. I hurried after her to the bathroom at the end of the hall, watching as she locked the door behind us. Then we stared at each other, waiting, feeling the tension between us and breathing it in, as if it were an aroma. Somehow, this moment was almost as exciting to me as what came after. Not quite, of course. Nothing really rivals the actual sex act, no matter what anyone says. But, every once in a while, the beat of anticipation before you start can do wonders for your heart rate. And, in those few seconds, mine raced forward, and I could hear the sound of my heartbeat pounding in my ears.

Then I stopped thinking, because Jenna was giving me an intense and easily decipherable look. A gaze that said, Stop waiting and start doing. Quickly, I bent on my knees on the tiled floor and watched as she hoisted herself up on the white porcelain counter of the sink, hiked up her dress and spread her legs. Stunned, I sucked in my breath at the view. She wasn't wearing any panties. That thrilled me, knowing that she'd spent the past two hours taping with no underwear on. Without giving me the slightest indication.

What a minx.

It was obvious that she'd gotten as turned on as I had by the reading. Her shaved pussy glistened with wetness, and I could see a silver ball nestled between the plump lips. I understood what this meant instantly: her clit was pierced. That made me even more aroused. I thought about how the metal ball would feel in my mouth, how I'd tug on it between my lips, tease it with the tip of my tongue, make Jenna arch her hips and press her pussy to my face. But, as I positioned myself for action, I heard a noise outside the door, the sound of one of the other recording artists heading toward the pay phone down the hall from the bathroom, and I remembered suddenly where we were. Making it in the bathroom at a studio. There was no going slow here. No taking our time. The one-stall bathroom would be needed soon, so I worked Jenna hard, worked her fast, and she responded exactly as I would have guessed. She ground her hips forward, gripped on to my hair and started to moan.

People would definitely hear her. Eliza. Baxter. They would know what we had done. 'Harder, Sadie,' Jenna suddenly murmured, and I instantly got over my potential embarrassment and continued with the wriggling dance my tongue was doing inside her satiny pussy. So what if people knew? That's what Jenna undoubtedly thought.

I'm a patient, considerate lover. I know what I like, and I know how to please. My mouth on her pretty cunt played all of those intricate games that women love best. I licked at her, tickled her clit, nipped at her outer lips and then her hidden inner ones. I delved into those secret, pink folds before spreading her open with my hands and sliding my tongue deep inside her cunt. Jenna moaned again, and then proved to me just how cool she was.

'I like your tongue against my clit,' she started, that famous voice a whispered caress that seemed to stroke me all over. 'Lap at it. Lick it. Make little circles.'

Automatically, I followed her commands, thrilled that she was talking to me like that, so poised and in control. Raising her hips forward, off the counter, she spread herself even wider, using her own fingers to part her pussy lips.

'Now lick from my cunt to my ass,' she demanded, 'all the way in one long stroke.' I did precisely as she said. My tongue tasted her, spread those silky juices along the valley between her cunt and her asshole.

'Talk to me' she said next, and this was my exact fantasy from the day before. As I'd imagined, I started to trace words with my tongue up and over her throbbing clit and then whispered those same words into her body. 'Dirty'. A little flip at the end of the 'y' to make her tremble. 'Sexy'. The 's' like a snake, the 'x' a fancy letter to write with the tip of my tongue, crisscrossing over that hot button of pleasure with a fierce little twirl. I spelled every naughty word I could think of, all of the X-rated phrases that we'd just finished saying in the studio.

'I'm going to –' she said, obviously on the very cusp, and at that precise moment there was a knock at the door. Baxter's voice called out, 'Ladies, you almost ready? We're on the clock.'

My lips were glossy with her abundant juices, and she was so close to climax, I could see it in her deep-blue eyes when I glanced up at her. Sadly, she pushed me away and slipped off the counter. 'Later,' she said, and we took another moment to get ourselves together, then headed back to the studio. *Was that it?* I could feel my pussy quivering with need, and I thought to myself that there was just no fucking way I'd be able to finish the job. But Jenna, still calm and collected, was way ahead of me. Back in the studio, she began talking with the technician.

'Baxter, the script is a bit personal, you know?' I heard her saying. 'I'm just going to rearrange the setup a bit. To get us more in the mood. And if you could dim the lights . . .'

He did as she asked, and I saw Jenna restructuring our taping environment, so that the partitions now shielded us completely from the window, and our microphones were side to side. The next section of the piece was completely different from the first. Rather than a give-and-take dialogue, it featured long monologues delivered by each actress, full fantasies spelled out in great detail. While one woman was speaking, the other only needed to make an occasional murmuring assent, an encouraging 'mmmm' or 'ahhhn'.

I knew in an instant exactly what Jenna was planning, and I made myself comfortable in the chair and started to talk.

**Marisa:** It's my number-one favourite fantasy. The one I return to time and again.
**Danielle:** Mmmmm.
**Marisa:** I've never told anyone before, but I guess I can tell you.
**Danielle:** Anything. You can tell me anything.

And then, knowing that her part was over for at least three and a half pages, Jenna slid down on her knees in front of me, silently pushing my skirt up and slipping the edge of my wet lilac panties aside. With my eyes focused on the script, I did my best to follow along.

**Marisa:** It starts with you and me having phone sex. You're at work. I'm here at home, and, while we're talking to each other, I'm playing with myself. My fingers deep in my pussy. Spreading myself open. Tickling my clit lightly . . .

As I read, Jenna did the actions. She spread my lips, tickled my clit, found out that hot spot and pressed her sweet face against it.

Baxter said, 'You're doing great, but I'd like you to reread that part, Sadie. From "Tickling my clit . . ."'

**Marisa:** Tickling my clit lightly. Running my fingertips over it. And the whole time you're telling me that I'm a bad girl, that you're going to have to give me a bare-bottomed spanking when you get home. Spank my naked ass until it's a blushing pink. Spank me until I cry, or until I come, whichever happens first. And then you describe the rest of the evening. The sex toys we'll play with. A butt plug for my ass, a pair of cuffs around my wrists, and one of those giant vibrators, the really powerful ones that sound like Harley engines, just pressed against my clit when I think it's impossible for me to come any more. After I've climaxed twice, you're going to lay me on my belly and lube up my asshole. Then you'll spread my cheeks wide and slide that butt plug deep inside me.

As I spoke, Jenna continued to lick between my pussy lips, and, as I said the words that were turning me on, she upped the intensity. Using her teeth to gently capture my clit she nipped me, nibbled at me, made me moan, in spite of my best intentions to stay professional for the read.

Baxter said, 'That's great, Sadie. That moan sounded so perfect. You've nailed exactly what the client wants, an almost innocent, unrehearsed realism. You really are letting yourself go. But let's try it again, OK? This time, wait until you finish the whole paragraph before you give that hungry moan. So, let's take it from, oh ...' He hesitated. 'Right after "Lube up my asshole".'

I reread as instructed.

> **Marisa:** Then you'll spread my cheeks wide and slide that butt plug deep inside me. I love the feeling of being filled like that. Having a toy in my ass while you finger and suck on my clit. It's dirty, somehow. Naughty, or something. I can't exactly describe why it makes me so fucking wet.

Now, Jenna wet her pointer and worked it under me, and into me, filling my bottom while I tried my best to find the next words on the page. But again all I could do was moan.

'You're really getting into it,' Baxter complimented me. 'And I hate to do this, to break the intense emotion here, but I need to go grab another disc. So just hold the thought, ladies, and I'll be right back.'

With a sigh of relief, I let myself slip down on to the floor with Jenna, and we got into a tight sixty-nine on the short grey carpeting. No longer caring. Not even thinking for a moment about any possible repercussions. Jenna's pussy was dripping and I slid my tongue deep into her hole, rubbing my face back and forth against the seam of her body as she rewarded me in the same manner. She continued playing with my ass as she ate from my pussy, spreading my bottom cheeks wide apart so that I could feel the cool air-conditioned breeze against my skin. Teasing and tickling, she slid two fingers up into my asshole, and, when she sensed I was about to come, she added a third, feeling the orgasm begin as I contracted desperately on her. The climax flooded through me like water let loose, from my pussy to the outer reaches of my body, sending powerful tremors of pleasure through me.

Jenna came a moment later, surprising me with the silent way her body shuddered. Not a screamer after all, but then, you never really can tell these things. By the time Baxter made it back a few minutes later we were in place at our microphones, much more satisfied, although a good deal stickier, than before.

Baxter said, 'OK, kids. We'll start at . . .' There was the sound of paper shuffling as he searched for his place. 'Oh, let's go from "suck on my clit", shall we?' As always, Baxter read the previous line with no problem. No hesitation or embarrassment. Because, after all, it was just a job. Right?

# **Reality Bites** Jude Phillips

It all started quite innocently over a chocolate truffle. No, that was not true: it was neither innocent nor about truffles. Ellie was trying to rationalise what she was doing on a train to Cambridge.

Her stomach lurched, and it had nothing to do with the motion of the train as it started away from the station. 'Oh, bloody hell, what am I doing?' The words picked up the rhythm of the train and kept repeating through her mind. Ellie took a deep breath and tried to get back to the rationalisation to calm herself down. Communication with Chris had begun as a spin-off, a bored moment when she had found nothing in her In Box. She knew of him, she didn't know him, he was just one of those friend-of-a-friend names in her electronic address book. She knew he wrote funny, dirty emails and she was intrigued. Curiosity. She just couldn't resist the urge and butted in. Ellie had introduced herself with a couple of lines that were purposefully ambiguous. She got the desired response: an equally ambiguous reply. Over the following days a series of cryptic comments had burgeoned into a complex repartee full of innuendo and double entendres. The truffles, so to speak, had taken the biscuit.

'How would you eat yours?' she had prompted.

'I would hold the truffle lightly between forefinger and thumb, and gently flick at its surface with my tongue, gradually increasing the intensity until I could feel the chocolate had gone, then suck the whole thing into my mouth and enjoy it melt.'

Ellie had melted. Sitting at her computer, she had tried to think of a suitable response and resorted to changing the subject. Of course the subject hadn't changed, just the metaphorical framework. From food to clothes. It went on for weeks, this talking about different things and always the same thing. Ellie had allowed herself to get carried away and now she was sitting on a train trying to recall exactly what she had said, how far she had gone, because it looked as if she was going to have to put her money where her mouth was. Fantasy was one thing, now reality was about to bite. She wondered if his teeth were as sharp as his wit.

Ellie settled back in her seat, looking demure. Her shin grazed against her overnight bag and she reached down and shifted it away from her, felt the solid weight of her clothes and concentrated her mind on her immediate fashion plans. She was comfortable travelling in the calf-length black skirt, the side splits just sexy enough to encourage her to walk with a swing, giving nothing away. The clothes for tonight – well that was a different matter. They would be eating in the hotel restaurant, that much was agreed, she hadn't been able to make up her mind on an outfit: everything was either too obvious or too uptight. That was why her overnight bag was packed to bursting, to keep her choices open. There was always the ultimate choice, of course: turn around and run away. Would she? Well, that rather depended on Chris.

Virtual reality was a dangerous thing. The trouble with emails was that you could fall under the spell of somebody's words. Far more immediate than letter writing, it was also a more manipulative medium than the telephone, allowing time for composition, for fine tuning so that the words were just right, and maintaining a distance that banished normal inhibitions. Face to face, out loud, she might not have been so ... Too late now. She had allowed email to manipulate her into a meeting, a meeting over which she felt her own control was precariously tenuous. The lack of control, the manipulation – these were a large part of the attraction; the fact she was actually submitting to it had been the result of an insane second of electronic bravado.

Ellie tried to concentrate on the rhythm of the train. Her mind ricocheted with the sound of the wheels on the tracks, between nerves and anticipation. She was trying hard to convince herself that this man had no idea what had being going on in her head and it would probably all turn out like any other affair: drinks, dinner, sex and cigarettes afterwards. Ellie found this thought disappointing and tried out the alternative: he knew what was going through her mind and her inhibitions would be blown apart. This thought horrified her; she crossed her legs, squeezing her thighs together as she felt the flesh at their juncture tighten and crawl. Oh, God, the train was slowing at the station.

As Ellie stood she realised she was damp, that peculiar sliding sensation that would quickly worsen as she walked. Bending to pick up her bag, she surreptitiously pressed her knickers into the dampness. She could smell her own arousal and hoped it was just her heightened awareness and undetectable to anyone else. She straightened up and took a deep breath, stepped off the train and stood motionless. This station was unfamiliar to her and she didn't know which way to turn. She didn't have to move. A voice at her side broke into her uncertainty, 'Ellie? I'll take that, shall I?' He took her bag from her hand and she found herself moving away from the train guided by a firm grip on her arm.

One choice had already been closed off. She couldn't quietly disappear from the platform. Ellie ventured a visual stock-take. He wasn't tall, though taller than she was of course – even her heels couldn't raise her above five foot two, and then they were dangerously high. Average build, smart-casual clothing, unremarkable. He looked down and caught her eye; she saw her own curiosity reflected. Well, of course he was curious, but there was something self-assured about his curiosity. She tried to match it with a relaxed smile but sensed the corners of her mouth twitch with nerves.

He walked her to the front of the taxi rank, where the driver opened the boot and put her bag inside and slammed the door with a finality that made her flinch. She opened the rear door and slid across the seat, and Chris followed, shutting the door himself. He sat back and turned slightly towards her, and his hand dropped on to her shoulder. 'You're nervous.' It was a statement and it was hardly deniable: she had jumped out of her skin at his touch.

'Of course I am. I don't –' She had been about to say I don't do this all the time, or at all, or something equally ridiculous and only half true. Of course she did take lovers, and there was always a 'first time' with all the attendant anticipation; it was the circumstances that were unique and unnerving in this case. She expected him to say something light, something to put her at her ease. It didn't happen.

Chris looked directly at her until she felt a blush rising. His voice was casual, and she found it hard to judge the level of irony when he spoke. 'What exactly don't you do?'

Ellie couldn't rid herself of the feeling that when he said 'exactly' he meant 'exactly, in detail, tell me everything'. She opened her mouth and closed it again, finding nothing she could say without lying or getting herself in deeper. The taxi pulled up in front of the Lancaster Hotel and Ellie threw the door open before the engine died. The winter chill hit her like a slap in the face and she realised how far she had allowed her sensations to slip away from her control during the short drive. Her focus had narrowed to the man next to her, and while she had been concentrating on how to defend or justify herself in words, and failing, the hidden corners of her mind had been conjuring images and ideas that had caused her to sweat and moisten. The expensive silk thong she had put on in a moment of self-confidence slipped uncomfortably between her lips and up between the cheeks of her arse as she swung her legs out of the car. She would give anything to fish the wretched thing down, but, feeling as if her every move was being examined, she gritted her teeth and left it.

The taxi driver's voice seemed to come from a great distance as he handed Chris some loose change with a cheerful 'There you go, mate.' And then he was gone. Ellie found herself taken by the arm once more and guided into the foyer. She was beginning to feel like an imbecile being manoeuvred from place to place. She cleared her throat and tried to feel more like an adult, and a consenting one at that. 'What name did you book us under?'

'Mine. I'll check us in.' Chris moved up to the desk. He had her bag as well as his own, so she followed. If she could just have her own things back she would feel more in control. With a sinking sensation Ellie saw both bags disappear with the porter.

They stood in the lift in silence, walked down a plush and hushed corridor, and Chris slipped a key in the lock of one of the identical doors along it. He walked in, held the door and shut it behind her. Their bags were on the stand beside the mirrored dressing table.

Ellie wanted a drink, a large one, but it was only half

past five. Chris turned to her and spoke. 'They serve dinner from seven. I thought we'd eat early. Time for a shower. Do you want to go first?'

Ellie did. She wanted to get somewhere private, strip off and get rid of the general grime from the train. She wanted to relax in hot water and rinse away the musky smell and the last sticky indictment that taunted her every time she moved. She wanted a change of clothes and probably a change of mind. She prised her wash bag out of the side pocket of her bag and bolted for the bathroom. She locked the door.

Ellie spent a good half-hour showering, drying and making up. She had been delighted to find one of those oversized bathrobes behind the door and the lock seemed to have been unnecessary. Chris hadn't tried the door. She emerged, a little more relaxed, wrapped and securely tied in the robe. What she saw immediately undermined her hard-won poise. Her clothes were laid out on the bed. He had been in her bag, rifled through her things, and quite clearly made her decisions for her. Ellie wanted to make a fuss, but it would seem so disproportionate, having a go at him for choosing her clothes when she had agreed to get on a train and spend the night with what amounted to a total stranger in the first place. She had put herself at a disadvantage and he was keeping her there. Chris raised an eyebrow. She said nothing. As Chris stepped through the bathroom door he spoke over his shoulder: 'I won't be long, then we'll go down.'

Ellie sat on the end of the bed, facing herself in the dressing table mirror. The mirror reflected her look of confusion, the bed and all her clothes laid out on it. She shrugged at herself and examined her clothes. Chris seemed to have some sense of dress, up to a point. He had chosen her short black skirt, of which she was very fond. There wasn't much of it for the price she had paid, but the quality shone through the drape of the cloth as it followed her hips and brushed across her legs just above mid-thigh. Chris had also put out the top she nearly always wore with it. Sleeveless with a deep V-neck, it smoothed into her body and ended just where the skirt began. All very well and good but that was where her choice and his parted company: on the outside. She would never normally wear stockings with a skirt that short and certainly not the ridiculous G-string that cut her in half if she moved too far. She looked longingly at her bag for a moment, and thought of switching underwear. She didn't – all a matter of proportion again. It seemed churlish and childish, possibly cowardly. So she just put on what was laid out. As she rolled her stockings up her legs and reached around to make sure the suspenders lay vertically down her buttocks, and nothing was twisted or caught, she glanced in the mirror. Oh, shit. She felt really self-conscious and exposed. Ellie grabbed her skirt and slid it on quickly. Adjusting her bra straps, so that they didn't show under the narrow shoulders of her top, she found her hands were shaking. She went straight to the minibar, took a miniature of gin and a can of tonic and poured. It was well after six now and nothing was going to stop her.

Chris walked out of the bathroom with a towel wrapped round his waist and took the glass from her hand. 'We'll share it, shall we? I wouldn't want you to think I'd take advantage of you under the influence.' She was speechless: he was a mind reader and a sadist. The two mouthfuls she managed to get burned into her stomach and hit her like a half-bottle. Alcohol and adrenaline made a powerful mix, but she certainly couldn't claim to be drunk. Chris dropped the towel from his waist and turned away in a fluid and confident motion. He took clothes from his bag and then tossed it on to the chair. Why did Ellie have the feeling throughout this that it was she who was naked? As soon as he was dressed Chris picked up the room key. 'Let's go, then.'

As soon as they were out of the door, Ellie wished they weren't. She walked awkwardly to the lift, fearing that the draught of the closing door might lift her skirt and, if she didn't walk as if she were balancing books on her head, bolt upright, her suspenders were going to show. More than that, she wanted to stay in that room and fuck. She had, after all, been waiting to fuck this man for days. That was what she was here for and, despite all the last-minute nerves, that was what she wanted. But the longer this went on, the more dominance he exerted without even touching her, the more nervous she became. Get it started, stop this tortuous waiting game, which was making her imagination run riot. The lift door closed on them.

Chris moved directly in front of her as she backed up against the wall. He looked straight into her eyes and lifted the front hem of her skirt. He lifted the lace triangle which lay over her pubic hair and slid a finger lightly down her slit. The tip of his finger dipped into her. 'Your cunt's soaked.' Ellie felt her cheeks flame and her eyelids started to close, trying to avoid the penetration of his look. He pushed his finger further into her and then the lift halted. Just before the doors opened he ran his fingers upwards over her clit, pressing the material of her knickers between her lips and pulling up. He brushed down the front of her skirt, took her hand and more or less dragged her from the lift.

The maître d' was the soul of English snobbery. Silkily, he enquired whether Sir and 'Modom' were guests and conducted them to a corner table near the window. Ellie felt a sudden urge to laugh: there was something surreal about her level of sexual arousal and the elegant restraint of the hotel dining room. Chris was smiling and she knew he was enjoying the same sense of the ridiculous. She was reminded forcibly of her state as she sat on the cool chintz of the upholstered dining chair. Her G-string pulled between her legs, her suspenders became taut over her buttocks and she surreptitiously eased her stocking tops higher to ensure the hem of her skirt covered them. She couldn't cross her legs, as she normally would, without flashing more flesh than was decent, so she pressed her knees together to try to ease the discomfort.

The menu was good and Ellie quite deliberately ordered the fresh asparagus dripping with clarified butter, not just because it was expensive but also because perhaps she could visit some discomfort on this man who seemed to be calling all the shots. She had barely taken the first spear between her lips, tilted her head back to catch the drips of butter, when Chris leaned forward and in conversational tones stated, 'I hope you like giving head as much as you like eating asparagus.'

Ellie nipped the head off the asparagus spear and then sucked the rest of it into her mouth, biting through at the base rather noisily. 'That's the trouble with asparagus, no substance.' She smiled sweetly. Ellie had reached that point of frustration and annoyance that triggered all her combative instincts. If he was going to play games then so was she. She had a nagging feeling that, rather like poker, if she was going to be 'in' then the stakes would be raised. She barely registered his response.

'I think I can come up with something more solid.' Chris carelessly buttered toast and spread the pâté he had chosen, and ate with evident enjoyment. As the waiter removed their starter plates with exaggerated courtesy, Chris rested his elbows on the table and his chin on the back of his raised hands. He looked at her for several seconds with absolute concentration.

'What have you fantasised would happen tonight?'

Ellie felt caught out again. He hadn't merely asked *have* you . . .?', to which she could have lied and said no. Of course she had fantasised, but she hadn't expected to be discussing her fantasies, certainly not over the dinner table.

'Oh, well, nothing in particular, just what you might look like, sound like, that sort of thing.' A half-truth: she certainly had been curious about his voice. Would it carry that ironic twist that had fascinated her on the screen? Would he look as she had imagined? He did, in fact, look much as she had envisaged he would. Dark hair, dark eyes and a slightly cynical cast to his expressions. Interesting rather than good-looking. The word 'fascination' occurred to her again.

'That's not all, though, is it? You must have imagined how we would fuck.'

'Fuck' was a word she was normally comfortable with. She preferred it to the romantic suggestiveness of 'make love', but here in the dining room it seemed more shocking and she couldn't help glancing around to gauge the distance between them and potential eavesdroppers.

'Oh, I don't think anyone's paying any attention.' Chris had correctly interpreted her reaction. 'So you can tell me: what have you been picturing as you lay in bed at night fingering yourself?'

'I haven't –'

'Of *course* you have. I want to know just what it was that turned you on most. Did I tie you up? Suck you? Hurt you? Is it straight? Is it kinky? Do you make it last when you masturbate? How?'

'I'm not going to tell you all that, not here.' Ellie

regretted two things: the pitch of her voice, which was panicky; and the 'not here', which she had tacked on in a sort of conciliatory way.

'Oh, I think you should tell me. Let's start with something simple. When we go upstairs after dinner do I undress you completely, in your fantasy?'

There was something persuasive about his voice, something so reasonable that she found herself giving way. Why shouldn't she play the game a little? If she gave him enough then dinner would be over and they could move on to action, altogether more familiar ground.

'OK. No, I think I slide my skirt to the floor. I step out of it. Then I raise my arms and you lift my top off. You push me backwards on to the bed and slide my knickers down my legs, leaving my stockings on. Then you lean over me and slide my bra straps down so that you can put your hands on my breasts.' Ellie hesitated. She intended to go on but, as she sought for the next words, Chris interrupted.

'I don't see it happening quite like that. Shall I tell you how I see it?' The question was obviously purely rhetorical, because he continued immediately. 'I think I lead you to the mirror. I'll move behind you, lift your top and unhook your bra. We'll both watch as I tease your nipples until they're hard, almost painful.'

Ellie was mesmerised. His voice was low and she couldn't break away from his gaze. The arrival of the waiter with their main course shattered the spell. Ellie had to lean back to allow her plate to be placed in front of her. She realised Chris had drawn her into an intimate space; the surrounding diners had been forgotten and their voices only now filtered back into her consciousness. She cleared her throat, found her breathing was too rapid and took a long swallow from the glass of cold white wine beside her plate. Her hands shook as she picked up her steak knife, and she wasn't in the least hungry.

Chris finished his first mouthful of steak. 'I might take the rest of your clothes off.' He paused as if in thought. 'Probably not, though. You'll watch as I slide that scrap of material aside, ease your legs apart and start to play with your clit. Looks indecent, doesn't it?' Chris cut another piece of steak. 'Doesn't it?'

Ellie's voice was barely above a whisper and, as she said 'Yes', she realised it didn't matter what answer she gave: what mattered was the acknowledgment of the visual image. He was making her share his voyeurism in her imagination.

Ellie tried desperately to eat. For several moments there was silence and, as she chewed and swallowed, the visual images kept repeating. Without volition, Ellie found her thighs tensing as, in her mind's eye, she stood stretching, striving to raise herself to purely imaginary fingers.

'The steak's good.' Chris's voice was smooth, soft. 'Tender, succulent, so moist. If I opened your legs now I'd find you were swollen and soft. I could bite into your flesh, suck you into my mouth. Do you want dessert?'

Ellie put her knife and fork together, politely. She picked up her napkin and wiped her mouth, took another swallow of wine. 'No. Thank you.'

Chris nodded at the waiter, signed the receipt and pushed back his chair. Ellie was still sitting, looking up at him, but she knew her eyes weren't focusing properly. She felt unsteady but knew she hadn't drunk too much wine. Chris moved behind her and helped draw out her chair as she began to stand up. Ellie smoothed her skirt down and slid her hand into the crook of his arm. She needed some sort of contact, support. Somehow she couldn't walk across the expanse of that elegant dining room without the reassurance of physical contact.

Across the foyer, into the lift. As the lift doors shut with a pneumatic hiss Ellie swayed. Chris put an arm around her shoulder. It was comforting and she relaxed into him as they ascended two floors. There was a welcome absence of words, until they were standing at the door to their room.

'I'm going to give you a safe word. You know what that is?'

Ellie nodded dumbly. She knew, but only in theory, never in practice.

'"Asparagus", since you love it so much.' Chris didn't wait for any acknowledgment as he turned the key in the lock. Ellie found herself thinking what a ludicrous word, and how stupid she would feel saying it. But its very existence immediately increased the tension and conflict in both her mind and her body.

Chris turned on the wall lights as they walked in. He drew her over to the mirror and she assumed he would act out his words as he turned her to face it. She found herself caught by his eyes, his face reflected in the mirror as he looked over her shoulder. 'Let's not be too predictable.' He murmured. He moved away from behind her and Ellie was at a loss what to do, so she just stood.

'Undress for me.' His voice came from further behind her and she half turned. He was sitting on the side of the bed leaning back. His feet were still on the floor, and he looked relaxed and slightly amused. Ellie gripped the bottom of her top and raised it over her head. She hesitated, wondering whether to toss it on the floor or try for a little self-possession and put it on the chair, where he had left his overnight bag. She chose the latter;

it gave her an opportunity to move away from the mirror. She stalked on her high heels, pretending an air of blasé disregard. He didn't react in any way, just watched. She slid her skirt down and unhooked her stockings, half expecting him to halt her. She wouldn't have minded keeping them on; she thought that would have been almost normal. The silence seemed to grow as she unhooked her bra and let it, too, drop. Taking a surreptitious breath, she eased her G-string down and stepped out of it. As she carefully placed this final item on the pile, her eye was caught by his open bag. Something in it reflected the light, but she couldn't see what. Ellie turned towards the bed.

'Sit down.' Chris stood and gestured to his vacant place. He began to remove his own clothes without waiting to see what she did. Ellie sat. She fidgeted, feeling exposed.

'Do you live in Cambridge?' As soon as the words left her mouth she wished they hadn't. She sounded as if she were making small talk at a party, and it was totally inappropriate. She was shocked when he responded in kind.

'Mmm, I live here and I work here.'

'Oh, what do you do?' Ellie felt trapped in the conventional responses and almost laughed.

'Well, let's see if you can work that out by morning, shall we?' Chris threw her off balance again – deliberately, she felt. He walked towards her.

'Ever seen a pair of these before?' She had. They were handcuffs. As he took her hand and swung them efficiently round her wrist she realised they weren't the joke-shop sort with a cute little key, but something altogether more businesslike.

'No. I don't think –'

'No, you haven't seen handcuffs? Or no, you don't think – what? "No" doesn't work in here. Only one word works.'

'Shit.' Ellie pulled back on her hand and made no impression whatsoever.

'Wrong word again.' For a fraction of a second Ellie kept up her physical resistance. She didn't trust him, didn't want to leave herself helpless, but she didn't want him to win, either. She relaxed her arm, leaving her hand in his.

'Other hand, please.' She mutely brought the other hand up. He took it and then, leaning over, pushed her back across the bed. She experienced a sickening moment of realisation as the other cuff closed on her free wrist. He had passed it around the ornate wrought-iron bedstead and she was not just handcuffed but immobilised. Like a diver arrested in mid-flight, she was flung across the bed with her hands raised in surrender over her head. Chris stood back and seemed to consider the arrangement of her body. 'Nothing to say?' He paused. 'I want you to be sure.'

Ellie crossed her ankles in a half-hearted effort to make herself feel less vulnerable. She wasn't sure of anything except that she would feel such a fool if she gave in and stopped it all. Chris seemed to think she had had enough time to consider her options. He walked purposefully over to the chair and drew it and his bag towards the bed. He tossed the bag carelessly on the floor and sat down as if he were going to engage her in conversation. Resting his elbows on his knees, he looked into her face just as she lowered her eyes to his erect cock. She flushed. In her confusion his nakedness and his erection had barely registered on her consciousness; now that they did, she knew just how badly she wanted to feel him inside her, wanted his weight and power and touch.

'Not yet. You have to show me how much you want it. What will you do for me? Anything?' His voice was at its most sinuous and his fingers slid delicately up from her knees to the top of her thighs. She could feel his fingers brush the first curl of pubic hair and come to rest.

'Please.' Ellie hissed between clenched teeth. Her knees parted and her heels dug into the bed. His hand traced down her leg and he pushed her ankle sideways. It dropped from the bed, leaving her sprawled and unsupported with her legs spread apart. She couldn't take her eyes from his face as he reached forward and thrust his fingers inside her. He turned his hand, curled his fingers and pressed. She began to rock her hips, unable to stop herself making humiliating noises of pleasure and greed, even as he smiled down at her and withdrew his hand. She let out a wail of fury. 'Oh, Christ, please, please, please.'

'Anything?'

She said it. She said the damn words. 'Anything you want.'

He grinned. 'Informed consent is so important, don't you think?' There hadn't been anything informed about it. She knew it, he knew it. But it no longer mattered. She was in too deep.

Chris reached down out of her eyeline. When his hand reappeared he was holding something long, hard and black. It made no sense to Ellie: it looked like a baton with a handgrip set at right angles nearly halfway down. He laid it on her stomach, its weight and solidity cold against her skin. Reaching past her face, he grabbed both sets of pillows and shoved them under her head and shoulders. She could see clearly down the length of her body. Her shoulders were pulled back and her breasts thrust nakedly upwards. A stripe of polished blackness divided her vertically from her breastbone to the junction of her thighs. The end of the baton seemed to nuzzle threateningly into her pubic hair and the thicker, deeply ridged handgrip lay crosswise on the soft skin of her stomach. Chris idly stroked the grip, turning it until it stood erect from her body. It fitted comfortably in his fist. He ran his thumb over the blunt thickness of the rounded end, protruding obscenely from his closed hand.

'You don't know what this is, do you? It has a very apt name, but I'll tell you – afterwards.'

The noise Ellie made meant 'after what?' But the words weren't there any more. Chris moved decisively between her legs. Her thigh muscles seemed to have turned to water and she let him raise her knees and spread her wide open with only the slightest resistance. He picked up the baton and slid it sideways beneath her thighs, the grip thrust up between her legs. He ran his closed fist up and down it, the back of his knuckles sliding between her lips and grazing her clitoris. For an absurd moment she felt as if she had a cock, as if she could feel his hand closed around it. She gasped, felt her cunt tighten.

'All you have to do is ask.' Chris leaned forward as if to hear her reply.

Ellie turned her head away. Pressing her face into the pillow, she started to plead again. 'Inside me, please, I want it.' Her voice was muffled and her eyes squeezed shut.

'Mmm, not good enough. You need to be clear. Is this what you mean?' She felt the end of the grip slide down between her soaking lips and press inwards, stretching the rim of her cunt. She felt a blaze of anticipation sweep up through her body, strained for more. For an instant she was filled. The hard polished surface slid easily, beautifully, into her and her throat opened to voice her pleasure. It was snatched away.

'Or is this what you mean?' The blunt end suddenly seemed harder, thicker, as it pressed against the tenseness of her arse. She resisted automatically and the pain was sharp.

'No.' Her voice rose in panic.

'I can make you want it. I can make you ask for this.'

'No.' She could hear the certainty in his voice but she didn't believe him. His hands moved over her, suddenly gentle and seductive, stroking over breast and thigh; his mouth traced down her neck, making her head tilt and her skin burn. His teeth closed hard on her nipple and she gasped and jerked as hot wires ran down to her navel. His head dipped between her legs and his tongue licked and his teeth grazed and nipped. Ellie knew everything was drifting beyond her control. She couldn't stop him; she couldn't stop herself. She whispered one word: 'Anything.'

Ellie's body tilted as he rolled her brutally on to her face. The handcuffs tightened and twisted on her trapped wrists. 'Get on your knees. Show me how much you want it.' Ellie dragged her knees under her, dropped her shoulders and thrust her hips up. Before she could question what she was doing, she was rewarded by rigid fingers thrusting into her cunt, making her squeal for more. She felt the baton press horizontally across her thighs, the thick grip rising up and spreading her buttocks, its textured surface rubbing across the sensitive rim of her arse. There was a flush of heat, and Ellie felt the knot of muscle give, open. Her body was inviting the invasion and she couldn't help herself.

'Now ask.'

'Please, I want it.' She felt the grip tilt and press into

her, the first thick inch drawing a ragged moan. Her body was confused, filled and empty; her cunt ached like fire and the ripples of exquisite pleasure drove her mad with need.

'You want more. Don't you?'

Ellie's answer came out on a long, drawn sob. But it was yes.

'I can't fuck you until it's right inside you, past the ridges of the grip, buried to the hilt. You understand that?' She felt the sudden increase in girth, the stretch that made her gasp and topple from pleasure to pain and back again. 'There's more.' His voice was so soft, so cruel. She felt a moment of sheer hatred. 'Once more.' Ellie's hands twisted painfully as she clawed at the bed, her breath coming in short panting bursts. She felt the length of the baton come to rest across her cheeks. In a red haze she felt his cock probe between her lips. She was so tight, so swollen that it seemed impossible that a man had ever fucked her before. He thrust hard into her; his body slammed into the bar across her buttocks and the thrust was repeated up her arse. His hands plunged under her stomach and, as he spread her lips apart, she started to scream. Her body bucked uncontrollably and her orgasm ripped through her. He pressed agonisingly on her clit and slammed into her again. She heard his own ragged noise as her muscles convulsed and exploded in waves of unrecognisable sensation. The red haze seemed to fade to black and she drifted away for moments.

In a blur of exhaustion, Ellie felt Chris release one of her hands, slide the intrusion from her, arrange her comfortably and stroke her sweat-soaked pubic hair. A mobile phone rang from the bag beside the bed. She was too exhausted to flinch at the sudden noise.

'DI Collier.' His voice was crisp, authoritative. 'On my

way.' He turned, leaning on his elbow. 'I shall need these.' He reached for the hand on which the handcuffs dangled and flicked them open. 'I'll leave the night stick – I borrowed that from uniform division. I don't suppose they'll ever figure out what for.' Chris's mouth twitched with amusement. 'Oh, and don't go anywhere. You're under arrest – for indecency. I want some more later.'

# **Rub-a-Dub** Maria Eppie

I'm lying flat on my belly, staring out through Janey's binoculars at the crashing, boiling, pounding sea. Every few seconds, a squall of rain spatters the picture window in front of me. The gale is making a deep moaning hum in the corrugated-iron roof. All pretty awesome and elemental. I should be moved and impressed. I would be, if it wasn't that we've had three days of it already. Thing about Scottish weather, you do get a lot. Wind, rain, mist; you can have a year's supply every twenty-four hours.

Even, like now, in midsummer. It's 11 p.m. and the sky is still light. I'm studying a tiny crack of bilious yellow on the far horizon, praying it's the harbinger of sun. Janey comes out of the shower, wrapped up in a fluffy towel, and squats in front of the wood-burning stove to dry her hair. The window immediately mists over. I snarl tetchily, 'Good thinking, Janey. The humidity factor *was* getting a bit low here.' She purses her lips and lights yet another aromatherapy candle.

Guess you can tell I might be a teensy bit irritated with Janey. Nothing to do with being cooped up in a one-roomed hut with a perpetually enthusiastic New Age Girl Guide. OK, I blame myself. Heading off for a week in the remotest corner of Scotland with someone you've nothing in common with does show lack of forethought, I suppose. See, I don't really know Janey and haven't exactly shared that many one-to-ones with her. Well, prior to this so-called holiday, none actually. The only thing we appear to share is that we're the last two single girls in our crowd. That, and a really close friend.

I was moaning at Close Mutual Friend about how I needed a holiday but didn't know who to go with. My various current squeezes were all fine for the usual stuff: dinner parties, tyre-pressure checking, casual sex. But, if anything, they were part of the problem, not the solution. I wanted a complete break. Mutual Friend immediately called Janey over and announced, 'Janey feels the same. You're both independent, grown-up gals. Hey, why not go away together?' I blustered a bit but our vacation counsellor cut straight in with the killer. 'You don't need guys to have a good time, do you?'

Hmm. I should have said something right there. Next mistake was to let Janey sort the arrangements. OK, we'd agreed that a girlie beach holiday would be just too tacky, being mistaken for a sad pair of Shirley Valentines by every waiter/gigolo *en la playa*, etc. And Janey said she didn't *do* sun. So when she started rhapsodising about the ethereal beauty of the North West Highlands, the roamin' in the gloamin' and the get-away-from-it-all calm, I uh-huhed and pretty much left her to it.

From what I knew of Janey, I was expecting some holistic, mind-and-body, beauty-spa retreat thang. I wasn't expecting the two-mile hike down a muddy track to the one-roomed electricity-less croft stuck on the edge of a rock-strewn hillside way out of reach of any mobile network. The perfect place to find yourself. Except, I don't need to. I know who I am. (I'm Kaye. I'm twenty-eight. I'm a sophisticated, urbane market analyst whose natural milieu is the kind of place where you lodge your platinum card behind the bar. Pleased to meet ya, mine's Veuve Cliquot, by the way.)

Janey, however, seems to have anticipated a week of us roped together on a mission of bilateral female self-discovery. (Some Janey facts I have learned since arrival: Janey *was* a Girl Guide. Janey is seriously into yoga. Janey sees no irony in starting each day with the Sun Prayer. Serene is the best way to describe Janey. I think she read somewhere that an overanimated face gives you wrinkles. She is very pretty in a demure, head-girlish way.) Basically, I guess Janey's miffed that I haven't fallen in love with Rub-a-Dub, just like her. It's just that it's a bit . . . well, intimate.

See, when I said one-roomed, I did not exaggerate. The Black House, *Rudh Dubh* in the Gaelic vernacular, is a converted cow-byre-cum-hovel. One long space with a kitchenette and shower at one end and a pair of mattress/divans at the other. It sounds squalid but it isn't. Rub-a-Dub, as I call it, is prettily restored, with the picture window cut through whitewashed stone walls to look out on the sea and chunky timber beams up in the roof space. If it wasn't for the weather, it would be just too cute. But there's the rub-a-dub: the weather. At least it's snug. The potbellied stove Janey's hunched in front of sees to that.

I take a swig of my McCallan and contemplate things. I suppose the weather's not her fault. I don't know if it's the candle or the reassuring afterburn of the peaty malt whisky that does it, but I start feeling a lot more mellow. Janey's towel has dropped and, bathed in the warm amber glow of the fire and the soft light from the candles, her porcelain skin does look really fabulous. (Another Janey fact learned this week: Janey hasn't been out in the sun since about 1982.) The logs are crackling away in the stove and we're all warm and cosy. So I call a truce. 'Hey, y'know, your skin's looking really soft and dewy. D'ya reckon it's the water?'

'Think so?' she asks earnestly, rubbing something oily

and no doubt essential over her tits. I'm a bit pissed and I find myself staring at the hands running over her glistening body. It feels weird. Even after half a week shacked up here, I hardly know her *that* well. My inner bitch resurfaces and I break the mood by adding, 'Really, you wouldn't think you were thirtysomething!' She looks so deflated, I feel mean. I pour a shot of McCallan each and mutter, 'Sorry, Janey. I'm bored.'

'No, you're tense,' Janey says firmly. 'Would you like some reflexology?' Well, she's wrong, I *am* bored. But never in my entire life have I turned down a foot massage, so I don't correct her. I'm wearing just a tee and knickers (that stove kicks out a lot of heat), so I roll over on to my back and plonk a foot in Janey's lap. Then bliss out and listen to the roar of the storm outside. I have been known to come by having my feet rubbed. Janey doesn't know this (obviously). As I said, I don't know her that well. Not enough to orgasm in front of, anyway.

OK, if she is my only available partner-in-crime then that one needs sorting. I need to know more about her. I ask, 'Truth or Dare?' Janey raises an eyebrow at me (black, very arched) and I pour out two more slugs of whisky before carefully capping the bottle, placing it on the floor and spinning it to point at her. 'C'mon, Janey. Truth or Dare, you must have played it!'

She rolls her eyes then replies, 'Truth,' in a just-humouring-you way. Right. I think I'll cut straight to the chase with this one. 'When was the first time you had an orgasm?' The eyebrows crumple and I think, shit, she's *never* had one, but then she says, 'Age six. Mum's dining room. Hard wooden chair. I perched on the edge and rocked myself off. So to speak.' She adds wistfully, 'I spent every moment I could on that chair, till Mum caught me. Then I was permanently banned from the dining room. Right, now it's my go, is it? What about you?'

'Fifteen, I think. With my finger one night in bed. I was a late developer, I guess.' Janey grins indulgently at me. I'm relaxing and actually starting to enjoy this. I didn't expect her to be this open. I drawl, 'What's the perviest thing you've ever done?' She does the eyebrow stuff again and repeats, 'Perviest?' '*The* perviest,' I insist, seriously. She racks her memory. 'Um . . . Well, I once had sex with identical twins. Does that count?' I start sniggering. I can't help myself. Head Girl Janey with two men? No! I dissolve in a fit of giggles. When they finally subside, she doesn't look offended, so I hang in there. 'OK, now the details . . .'

She shrugs. 'They were both trying to date me separately. It was all a bit competitive, so I said they could take me for a meal, but jointly. When we got back to mine, I let them in for a coffee. One of them, we'll call him twin A, was in the bathroom when his brother, B, jumped on me. I had a strappy low-cut dress on, no bra, and he just pulled it down and started sucking my breast. Next thing I knew, A was on the other one. So there they were, A and B, sucking away. I've got very sensitive breasts. I thought, Oh, what the hell. I shimmied off my dress and told them to get naked, too.'

I nod, entranced, while Janey continues serenely. 'Well, they were identical in every way. Totally. Nice bodies too, but *so* competitive. Say, A would lick my clit. Well, B would have to lick my arsehole at the same time. And, as soon as one wanted to penetrate me, the other had to do it too.'

I'm shocked. I didn't know Janey even knew the word 'arsehole'. She continues, 'They wanted to have my cunt simultaneously but the mechanics were too tricky, even though I was wet as hell. So we compromised. A had my cunt and B my arse. I thought it was a very holistic solution.' My brain is reeling. I've never had two cocks at once and, looking into Janey's demure face, I can hardly really believe she has, either. She just says brightly, 'All right, Kaye, my turn.' She studies me. 'Tell me the weirdest way you ever had an orgasm.'

Ah, *touché*! But I'm known for my lack of coyness. Definitely a WYSIWYG kinda gal. I come straight back. 'Well, y'know, having my feet rubbed, I think,' I say insouciantly.

'Oh, I don't know if it can really do *that*,' Janey says with her innocently musical, English schoolgirl laugh.

I expect the foot business to cease forthwith, but I think she actually intensifies her rubbing. I'm confused. I'm stretched out seminaked while an equally undressed footmaiden anoints and massages my feet, even though I've told her it makes me come. (OK, only twice and with a particularly sensuous, experienced lover, but she doesn't know that.) I've got a horrible feeling I'm on the edge of a *faux pas*. Has Janey really heard what I've just said? Perhaps it's her way of being friendly. I decide to ignore everything, too, and carry on with the game. But I can't put another question together because my head is full of the lewd and sexy images Janey has stirred up there. I've gone silent but Janey doesn't seem to have noticed. Her fingers continue manipulating, working their way along my sole. Oh, God, that's it. That's the spot. With the heat from the stove and the warm, tingly sensations being generated in my feet, I'm starting to feel woozy. In a whisky-fuelled, essential-oiled way. There's a luxurious ache radiating from my nether regions that's very similar to one that sometimes radiates from a more central part of my anatomy. I'm not sure I should be feeling like this, but I can't form the words to tell the footmaiden to stop.

But she does. Without a word, she releases my foot and stands up. I feel a terrible surge of disappointment as Janey goes into one of her stretch routines, folding herself at the waist so her elbows touch the floor. Her towel slips off, revealing a slim, girlish figure. Then, she unwinds herself and flops down on the mattress next to me, saying 'Hey, look, a sunset!'

I roll over and look out to sea. The storm's abated and the clouds have broken up. An unfamiliar red orb is hovering over the distant horizon. Janey lies next to me, not invading my space. She is so natural and unself-conscious about being naked, I feel a twinge of guilt. She's been trying to make up with me. And it's worked. An hour ago, this girl irritated the shit out of me. And now? It's like we're old friends. I relax and sleepily enjoy our lying together, companionably sipping whisky, while we watch a fiery sun sink imperceptibly into the waves.

I wake up to find my crotch shoving itself into the mattress. A vague memory of some dirty conversation and some frustratingly unfinished business with feet has stimulated a dislocated horniness. It slowly focuses into a familiar ache between my legs. I'm all bunched up, untidy limbs, my arm strewn over something soft. It's Janey, stretched out neatly next to me. I lift my arm away but she doesn't stir. Well, Janey may be out like a babe but I know that, unless I do something, I'll be tossing and turning for the rest of the night.

I slip a guilty hand between my thighs. Surreptitiously, my fingers find my cunt. It's hot and moist. I hold my breath and stretch my thighs wider apart, careful not to brush against her. I tentatively circle my clit with my eyes fixed on Janey's sleeping form to check she isn't about to wake up. In the crepuscular light, she looks like an elegantly underlit *Vogue* photoshoot. I can see her pouting rosebud mouth, her small pointy breasts, her nubile waist, her mysteriously dark bush. I imagine those twin cocks penetrating deeply. Now this *does* feel deliciously pervy.

My fingers move faster and my body tenses. My mons is pushing up to meet my hand and I'm starting to pant now. I'm terrified that Janey will wake and catch me but, somehow, the thought makes me hornier. I almost will her eyes to open. And then I come, trying to hold the long soft moan in my throat, with just a little unsatisfied aching for something else: perhaps those twin cocks I can't stop thinking about.

When I next wake, I'm alone and covered by a duvet. I can hear Janey in the shower, again. The room smells of whisky and jasmine and woodsmoke. And outside the sun is shining. Fluffy white clouds scud across a seriously blue sky. I can't believe it! Where before there was a misty expanse of rock-strewn turf, disappearing forlornly upwards into grey cloud, there is now mountain. The kind of dramatic, pointy-peaked mountain you drew as a kid. Time to walk off that hangover.

Even though Janey was up before me, I'm ready ages before her. This no-sun thing is incredibly high-maintenance. I spend twenty minutes sniffing the tangy, champagne air, while she decides which hat to wear. 'Janey,' I snap, 'it doesn't fucking matter how much sun block you put on: one day you will get old and die. Now can we please go?'

I think Janey walks faster than is strictly necessary out of spite. She's got much longer legs than I have and

I practically have to trot to keep up. Still, a fast pace means not enough puff left for talk, which is fine by me. I'm not really sure how to deal with last night. That was us making friends, wasn't it? Janey is in Girl Guide mode and has taken charge of map-and-compass drill. When we pause while she checks our co-ordinates, I take the opportunity to commune. A bank of blazing yellow gorse scents the entire hillside vanilla. The mountains pile up before us while, far below, the sea is lapping at the rocks in our bay. The clouds have disappeared and the wind has dropped. And there's not a soul in sight!

We climb on for the rest of the morning as the slope becomes steeper, the terrain rougher. A wisp of a waterfall snakes over a long rocky outcrop way ahead. Forty minutes later, we are scrambling and heaving our way through a narrow cleft in the outcrop. This seems serious stuff to me, not one of those 'toning strolls' Janey blithely talked about before the holiday began. My shins are getting scratched to buggery. It's painful breathing and sweat is cascading down my back. The temperature has soared and I've drunk all my water. Unfortunately, I haven't got the energy to complain. Not that the Patrol Leader would bother: she's already twenty metres ahead and steadily leaving me behind.

When, eventually, I stumble over the crest, superheated, dehydrated and drenched in perspiration, I'm hit with a mirage. A sparkling stream meanders across a pristine alpine meadow, its short, emerald turf scattered with boulders. The meadow is surrounded by buttresses of rock, a sun trap. It's like stumbling across a private Eden – and guess who's playing Eve. Yup, Janey.

I walk up, open-mouthed, to where she's splashing around completely nude in a pool, and stare at her. Sweat dribbles down the cleft of my bum. It dawns on me that Janey may conceivably have the right idea. I wrestle off my boots and tentatively poke a sweaty toe in the gurgling, peaty stream. Icy! Janey laughs kittenishly, 'Kaye, don't get coy. There's no one for miles.' I look around. She's got to be right. We're seven hundred metres up and we haven't seen a soul all day. I strip and launch myself into the pool. Like the plunge at a sauna, it's *so* cold you actually don't notice. The dark water feels soft and clean. I am instantaneously rehydrated. We flap about like a couple of mountain dryads, splashing each other and whooping and exalting in being naked. 'Isn't it amazing?' shouts Janey.

It is. The bottom is rocky, but soft. Over the years, the burn has scooped the stone into curvaceous little rills and these have become overgrown by a velvety, mossy growth, covering the rock like sponge. It should be slimy, but isn't. It's incredibly tactile, like a giant, downy, pubic-hair-covered mons. I find a little channel and wriggle back, allowing the stream to cascade over my head and shoulders and funnel down into my pubes, while I watch the Water-Sprite-formerly-known-as-Janey play in her grotto. She seems so right in this environment. Somehow, this is really her.

She scoots around the pool, walking on her fingers like a crayfish, slithering over exposed boulders and plunging into the deeper parts. 'Mmm, this is nice,' she murmurs, lying flat on her tummy and undulating against the stream bed. She looks at me, her face illuminated by a strangely intense grin. Water Sprite is doing curious humping shimmies that make her white arse bob in and out of the water and something tells me it ain't aerobics. I watch while she grinds herself languorously into a mossy boulder. I'm astonished but transfixed. Head Girl Janey has totally gone, replaced by this mysterious nymph who is staring at me with her sexy, sparkling eyes.

My nipples are so hard they hurt. I'm extremely aware of the meltwater sluicing over my own clit, despite the fact that it should by rights be frozen off. The Sprite is thrashing hard now, her mouth pouted, a frown of concentration across her forehead. Her breathing gets shallower and she starts making little panting 'Oh, oh, oh' noises as she abandons herself to vigorous, forceful shoves of her hips. I'm gripped by a desperate desire to see her come. She's just reaching the very cliff edge of orgasm when the moment is shattered, devastatingly, by a politely quizzical 'Hello?'

Two figures are silhouetted against the sun. Janey's twins? Fuck! Maybe this *is* all a mirage. Maybe I'm still asleep in Rub-a-Dub. I pinch a nipple. It hurts! Nope, I'm awake and these are just two regular climbing guys. Sprite has comported herself and is splashing water over her shoulders, pretending she's just taking a quick dip for her health. I slip under the pool surface and watch. Somehow, I don't feel embarrassed, more curious. The new arrivals are mid-twenties and not bad-looking in a rugged, outdoorsy way. Probably extremely fit. One of the guys is a dark-eyed, beardy Celt, the other, a floppy-haired blond with a handsome, open face. I'm curious whether they might be hot and bothered, too, after their climb, and might like to join us nature gals in our little pool party. Dress informal. Dress minimal, in fact. I splash a pretty foot enticingly and smile a wicked smile at my partner-in-crime.

Apparently not. There's a shuffling, tongue-tied silence while the guys harrumph a lot. Then, after a rather condescending, 'Don't let your body temperature drop too much,' the mountain men turn and stomp away summitwards. I watch their hard round buttocks disappearing up a ravine, perplexed and disappointed that they seem more anxious to conquer mountain peaks than mountain nymphs. All that stamina wasted. Did we say something wrong?

'Hungry?' asks Janey.

'Mmm, very!' I purr, and turn to find her fully dressed, be-hatted and presiding over a tartan-blanketed feast. 'Lunch? I thought we were indulging in *Carry On* innuendo.' I frown.

Janey swallows a morsel of sandwich and says, 'Oh, you mean hungry for sex? Didn't you come last night?' She knows? I feel my face colour. Janey studies me serenely. 'You're looking a bit red, Kaye. You really ought to cover up.'

Is she taking the piss? I clamber out of my splash pool, bitching, 'What about you?'

Janey shakes her head. 'Waterproof sun block. But *you* are about to exceed your burn time.'

I meant, 'What about you fucking that rock?' but I let the subject drop and turn to eating.

After we've scoffed everything, we continue scrambling up the mountain. We've devised a system where Janey bunks me up the bigger chunks, then I wedge myself into a crevice and haul her up. Y'know, team work and that. The mountain men have gone missing, I'm glad to say. They'd probably tell us off for doing it wrong and start giving instructions. Janey and I are doing fine and dandy by ourselves. We reach the saddle and, while we gasp for air, Janey suddenly asks, 'Do we go all the way?'

I take a deep breath. 'Do *you* want to?'

'Well, ye-es,' she pants, staring at some clouds, 'but the weather's closing in.'

I need to sort something here. 'Janey,' I say, 'we *are* talking mountain climbing?'

Janey smiles enigmatically and takes my hand. 'How about it, all the way?'

I swallow and nod.

Janey leads me to where the saddle narrows to a tightrope-thin edge and says, 'If we cross this col, we can do the summit and take a short cut back.'

The ridge is about a half a metre wide. The difficult bit is the dizzying drop on either side. She goes first, making it look too easy. My turn. I concentrate on Janey's serene smile of confidence as I edge slowly towards her, trying to ignore the fearful, fluttery feelings in my cunt. I stumble across into her arms and she half carries me on to a rocky plateau and that's it. You can see for forty miles in every direction. We're on top of the fucking world!

With the blackening sky, Janey suggests we leave pronto by the most direct route possible. We negotiate a way through a narrow gully on to a huge scree-strewn slope. We're picking our way downwards when the weather breaks. Maybe it's the team spirit, maybe the adrenaline, but neither of us seems to care. When I glimpse a couple of blurry, rain-shrouded figures below us, Janey focuses her binoculars. The mountain men, waving furiously. Five minutes later, we're on them. There's another embarrassed silence till they reveal they have A Situation. Overconfident scree-running in driving rain doesn't seem the cleverest of ideas to me. And the results – a wrenched knee and a severely twisted ankle – are both major problems under current circumstances. We fight the urge to lecture them and grab a boy each. Then we set off: two three-legged teams sliding arse over tit down the rain-lashed mountainside.

I say sliding, because, as soon as we stumble off the scree, we hit the peat and we're rolling around in mushy brown boggy stuff. I've got hold of the Beardy One by the waist, and a fine hunk he is, too. I know this, because he has landed on top of me twice, with much stiff-upper-lipped grimacing at the agony from his ankle. Janey is meanwhile hopping along with Blondie. I occasionally glimpse the pair of them floundering in the peat, desperately snatching at each other like a pair of horny anoraks. The whole episode has acquired a surreal intimacy.

After much slopping and sliding, groping and groaning, we make it to the safety of Rub-a-Dub. We stumble in from the sheeting rain and Janey assesses the situation. There's nothing intrinsically life-threatening about the boys' injuries, in her opinion – they just need to rest up. As everyone is totally plastered in muck and soaked to the skin, we suggest the boys clean themselves up while Janey and I do homey stuff like lighting the fire. I'm determined to ignore their injury-hampered attempts to undress at the far end, but all their crashing around distracts me and I can't help clocking a few details. Like the fine set of pecs on blondie David and the impressive six pack on Tam (the Celt). Must be a mountain-fitness thing. Y'know, broad shoulders from humping rucksacks everywhere, pert bums and solid thighs from pumping up those lofty alpine slopes, deep chests from exertion in that pure thin air.

When their tight, round buttocks finally slip into the shower, I get a first opportunity to discuss the situation with Janey. I think it's time to junk all that 'don't need men' bollocks and connect. 'Which one would you, um...?' I whisper tentatively. I'm happy to let Janey have first choice.

'Oh, I wasn't thinking of pairing off,' Janey says airily. 'Were you?'

I bluster and splutter a bit. Well, the thought did cross my mind, as I'd assumed it had hers, but obviously I've got it wrong again. This girl is so hard to fathom, I give up. Why did I come on holiday with an ex-Girl Guide?

By the time I get to shower (last), the guys are

sprawled over divans either side of a roaring stove. Tam, in Janey's rather snug-fitting spare trackies, is having his ankle strapped while David, very fetching in a minuscule pair of her shorts and a crêpe bandage, is studying her handiwork, obviously impressed. No doubt Janey got some badge or other for her skill. Otherwise, they're still stripped to their manly waists. Oh, what a waste. Janey stands and says brightly, 'That should do. Well, what can we do now, then?'

'Play charades?' I shout sulkily and dive under the jet. As the warm water sluices my naked body, I'm frustratingly aware of the hunks reclining half naked only metres away. My cunt is, too, I realise as I soap my groove. It's sopping wet (and not from rain) and eager for action. I slip a finger into the juicy slit and circle my clit. This is only making things worse. I'd love to sort myself out but this is hardly the moment for another episode of exhibitionism. Reluctantly, I stop. When I emerge, even more bad-tempered, from the shower in an ancient, baggy Fair Isle sweater, Rub-a-Dub is like a sauna. I'm towelling my hair, so I almost don't notice the empty whisky bottle on the floor that is pointing directly at me. 'We're playing Truth or Dare,' says Janey. 'Which d'you want?'

I'm not at all sure where Janey's coming from here. The guys are both looking annoyingly hot, their torsos gleaming softly in the warm glow of the candlelight as they pass a fresh bottle of McCallan between them.

'Dare,' I almost snarl and grab a swig as the whisky passes me.

'Fine,' she replies, 'dare it is. Now I can't help feeling you're a little stressed, so my dare is a really nice one. I dare you to have a foot massage.'

I plonk myself down and stick a foot out suspiciously.

Kneeling in front of me, Janey anoints it with her essential oil and begins to rub. She must have magic in those long slim fingers, because, soon, I've slumped back, silently enjoying her attentions while I glug some malt. Janey strokes and tickles each foot alternately, while prattling away to the guys about traversing cols and summitting peaks. I'm becoming aware I might have to be careful I don't summit, too. I manage to rouse myself and say pointedly, 'Janey, I think we should keep playing the game. Fuck the bottle, you go next. What'll it be?'

Janey hmms to herself, then says, 'Truth.'

Hah, got her, I think. 'OK,' I say. 'What exactly were you doing in that pool? When Tam and David interrupted?' I notice a quick, covert glance between the boys.

'Oh, I was thinking about you, Kaye,' she says, still stroking my feet. She turns to Tam. 'She'd orgasmed in front of me last night and I kept thinking about it. It made me feel nice. So I started, you know, rubbing myself against one of those moss-covered rocks and then my clit got quite stimulated. I wanted her to see *me* come. I thought she'd like it.' She concludes, 'I was just about to, when you two arrived.'

There's nothing to hear but the rain drumming on the roof and the hiss of the stove. And the thumping of my heart. How dare she tell? My belly is doing somersaults with all sorts of emotions but the link between my brain and my mouth is severed. Janey hasn't stopped foot rubbing once and the twinges in my tummy are joining up with twinges lower down. Maybe I gave away too many secrets last night, because she seems to know exactly how to immobilise me. She looks me in the face, her eyes twinkling. I remember that twinkle from the mountain. Then she turns to David, 'Your turn, David. Truth or dare?'

He shrugs. 'Truth?'

'OK. Have you and Tam ever fucked the same girl? At the same time?' she asks.

David's cheeks do a fetching impression of a Scottish sunset as he stammers, 'No,' drawing the word out till it merges into a shy grin.

I realise that one of Janey's hands has moved up my legs, her fingernails gently circling my inner thigh. There's an electricity flowing from her touch that's more potent than anything I've ever felt before, generating little trails of energy that reach right into my cunt. I want to squirm away, but my muscles have stopped obeying orders and I'm lying there with my legs slightly apart, nearly revealing that I'm not wearing any knickers. I don't know if the boys have noticed.

'Tam,' she says, 'truth or dare? What'll it be?'

He strokes his jet-black beard and laughs. 'I'm up for a dare.' The boys are obviously getting into the game.

'Brave man,' says Janey, turning to me. 'It's Kaye's turn to choose.'

As I try to think, Janey slips her hand quite naturally under my sweater and her thumb just flicks my lips. I find myself staring wildly at the boys' crotches. There are taut bulges in both the borrowed items of clothing. Janey's gently rubbing the top of my slit. The sweater has ridden up, exposing my cunt. I swallow. 'I dare you to take your cocks out and rub them with the oil.' I add hoarsely, 'Both of them.'

Wordlessly, Tam kneels up and shucks Janey's trackie bottoms carefully over his ankles. A large, handsome cock springs out, surrounded by a Caledonian forest of hair. He slowly dribbles oil along its length. Then he takes it in his hand and pulls the foreskin firmly back, allowing the deep purple tip to push out. He massages the oil into it, his black eyes burning into mine. His beautiful, dark cock swells right up to his six pack. Then he leans across me, his luscious erection swaying almost into my face, and yanks David's shorts over his thighs. I'm hypnotised by the sight of another fat cock, this one surrounded by a mass of downy blond. Tam takes it in his hand and David groans as it stiffens. I reach out and steady Tam's swinging hard-on, stoking his black-haired balls while I watch him masturbate David's cock slowly and purposefully till both are huge and swollen and anointed with oil. I pull my sweater up, exposing my tits, and draw Tam's glans tantalisingly across my nipples, smearing them with oil and pre-come till they glisten in the candlelight. David is sprawled out naked on a divan, a monumental erection springing out of his groin. The heat coursing through my veins is hotter than the fire roaring up the stove chimney. My thighs have fallen wide open and someone's fingers, I don't know whose, are teasing my cunt hole and I'm feeling luxuriously, opulently sexual. I hear Janey's voice over the thumping pulse in my ears: 'Well, Kaye. All the way, to the top?'

I try to move my lips but someone's mouth meets mine in a hungry, unyielding kiss that slowly pulls away. Janey's voice whispers fiercely in my ear. 'Two cocks, do you want to?'

I groan in assent. I'm gently pulled on to my knees, then manoeuvred on top of David's erection. It slides right up me to the hilt. I sink on to his broad chest and squirm myself into his tense, muscular body. I feel fingers lubricating my arse and I lift my hips to let them enter. Then something hard and swollen stretches the hole with its girth. I feel a weight on my back and jet-black hair drapes the side of my face. Someone lifts my own hair and I feel Tam's beard tickle my neck as his teeth begin to nibble at the nape. His hot breath burns my skin. He starts to build a rhythm, pulling in and out slowly and taking me with him, so my cunt is simultaneously drawn along David's cock. Far, far away, I can feel a delicious pressure on my feet as Janey continue to massage, one hand on each foot. I think of her eyes looking at me in the pool. I remember my images of her, taking the twins' cocks, when I wanked last night. I think of me wanking while watching her. I think of the boys' gorgeous cocks taking me now, and, suddenly, I'm there, there at the top. Right on top of the fucking world!

It was another two whole days before the storm subsided. That, combined with the boys' injuries meant forty-eight hours holed up with them (so to speak). Janey and I didn't waste the opportunity we had to improve our mountain craft, oh no. Plus, we all learned a lot more about creative teamwork. Y'know, group dynamics and such. Two into one does go, very nicely, thank you, as does three into one and two into two as well. I learned a lot more about Janey too. She's not a WYSISWYG girl. You have to look a bit closer to find the real Janey. Like the mountain, she was there all along but I just couldn't see her. We're pretty good friends now. As Janey says, we rub along together perfectly.

# **Neighbours** Terry Batten

I don't know my lover's name. It's not a *Last Tango in Paris*-type scenario: it's a little more weird than that.

I first 'met' him some weeks ago now. I was sitting on my balcony, surrounded by candles, cocktails, wine, and two of my friends. My balcony does not have a view: it looks out the back of my flat, and onto the back of other flats, so we were quite sheltered. It was a hot night – it always is here in August, which is why most people just get out of the city, and also why there weren't any other lights around. No flickering of a TV set, no lights dimmed by curtains and mosquito nets, no sound of radios or hum of soap operas. And then there was a light. None of us noticed until the man appeared, naked – and visible, through his open window – from the knees up. Jennifer gasped in astonishment and pointed him out to her boyfriend and to me. 'He's not . . .' she said. 'Oh my God, he is!'

We all looked to see if he really was, and, sure enough, his right elbow was pounding away.

'Do you think he can see us?' asked Jennifer.

'Surely not!' exclaimed her boyfriend, Gavin. I agreed with him. I didn't think it would be possible to see us in the dim light that our candles gave, and he was a fair distance from us: we couldn't make out his features, or tell whether he was old or young.

We watched him, fascinated, as he completed his task, and ended spectaculady by staggering backwards and collapsing. We laughed, and got on with the more serious business of drinking.

'Half an hour later he was back again, and this time we decided to make him aware of our presence. We waved and cheered, and he promptly disappeared, light swiftly following. But not for long. He came back, peering round the wall and out of his window. He started with just a part of his face, but his elbow's frantic movements were also obvious. As he got himself more and more excited, he became more confident of himself, and once again stood full frontal, working his organ into a frenzy.

We thought it was funny, even the second and third times. Jenny even suggested *I* go and give the man a hand, so to speak.

The next day, though, we were a little more concerned.

'Be careful,' said Gavin, as they hugged me goodbye.

'Your neighbour was kind of funny when we were all together having a drink, but the guy must be some kind of pervert. I mean, he knew we were watching him.'

'I guess that makes us perverts too,' I said,

'Ye-es,' said Gavin, 'but, even so, I would be careful when you're on your balcony.'

I came out on to the balcony every night after that, just for a few minutes, but I didn't see him until the third night. I watched him, in the dark. I don't believe he could see me. The next night, I lit all the candles on my balcony, and sat there with a book, waiting.

Eventually he appeared, and started his ritual. I stood up to watch him, and started to touch my own breasts, squeezing my nipples between the fabric of my dress. As my mystery neighbour began to climax, I wet my fingers in my mouth, licking two of them all around, and placed them under my dress.

My neighbour finished his stunt, and collapsed, turning his light off, and I disappeared into my room, and continued to pleasure myself until I shuddered into a climax.

The next night, I was ready for him. My dress was almost transparent, and I had arranged a pile of cushions, so that I could lie down, and watch my neighbour at the same time. The candles lit, I watched his window, and waited.

He appeared in his window, with a soft glow from his faint light behind him. He looked out over at me, and started to pull on himself, watching me. I touched my nipples again, then licked the tips of my thumb and forefinger, and used them to squeeze my nipples, until my breath could be heard, and I'm sure he heard me. He slowed down, as I moved my hand underneath my dress, and pushed the fabric up to reveal lacy underwear. I pushed into the lace, and played with it, as my other hand caressed the soft mound that was there. Eventually, I slipped the panties off, and tossed them to one side, with a groan that was audible all around the back of the flats.

I pulled my dress off, too, and lay there, naked in the candlelight, carressing my body, teasing my nipples, then rubbing my clit, all the time looking at my neighbour. He watched me, too, as he pumped away. I slowly put my middle finger into my open mouth, and then closed my lips around it, pushing my finger in and not quite out, in a steady rhythm that I followed with slight upward thrusts from my pelvis. My neighbour paused in his endeavours, placed his hands high on his window and pressed his penis to the glass. I placed some cushions under my backside, raising my sex up towards him. I took my finger from my mouth and slowly inserted it inside me, as my neighbour grabbed his rock-hard cock, and the two of us moved in a rhythm, as one, despite the distance between us.

When we had finished, he collapsed out of sight, and his light was extinguished a few seconds after. I lay there on my balcony, twitching sporadically as my orgasm tailed off. I lay there alone for a long time, until I finally gathered up my cushions and went to bed.

The next night, he was waiting for me when I came out on to the balcony. My hair was held up in a loose ponytail, and I was wearing a tight, cropped, vest-type T-shirt, and very tight jeans shorts. I had a spray bottle with me, and started by spraying my plants. I'm sure he thought I wasn't going to play that night, but then I started to spray my breasts, and soon my top became transparent. I sat on a chair, and continued to spray myself, as he watched me. He put one hand on the window, and with the other he started to touch himself lightly.

I spread my legs, put both my hands at the top of my inner thighs and started to rub upwards, over the jeans towards my navel, and then down again to my thighs. Then my left hand travelled over my body to play with my breasts, as my right hand grabbed the fabric of my jeans, pushing the hard rough seam between my legs closer to my body. Suddenly my left hand flew down to grab the wrist of my right, and I flung my head back over the back of the chair, closing my eyes. My hair came tumbling out of my hairband, and my mouth started to open, and not quite close, repeatedly, as if I were stifling back a groan, or as if I were giving pleasure to someone. I moved my head up slightly and opened my eyes, looking straight at my lover, with a look so full of sex that he should have come right there and then. The distance between us did not allow him the pleasure of seeing that look, but nonetheless he was excited, and he grabbed his stiff cock firmly, and started to ease his hand up and down along the length.

I unbuttoned the top button of my shorts, then the next, and then I slid my hand in and made my way down. He could not see what my hand was doing, only the way my body thrust itself upwards, pushing my breasts up, the nipples rock-hard and visible through the flimsy top, and my left hand reaching up and behind me, grabbing on to the wall for support.

After a while, I stood up, hand still firmly in place, and faced him. Slowly I withdrew my hand, and gently sucked on my moist fingers. I replaced my hand, and bent my knees outwards, lowering myself down towards the ground, hand moving rapidly as I did so, then I slowly rose up again. As I stood up, I put both hands on my hips, and pushed my shorts down to my feet. I was naked underneath, and my wetness glinted in the candlelight.

His breath was coming so short and rapid that you could see it on his windowpane. Perhaps that was why he opened the window. He stood there, his penis looking out over the window, and he was so full of lust that for a moment I was afraid he would fall, but he grabbed the top of the frame with his left hand, and continued his strokes with his right.

I sat back down on the edge of the chair, and leaned back, lifting my feet up to rest on the edge of the knee-high iron rail that walled in my balcony. From under the chair, I pulled out a large, pink, penis-shaped vibrator, and I used it to caress my entire body. Starting under my chin, I made my way up to my face, and teased my mouth by letting the vibrator brush my lips, threatening to push its way in. When it finally did, I lapped at the phallus, while my left hand teased my nipples. Then I trailed the vibrator down to my breasts. and switched the machine on, allowing it to vibrate gently against the wet cloth that was stuck to my nipples. I sucked on the vibrator again before allowing it to travel downwards to where my sex was waiting, pulsating in anticipation.

My lover struggled to hold down his climax as he waited for my vibrator to penetrate. I looked straight at him again as I pushed the plastic cock into me, and I allowed its size and pulsations to bring me frantically to a loud groaning orgasm. He let go as my thrusts became more frantic, and our groans raised up into the night air, and joined together as one in a way our bodies never could.

And then he left me, as he does every night after orgasm, melting into the darkness of his room. He leaves me, lying or sitting on my balcony, leaves me with the afterglow of sex to comfort me. And the truth is, that's all I require from him. I don't want to know his name. I don't want him to hold me in his arms, or tell me that he loves me. I don't want to have to talk to him. I like the feeling of being in control, deciding when I want to play with him, how I am going to be pleasured. I feel as if I am in control of him; I have taken control of his fantasies. I want to enjoy our strange relationship for the short period that it will last. And even there I am in control, because only I know I am moving on soon, to a flat with a better view.

# Under Wraps Kit Mason

Every morning, for Maxine, dressing was a ritual. With her flatmate Sarah, she would lie on the bed contemplating the open wardrobe. Freshly showered, a tiny dusting of talcum powder on breasts and bottom, she would choose the underwear first. For Maxine now the day had begun to take form, the delicious constraints of fabric, strap and buckle taking over.

Standing in her underwear, translucent black bra studded with tiny pink roses and string stretching pleasurably over anus, Maxine bent over to select a pair of high-heeled sandals that belonged to Sarah. Shoes were the only articles of clothing they could share: Sarah being tall and slim, and Maxine usually unable to squeeze her curves into most of Sarah's tiny dresses. Maxine's tastes in clothes were eclectic. Designer clothes seemed pointless to her. What was important was dressing every day as if for a drama. Sarah looked up from the bed.

'So who are you going to be today?' she asked, with one eyebrow raised.

After much deliberation Maxine chose a grey silk blouse with a straight skirt split up the front. The high-heeled, strappy sandals and long elegant coat combined to make the look slightly reminiscent of the forties.

They both emerged from their pigsty of a flat (housekeeping was not high on their list of priorities) sweet and fresh-smelling. As usual, Maxine and Sarah went their separate ways at the corner of the street – Sarah heading for the city and Maxine for the little arcade in the shopping centre.

That moment every day felt like a liberation, rich with joy and possibility, people and shops and clothes. On the way to work, pinched-looking men in suits roamed her body with inquisitive eyes as if they were starving and she were a feast. She wanted them to taste her joy, to draw their heads to her breast and let them suckle there at her abundance, sharing her sense of life. She'd grown tired of honest straightforward fucking, the bump and grind of earnest young men. She was looking for something complicated, somehow, dressed up and fancy – Marlene Dietrich encased in satin, looking into the camera with one raised eyebrow.

There was something about the exclusive otherworldliness of the arcade that made you feel as if you were entering another universe. It felt something like swimming underwater: the daylight came down only after being filtered through frosted glass and sounds seemed muted and muffled. The lingerie shop where she worked always reminded her of Zola's eulogy of girl's underwear on sale in Paris: 'It looked as if a group of pretty girls had undressed piece by piece, down to the satin nudity of their skin.' Either that or, with all its striped wallpaper and gilt, a kinky version of a Doris Day movie.

The old-fashioned glamour of the shop was the perfect antidote to the club scene that took up so much of Maxine's weekend. The sweat, the heat, the intense music and the near-naked bodies were one kind of energy. The rustling enclosure of the corset held another kind of repressed energy, somehow more exciting because it didn't reveal itself all at once. Maxine had always harboured a lust for the expensive stuff – now she was surrounded by it. The silk and lace whispered as she walked by to open drawers that revealed tiny, exquisite items, the price tags seemingly out of all proportion for such pieces of flimsy.

Corinne, the owner of the shop, had noted how the sales of underwear sold to men had gone up tenfold since Maxine had been working there. Her lush sense of availability seemed something of a draw in such an intimate environment. They bought ostensibly for their wives, their partners' measurements being kept discreetly on a Rolodex under the counter.

'Ah, yes, for Mrs Edmunds, a 34C. Is this the sort of thing she might appreciate?' And Maxine would spread a boned and fluted basque out on the counter, arranging the little panties that went with it prettily underneath.

'See, of course this is all silk. Even the lace is made of silk, and if Sir would care to feel . . . ?' she would say impishly. Maxine made sure she bent over so the top of her cleavage could be seen and the man would finger the lace with shaking hands.

One of the drawbacks, if it can be called that, of being so constantly aware of her body, of feeling flesh so firmly pressed by clothing and nubbed lace chafing at her, was that Maxine felt almost permanently half aroused. Sometimes this was a mere itch but other times it became an urgent need. Gazing out at the shifting crowds outside the shop window, she would reach down and hook her finger through her knickers, softly patting her swollen clit until, with a rush of honey wetting her seat, she would come almost imperceptibly.

This was an art she had developed over the years. She could come quickly and easily by a variety of different methods she had devised. Sitting on the arm of a chair could be very fruitful and, once, she had made herself come on the tube in front of at least twenty people simply by letting her bag swing back and forth to the rhythm of the train, each nudge sending her into greater silent transport. The only sign of orgasm was a practically imperceptible sigh.

So when he entered the shop she had reluctantly to withdraw her hand from between her legs, fingers wet with dew, leaving her body aflame. His largish head, light-blue eyes and muscular legs looked vaguely Germanic and also slightly familiar – she was sure she had seen him around before. Unlike most men who made straight for the counter, as if they were on a sinking ship and they needed to reach the life raft, he took a minute to look around. Maxine studied the way his dark, long overcoat skimmed over his large body as he studied a glass case displaying knickers. Underneath he wore a rough tweedy suit and fashionably long shirt collar. He swung round abruptly catching her staring.

'I want to buy something for my wife.' His voice rose seductively from his chest rather than his throat. He put both powerful hands on the counter, invading her space.

Maxine felt a stab of disappointment. 'Do we keep her details on file here?' she enquired, a touch frostily, and peeved that he dared to have a wife and a life of his own.

'Yes, her name is Mrs Chadwick, the initial is K. We have been customers here for some time.'

Conscious her body was still in a state of excitement, she leaned down to retrieve the details from the Rolodex. She saw from the corner of her eye that he was looking down her front and she became suddenly aware that it was likely that the fiery flush of excitement was still marking her neck and bosom.

'May I ask if it is an anniversary or birthday you are buying for?' she asked nosily.

He smiled enigmatically. 'Something like that,' he replied, his eyes running up and down her body.

What a strange job, she thought to herself. Here she stood, selling the kinkiest of expensive underwear as if it were cabbages or wallpaper. The fact that women would fold themselves into little items of silk and lace and their partners would pull the crotch to one side to reveal their slits was not spoken of. The fact that nipples could be glimpsed tantalisingly through translucent fabric and pubic hair was glimpsed in enchanting tufts through a froth of lace was completely ignored. Up until now, Maxine had never been so conscious of what it was she was actually selling. She could almost sense that he knew, could read her filthy thoughts, and realised what she had been doing when he stepped into the shop and how her nipples were aching to be licked and her fanny teased and played with.

He shifted his gaze to something pinned up behind her. It was a full-length rust-coloured corset with tiny ribbons all down the front.

'What about that?' he suggested.

Maxine turned to take the garment from its padded hanger and laid it on the counter. Mrs Chadwick floated invisibly between them. He held the garment in his thick fingers and stared at Maxine's body unashamedly. She had never experienced such intense flirting with so few words.

'I like the shape of this, its curves. But have you something similar in a pale pink, like the colour of a shell?' he asked in a formal tone, which only served to heighten the feeling of illicit naughtiness to the situation.

Unusual in such exact specifications, men usually proffered their credit cards and then turned and ran. But he was obviously trying to draw the experience out. Maxine was more than happy to go along with it. She dug out an ivory corset with a very pale-pink sheen to show him. He looked at the confection before him and then at Maxine, as if mentally picturing her wearing it.

'Look,' she said wickedly, 'this style features an opening down the front instead of the back, using these hooks and eyes.' She popped a couple open between the cups for effect.

'It's beautiful.' He spoke quietly with an air of a man who appreciates such things.

He seemed about to say something else when a couple of youngish women came into the shop, making the doorbell clang noisily.

When Maxine left for lunch, she heard a soft whistle from down the side alley that led to the back of a row of shops, and she somehow knew he would be waiting. His long overcoat was unbuttoned and he did nothing to attempt to hide the mound of his erection. Simultaneously as his mouth fastened on to hers he drew her hand to feel his rock-stiff cock. She traced her fingers under the rough fabric of his trousers like a pickpocket, a delicate, talented street thief, and his breathing began to intensify.

At the other end of the alley people passed back and forth. He leaned one arm against the wall and let his coat fall in front of them, like a curtain. The golden lining made a rustling sound as it drew around them. He stroked her breasts through her blouse, the fabric grazing the stippled lace underneath. Slowly he opened a couple of buttons and pulled at the edge of her bra so that one nipple peeked over the top. When he tugged it between finger and thumb, it puckered up almost instantly.

Breathing hard, Maxine leaned over and glanced over his shoulder. Anyone who bothered to look down the side passage would assume they were involved in a passionate argument or locked into an embrace. She was too far gone to care, anyway: she was now in a state of turmoil, and could feel her lips hanging down, wet and stiff and heavy, in a state of greedy wantonness.

He moved his fingers down over her stomach, tracing the shape of her pubic bone, and put his hand carefully into the front slit of her dress, which conveniently reached nearly to the top of her thighs – one reason she had chosen it. As he put his hand between her legs his nostrils quivered, as if the action had sent a whiff of juicy female odour wafting up.

The click, click of heels in the background started to form a rhythm in her head and gave time to her breathing, which was so heavy now that she was sure people could hear it for miles. He parted the slit in her skirt, revealing her most flimsy panties – practically a triangle of gauze on a string. Through the white gauze her fleshy lips were very visible, her sticky wetness gluing them to the fabric. He sighed happily as he looked down.

He began to tease her clit through the material and Maxine had to bite her lip in an effort not to scream. He rubbed away with the tip of his finger and it was as if the whole of her body was concentrated into one point, as if all that existed was a few millimetres of clit and his probing finger.

As her knickers became wetter and wetter they began to chafe delightfully against her labia and her arsehole. Her breathing became frenzied as he took one of her earlobes into his mouth and bit it gently, the rough fabric of his jacket grazing her nipples. As her desire escalated, her stomach began to contract and she came in a welter of wetness, putting her hand over her mouth to suppress the noise.

Taking a shaky breath, she saw him looking hungrily, almost pained at waiting for his own exquisite relief. Feeling her way down, she unzipped his trousers and his cock sprang out indolently. He was wearing nothing between himself and the coarse tweed of his trousers. It was already hard in her hand, but as she gave it a first few tentative strokes, it became even more taut, straining almost to bursting.

Maxine looked down and gasped: the sight of his huge cock rearing out from his suited attire had to be the horniest thing she had ever seen. She grasped it with renewed enthusiasm and began stroking it the whole length, his purple bulb becoming visible each time she drew his foreskin back. It took only half a dozen strokes before he closed his eyes and groaned softly as he disgorged his load into her hand.

After a few microseconds the world seemed to return. He quickly zipped himself up and did up her blouse buttons. He leaned over and kissed her deeply with what seemed like immense gratitude before turning on his heel and leaving. Maxine was left standing with a beatific smile on her face and a handful of come.

'You did what?' exclaimed Sarah later that evening. They always shared their sexual adventures as they did their shoes.

Giggling over a plate of pasta and a glass of wine at the cramped kitchen table, Sarah could hardly keep the admiration from her voice. She took a big swig from her glass.

'I want to know every detail.' The telling must have made her hot under the collar, because Sarah disappeared rather abruptly, presumably to wake the slumbering man in her bed, judging by the sounds coming from her bedroom.

Maxine waited for him to return all week. This was new to her and she felt annoyed with herself that she was bothered that he didn't show. But towards the end of the week she was starting to go mad with expectation and frustration. The incident had burned its way into her memory and her body ached for more. 'It's not as if I want to marry him: I only want to fuck him,' she muttered to herself, as another day passed without his putting in an appearance. She even volunteered to take on more shifts.

'I need the money, and, besides, I've nothing better to do,' she lied to Corinne, who was rushed off her feet setting up another shop and seemed quite grateful.

'There's new stock coming in on Friday. Can you put it straight on display? Apart from that it's all yours, love,' she said, dropping the keys to the safe into Maxine's hand.

The delivery arrived on Friday morning before she had even opened up the shop, and she began slicing the boxes open with a Stanley knife, aware of the fragility of the contents. Maxine gasped as she took each piece out. It was simply the most exquisite lingerie she had ever seen. She reflected how gorgeous it was to walk around with the secret knowledge that you were wearing such delicious, hidden garments.

It all seemed designed to tease: basques, made of sheer black net and scalloped lace, were laced up the front, leaving bows dangling enticingly between the breasts; knickers were little silk snippets tied at either side; bras were embroidered gauze in the 'balconette' style Maxine loved so much, designed so the top of the bra skimmed straight across the breasts and pushed everything up in a voluptuous style. Even slips – slips that Maxine had always associated with the Women's Institute – were entrancing, made of gauzy lace at the breasts, held up by spaghetti straps and flaring out in filmy material, baby-doll style, just long enough to skim the thighs.

Since she'd started working here most of her wages seemed to be eaten up buying the same stuff that she was selling, and Maxine sighed as she saw another wage packet going back to her employer. Still, it was worth it, and she began sorting the items, putting to one side those she was going to keep herself.

Impatient to admire herself, Maxine took everything she'd chosen through to the changing room, a little space at the back covered by a heavy red and white striped curtain. She flung her clothes on the little curved, velvet couch and hooked herself into the basque, enjoying the way her breasts spilt generously over the top. The knickers slipped on like a whisper and she finished off the whole effect with a pair of hold-up stockings, encrusted with lace around the thighs. Maxine admired herself in the mirror, turning and looking at the ensemble from behind, her bottom peeking cheekily from its constraints. She dressed quickly. Her starchy, white blouse and schoolgirlish navy skirt made a naughty contrast with the fuck-me underwear. She squirted herself with the perfume that was kept there for customers, letting it run down her arms.

After opening the shop she set up the new displays, laying the bras and knickers under the glass counter. She decided to use one of the basques for the front window. It was while she was dressing the strange, truncated mannequin in the window that she became aware of being watched, just a sensation from the corner of her eye. She leaned over so her full cleavage was displayed, aware of the image she was creating as she laced the tantalising garment tighter around the mannequin's unyielding body.

The bulge in his trousers was visible already, the hunger on his face blatant. He wore a silky suit, a crisp, white shirt and the same long coat as before. Not handsome exactly, certainly not a pretty boy, but powerful as if he were made for sex. Maxine let him in, locking the door and flicking over the CLOSED sign in one movement. The world would just have to wait for its undergarments.

'I've been past many times,' he said, 'but every time the shop's been busy. I wanted to clear everyone out and fuck you on the floor. I watched you for a while each time.' He sounded breathless.

She pictured him in the shop doorway across the way, masked in the shadows, avidly watching as she bent over to adjust some little piece of lacy nothing on its wire rack. She revelled in the attention – of being spied on.

'I've been so busy, I've hardly had time to think about it,' she lied. She felt that his erratic appearances needed some payback; she didn't want to melt in front of him at first sight.

He ignored this and went on. 'Every morning I've woken from a dream about you. You're on a fashion runway and you pause as you strut by me. The dress you're wearing is eighteenth-century, the kind that pushes everything up and is constricted round the waist,' he added inconsequentially. As he spoke he came closer and Maxine caught his clean, masculine smell, which reminded her of berries and wood bark.

'You start to slowly strip off your clothes, taking time to unbutton and untie everything. When your dress comes off you're wearing the corset I bought the other day. Everyone in the room can see, but they know it's just for me.'

'What happens then?' Maxine could almost feel the dress rustling around her legs.

'You perch on the edge of the catwalk with your legs wide open and I start to eat you. I can almost taste my dream. Everyone's watching, craning their necks to get a better view. They know something wonderful is happening. You lie back and open your legs further and everyone in the audience murmurs in appreciation. I wake up in a state of rather obvious excitement.' He said the last bit cheerfully, the crow's feet crinkling round his bright-blue eyes.

Swept along by the images, Maxine could feel the band of constriction around her waist and her cunt as if agitated by his tongue.

In the changing room, underneath the smell of the perfume she'd doused herself in only hours earlier, was the sweet, earthy scent of women's bodies. His nostrils quivered as he entered and breathed in the odour. Afraid that any hesitation between them might break the trance, Maxine positioned herself in front of the mirror and knelt down in front of him. Unbuttoning his fly, she noted that again he was without underwear, allowing the thick, soft silk of his trousers to chafe his shaft tenderly.

Pausing a moment to breathe in the hot scent of his bulging groin, she fixed her mouth to the end of his knob and began to suck gently, savouring his salty maleness. He groaned and tangled his fingers in her hair, pushing her head forward to gently encourage the pleasuring. As she licked and sucked, Maxine swivelled her eyes so she could see them both in the mirror. The picture that greeted her was so blatant and dirty that her fanny quivered and contracted in pleasure.

He stood there fully dressed, just his cock, red and hard, sticking out from his flies, Maxine's mouth stretched over the end, sucking and nibbling as if on some rare delicacy. His eyes followed hers, and, obviously fired by what he saw, he moaned and ran his finger around her stretched and taut lips.

Curious about the rest of his anatomy, Maxine eased his trousers down his thighs, which were tense with the strain of thrusting his cock forward. Taking a moment to admire the expensive fabric that rustled beneath her fingers, she unclamped her mouth from his knob and ran her hand down to cup his balls, which were hard and tight. She peeked into the mirror again as she gently squeezed his balls. God, his cock was beautiful, truly beautiful, arching proudly forward, ribbed and tense with the end blazing purple and angry.

Wanting him behind her, Maxine stood in front of him so his cock nestled into the scratchy softness of her skirt between her bum cheeks.

'You look like a naughty schoolgirl today,' he whispered into the mirror, 'in your little white collar.'

'Why don't you see how naughty I can be?' goaded Maxine.

With shaking fingers he undid the buttons down the front of her blouse so she spilled out, and pulled up her skirt revealing her stocking tops and knickers. They both admired her in the mirror, hair falling over her shoulders, cheeks looking as if they'd been smacked and her dark bush strapped down by the triangle of fine mesh that made up her knickers, ready to spring up and be played with.

'A *very* naughty schoolgirl?' he suggested, squeezing her laced-up breasts together as he drank in her underwear. 'Kneel on the couch – I want to see you open up.' He sounded breathless.

She moved so that she was kneeling on the velvet couch, arse in the air. Exposed, excited, her cunt was truly hungry now so that her juices were seeping through her knickers. He looked down and firmly flicked the string on her knickers so it bit into her arsehole and sent waves of excitement through her body. Pulling her knickers to one side, he let his cock nudge her opening, nestling his knob end against her outer lips.

In the mirror she could see him looking down, contemplating the sight of her slithery slit. He was panting like a dog now. He pushed his way in just a tiny bit, teasing her and thrusting just enough to send her crazy. She waggled her bum in the air, trying to push him further in.

'Your arsehole looks like a beautiful little flower,' he said, softly.

Tenderly he held each of her arse cheeks, separating them, pulling her wet slit even more open and admiring the stretch of her anus. He stuck his finger in his mouth and coated it with saliva, then used the moisture to gain access to her arsehole. Gently he inserted his finger, admiring the effect of himself occupying both of her precious orifices.

As she saw him look down once again in the mirror she thought, not for the first time, how lucky men were that they could see everything.

'I want to see,' she gasped. Pulling out, he turned around so she could view everything in the mirror. This time he entered her fully and she saw his rigid cock disappear right up to the hilt and then emerge gleaming and coated with her juice.

The dimly lit room had taken on the aura of a peep-show booth, the images in the mirror being the offering for sex-hungry clients. It was almost as if, should the curtains part, rows of Victorian gentlemen would be revealed, watching their performance appreciatively. Maxine exclaimed, 'That looks so dirty.' She pushed herself higher. 'Open me out, fill me right up,' she gabbled incoherently, groaning for more.

The textures of skin, lace, wool, satin and Maxine's heady juices merged in glorious union with hooks and eyes, buttons and secret openings. He leaned forward and fumbled with her corseted breasts and then tugged on the bow between them, finally pulling them free. 'Let me see those creamy white tits,' he panted.

He cupped them both from underneath, squeezing the nipples hard – nipples that were almost as sensitive as her clit. Waves of deliciousness ran up and down her body, pleasure running from her tits connecting with her fanny and her arsehole, which were contracting in pleasure.

Looking at his face, Maxine could see he was on the verge of coming. She slipped her finger between her legs to find her gleaming clit. The little button that she loved and treasured so much was standing out puffy and hard. Between finger and thumb she began to rub herself furiously, each stroke intensifying the electricity in her body.

Finally, one look in the mirror sent her over the edge, his finger pulling her knickers to one side, skirt up around her waist. His cock was stroking in and out between her legs, her tits spilling out of their constraint and bouncing heavily with each thrust, her finger busily stroking her delicious clit. The image conjured up a naughty Victorian drawing: he fully clothed, cock shafting from his heavy coat and suit; she stripped to her underwear – like the master and the maid caught in the act. She came with a heavy sigh of joy. Afterwards she idly wondered whether it could be heard from the street. Almost instantly he gave an enormous grunt and, with a final slam into her, he came, legs flexing with each wave as he pumped every last little bit of spunk inside her.

The changing room stank of sex for days afterwards and, every time she wanted to remember the most delicious fuck she'd ever had, all she had to do was to go in there and fill her nostrils with the smell. The memory made her slide her hand inside her blouse and play with her nipples, which hardened into tiny pebbles. But soon the ripe odour began to fade and all she was left with was a cunt that felt permanently creamy and ready, which no amount of masturbation could seem to satisfy.

Even flexing her plastic on a new skirt that buttoned all the way up the back and hobbled her ankles, a plunging bra that squeezed her tits together and leather boots that zipped up the side didn't help. She could just envisage them fucking in it all, her legs wrapped around him, heels pressing into the flesh on his back.

It really pissed her off that anyone could create such heart-stopping longing in her. As usual it was Sarah who took her in hand.

'Get his wife's details off that file in the shop and find him that way.' She was clearly losing patience.

'But what if he doesn't want to be found? I don't even know his first name,' Maxine moaned from the sofa, slices of cucumber over her eyes, enormous gin and tonic in hand.

'Then fuck him,' Sarah said practically.

So, feeling like a stalker, Maxine turned up at his house the next day wondering what her cover story was if Mrs Chadwick were to answer the door. She retrieved a clipboard from the chaos of the back seat of the car and mouthed to herself in the mirror.

'I'm doing a survey on . . . on orange juice. You could enter a prize draw to win a week in Florida.' She looked down at her pointy, extravagantly heeled, naughtily peep-toed shoes for comfort. What she really wanted to say was, 'Hi, I'm Maxine. I want to fuck your husband's brains out, whoever he is, because he has the most delicious dick in town, and if you don't like it . . .'

Feeling distinctly creepy, she approached the house, which was a hideous mock-Tudor semi. Something about its suburban smugness really infuriated Maxine and she rang on the bell loudly, keeping her finger pushed on the button for far too long. As she took her hand away he opened the door, obviously about to go out.

'Come in,' he said quickly. In the hallway he couldn't take his eyes off her. 'I've had so much shit to sort out first but I was coming to see you, I really was, this morning.'

Although she was nearly panting at the sight of him, she felt he needed a little punishment, so she slipped off her coat to display her outfit, wanting him to have to look but not touch. Underneath she wore a tight little virginal T-shirt with a flaring skirt – she'd had Sandy from *Grease* in mind when she'd dressed this morning. He seemed to like the look because he eyed her as if she were a luxury sweet he wanted to gobble up straightaway. Her eyes flicked to the back of the house.

'She's gone. We're putting this pile up for sale tomorrow,' he said, and slid his hand over her breast. Maxine decided he'd had enough punishment and began to unzip his flies.

'Why did she go?' she asked, not much interested.

'Because of that,' he said, nodding down.

At that moment Maxine put her hand over his rapidly hardening cock, revealing what she'd kind of known all along. Under his dark woollen suit he wore tiny, pale-blue, lacy knickers which restrained his bulging cock to the point that they were almost ripping. The ultra-feminine film of lace contrasted magnificently with the thick, purple end of his dick, which was rearing over the top. Joyfully, she traced the shape of his cock through its lacy confines, almost laughing out loud in disbelief at the other woman's folly.

# Desirable Residence
## Primula Bond

The interior of the house was pitch black. This was how it would have been when it was originally built, in the days before electricity. All the plasterwork details on the walls and doors edged out of the orange street light, which elbowed its way past her to pierce the gloom. The front door creaked open to reveal a man who seemed as indistinct at first as the building around him. From where Fran shuffled her feet on the worn doorstep it looked as if he was floating a few inches above the hall floor.

'Rather awkward, I'm afraid, with no illumination.' He cleared his throat as if he hadn't spoken for months. 'Perhaps you'd rather come back tomorrow, when there's some light. Can't see the detail on a dark evening like this.'

She shook her head with what she hoped was a businesslike smile and stepped inside. He flattened back against the wall. The front door groaned closed again. The air whispered up, jostling and enveloping her. She should have been spooked, the way the dense shadows dragged at her, but instead they enticed her. The curving stairs led her eyes upwards, daring her to explore.

'Now I'm here, I'd like to look round.'

He dipped his chin in a kind of bow, and hunched one shoulder to gesture her through some double doors and into a cavernous room, which smelled of wax and was bare except for a fire flickering at the far end. Three French windows gave over ornate balconies on to the oddly quiet street. Her shoes squeaked on the parquet as she circled slowly.

'All the furniture has gone. I've had to lurk in the attic,' the man explained. 'Now I find it heartbreaking to leave.'

Fran stopped twirling and peered over her shoulder. He had stopped behind her, hovering by the fire. Slowly he traced the outline of a marble leaf on the mantelpiece. There was an old mirror hanging there, so tarnished that the back of his head didn't show in the glass. The fluorescent lamplight from outside was dulled as it tried to compete with the flames twisting sluggishly in the grate.

'You've been camping in the attic?' she asked, taking a step nearer. 'I thought this was vacant possession. That's what your office told me. I arranged to meet an estate agent here at seven. I know I'm late, but I had to rush home to change. I'm on my way to a fancy-dress thing. Historical costumes, the invitation said –'

'I am Marcus. This house is mine.' His voice was stronger now and he rested his elbow on the mantelpiece like the aloof hero in a period drama.

'Perhaps I'm intruding,' Fran apologised. 'I didn't know the owner would be in residence. Mr James said he had keys. I expect he'll be here in a minute –'

'I knew you were coming,' he interrupted, smiling. All she could see in the gloom was a flash of teeth and a diamond of saliva reflecting light on his lower lip. 'No inconvenience at all.'

'That's OK, then.' She felt her lips stretching in an answering smile. He was so still, like a statue, yet not stony. Calming, like a balm. Her eyelids felt heavy with peering through the twilight and blinking against the heat from the fire.

'You've restored it beautifully.' She waved her arm around. 'Early nineteenth century, I'm assuming. Have you any candles? We could at least light it the way it was meant to be.'

'The year is 1800.'

Inclining his head in another odd bow, he backed towards the corner and melted away. The walls in this room were wood-panelled, and she liked the idea of secret doors and passages to vanish through. Think of the house parties! She unbuttoned her heavy coat and as it dropped to the floor a cool draught whisked over the surface of her skin. There was more than usual of it on display. Tiny hairs rose and prickled as the puffy sleeves of the Empire dress slipped off her shoulders. Her breasts this evening were hoisted unnaturally high in the narrow bodice, resting on a row of stitching, which gathered the fabric in to her ribcage and under her bosom, presenting the curves of her tits like two pale melons on a dish. The lace framing them shook each time she took a breath, and the melons bulged in uncomfortable rebellion against the tight seams binding them in.

The dress she had hired for the party was the genuine article, right down to the yellowing buttons and snagged muslin. She had no idea if this was the costume of a lady or a servant girl. How did people back then survive in such awkward clothes? The design forced you to stand ramrod straight. You could only move or swivel in tiny movements like a geisha. The effect was dainty and virginal, yet thrust the bosom out into people's faces. Even boy-chested girls would have looked like Wonderbra models, and as for women like Fran with breasts famed for their size throughout the West End . . .

Now that they were exposed, practically bare and

brazen in their unaccustomed finery, all she could focus on was those white mounds, how everyone at the party would stare at them rising like ripe dough from the embroidered bodice, and how soon it would be, if she sneezed or laughed, before they lifted and overflowed from their constraints, bouncing into the limelight for everyone to see and feel. She could stand there, the dress disintegrating round her with the force of her body bursting out of it, people crowding round to grab and fondle. Men would be unable to resist squeezing and nuzzling at her breasts; women would kneel to sniff the sudden blackness of her pussy brazen beneath the prissy costume. There would be a few fronds of muslin and lace left, clinging to the sweaty patches under her arms and inside her thighs, then these would peel away like burning paper to drop off and leave her bare as Venus, arms and legs open to embrace her greedy public.

Her nipples were already burning from where they kept grazing the rough lining of the dress, and her thoughts stoked their prickling heat. There was no bra that would fit under this dress, and the chill in the room shrank them, her personal radars, into sharp points. Hidden below the lace border, they started to demand attention. There was only a scrap of old material between her nipples and the world. She was impatient now to get going, show herself off, make real her imagined scenario, but she hadn't finished with the dark, silent house. Or it hadn't finished with her.

Fran raised the long white dress over her ankles and skipped and shuffled across to the mirror. Somehow that was the only way she could move in the satin slippers, and she wanted to glance at her assumed self.

Her reflection was clear, dancing in the firelight. The ringlets she had rigged up with her curling tongs were quite effective in this flickering light. She had knotted the rest of her hair on top of her head, which elongated her neck like a swan's, extending out of the broad swell of her billowing breasts. She looked like a publicity photograph for the latest dramatisation of Jane Austen. Demure, but oh so dirty.

'Not only candles, but wine as well.'

He was right behind her, setting a silver tray and crystal decanter down on the floor. Her fingers played coyly across her lips, and her tits rose higher out of the dress as she tried to steady her breathing. She spoke at herself in the mirror.

'You must excuse me looking like this. It's for a party. The dress didn't feel so small when I tried it on in the hire shop.'

'The gown is just right for the occasion,' he answered, not looking at her but throwing some thick brocade cushions into a pile in front of the fire. She turned, and he held out his hand. 'Now you belong here.'

'Perhaps just one glass, then. Women in those days didn't sprawl on the floor like this, did they?' She laughed, grasping his cold fingers as she lowered herself carefully on to the bed of cushions. Her limbs felt stiff, and instead of lounging down carelessly as she would normally, she tucked her feet sideways under her and sat upright like a ballerina, holding her glass in front of her like a ceremonial sword. She glanced at her wrist, but she'd left her watch off to add authenticity to her costume. There were no clocks and nothing but the darkness to indicate that it was night. She sipped from the heavy crystal and the wine lapped immediately against her skull.

'There is no one to see us now, so nothing matters,' he answered, kneeling down opposite her. He filled his own glass with the dark red liquid and examined her with his head on one side. The stillness of his angular face struck her as strangely mournful, though his eyes glittered black and restless. His wild hair looked as if it might be full of cobwebs. She remembered he had, after all, been roosting in the attic, and maybe his plumbing skills didn't extend to sorting out the hot-water system. Nevertheless his shirt was dazzling white, loosely open over his chest and ruffled over the buttons and the cuffs. His long legs were encased in tight breeches and a bubble rose in her throat as she saw that they were fastened into leather riding boots.

'I don't believe it!' she choked, swishing her glass wildly and covering her mouth again with her other hand. 'The clothes! You're going to the same party!'

He drew a large handkerchief out of his sleeve and waited for her to stop cackling.

'You've spilled some,' he murmured, leaning close and wiping it slowly across her stomach. She peered at what he was doing, and saw a dark splash across her white skirt.

'Shit!' she hissed, grabbing the cloth off him and rubbing furiously. 'It won't come off. This dress isn't mine!'

'It looks like blood,' he remarked, lifting the hem of her dress towards his nostrils. 'Smells like it, too.' He let the dress drift back over her upper thighs. He dropped on to all fours like a hound and swayed over her.

'I can't get it off,' she protested weakly, flapping the handkerchief. 'It'll stain.'

His hands flattened on either side of her thighs, pinning her to the cushions.

'I'll lick it.'

For a moment his face hung white and suddenly fierce, inches away from hers. Fran was shivering, she realised, but not from fear. She was cold, that was all. The heating in the house was obviously nonexistent, something that would have to be fixed, like the lighting, and now he was blocking the heat of the fire. Her legs were stretched on either side of his poised form. Her arm still held the offending wineglass aloft and her other hand, clutching the handkerchief, came down behind her bottom to support her weight.

A log cracked in the grate and she flinched at the sound. He darted forward. She wanted to keep him sweet, but she tossed her head to one side, in case he wanted to snatch a kiss. But his mouth locked on to the sinewy edge of her throat. His lips were cool, attached for a moment like a vice on that spot, but then his tongue came out, slim and slippery, slicking swiftly just above her collarbone so that she automatically hunched her shoulders against the tickling sensation.

'I think you must be mistaking me for someone else!' she gasped, wriggling aside.

He backed away, frowning, his mouth shining and wet.

'Not at all. I know exactly who you are.'

'In that case, I'm flattered, Marcus, but you must realise that I am not accustomed to being licked by strangers –'

Fran gave a piping laugh to cover the intoxicating mix of discovery and excitement. She wanted this house, and now she wanted its owner. She waggled her fingers at him in the dainty new mannerism she seemed to have acquired along with her borrowed dress.

'Well, now that you have been, I am afraid you are beyond redemption,' he answered, his face calm again but still close as she shifted her legs under him and tweaked at the dress. He cleared his throat. 'That is to say, your dress is ruined.'

Fran sat back on her ankles, plucking at the red patch. It already felt dry, and permanent.

'Nonsense,' she asserted. 'These fabrics may be old, probably as old as the house, but look how pristine you keep your shirt –'

'True. But you did not come here to do laundry, did you?'

Fran snorted and got ready to stand, aware that her cleavage was low and thrusting as she bent over. She paused in that position, suddenly unwilling to move.

'I came here to view your property,' she reminded him softly, watching his hair lift under her breath. 'I might want to buy it. But I ought to clean this bloody dress first. Come on. We can find some soap and water while you're showing me the rest of the house. That's if there *is* any water.'

He shook his head, and she had to laugh again, bent over as she was. He reached up, sensing her surrender. He grabbed her arms and pulled her down on to the cushions.

'There's still wine on your neck,' he murmured, drawing his tongue across his teeth. 'And it still looks just like blood.'

He laid her down and let one leg slide up under her dress, pushing her knee sideways.

'Still want to see the house?' he murmured.

'Later,' she replied.

He continued his journey, moving his breeches smoothly between and parting her legs, rucking up the flimsy fabric so that it barely brushed over her fanny. Fran's cunt twitched violently as the draught between their two bodies kissed it. Knickers didn't come with the outfit. Her pussy lips pouted against the pressure of his groin through the wisp of material still covering them.

'And my dress?' she whispered.

He looked down then, frowning as his eyes feasted on her large breasts displayed on their fabric shelf, then moved on over her stomach to where the dress was wrinkled over her splayed legs. She couldn't move. He took the wineglass out of her hand and tipped some of its contents into her mouth. Some of it dribbled over her chin, and again he licked it off with long swipes of his tongue while she swallowed and felt it flow through her chest and into her head, spirals of intoxication. It wasn't like wine: more like a thick dark potion, and sickly sweet.

'This will stop you going to the ball.'

With a mad grin he held the glass, tipping it slowly, so that a stream of wine threaded through the cold air and landed all over her breasts, drops splashing all over the cushions, all over her doomed dress. A scream of protest wound up from her at the thought of the expense, not to mention the impossibility, of washing all that white muslin. He threw the glass aside, letting it shatter in the fireplace.

'You no longer look like a lady, anyway,' he muttered, bending at the waist so that his nose dived between her tits, his breath rasping over the acres of skin exposed there as he lowered himself over her.

Fran sank back, defeated by the tingling in her breasts, and flopped on to the cushions.

'Perhaps I should just take the dress off,' she suggested, grabbing his head and shoving it into her cleavage. Though it looked thick, his hair was as fine as water between her fingers, but his teeth were strong, nipping across her breasts towards the straining nipples still trapped in their lace prison. He tore at the dress and a delicious rending of cotton split the silent air. Her breasts sprang free, filling up with desire as they met the air. Fran arched her back and he pushed the breasts together so that the nipples stood side by side, rigid in the cold, and the tips of his sharp teeth glinted briefly in the firelight before clamping round one taut bud and biting it, hard.

She shrieked out as the pain shifted into pleasure and her legs parted automatically beneath him. She reached round to his buttocks, smooth as buckskin and muscled beneath the breeches, which clung as if he had been sewn into them. He was still kneeling and her fingers groped round to the front of his trousers, where a row of tiny buttons marched up his groin, barring the way. Her fingers were stiff with cold. She rubbed them over the tightly fitting material, searching for warmth and for the thick shape of his cock, but she couldn't fix on to the buttons or anything else remotely solid.

As if realising this, his hands grabbed her wrists, pinning them above her head. Fran was no longer in the business of resisting. His mouth continued to work on her nipples, and she brought her knees up round his hips, grinding her moistening pussy up against him. The dress wrinkled round her waist and her bottom felt cold on the floor as her legs tried to grip his bones, but all they found was air, as if they had no strength.

He was like a mirage, slippery and unmanageable, yet his mouth was determined, sucking like a baby's, taking in the point of the nipple and all the puckered skin around it. His teeth were sharp, drawing ragged gasps out of her as they pulled and tugged and the cold air shrank her skin into needles of sensitivity. Fran's cunt was melting. She couldn't tell if she was imagining the friction of her open labia against his breeches, or if she was willing the sensation to sizzle through her, but either way she could hear the wet kiss of her pussy lips as she let her legs drop lazily across the musty-smelling cushions and let him suck, bite and swallow as if he were devouring her.

Suddenly he lifted his head from the red raw nipples and sniffed the air like a dog. His eyes glittered over to the windows, then back at Fran, stretched out in the dying firelight.

'Don't dare stop now,' she moaned, scarcely familiar with her own voice. 'Do it, just do it to me!'

He bared his teeth in a wolf's grin. Delicious fear stirred in her belly then, but it was chased away by her own ferocious excitement and she arched herself at him again, half closing her eyes to try to recapture the ecstasy he had started. As the flames filtered through her eyelashes she saw his teeth ranged behind his lips, sharp and white like fangs, and she laughed out loud at the craziness, laughing louder as he bent close and sank them into her neck. Then she screamed as she felt the juicy pop of pierced flesh under his mouth, as if he were biting a grape, not hurting exactly but it was as if he'd also unscrewed the top of her head, letting cold dark air and hustling voices rush in; and, as a sticky trickle of liquid oozed towards her collarbone, Fran's screams spun away into the corner of the moonlit room.

Marcus was sliding off her like a snake's skin. Her tits wobbled in protest as he released them, flopping softly against her arms. She floundered as she tried to drag him back, but her hands clawed at nothing, and all she could see was the redness lining her closed eyelids.

The leather brogues clicked briskly along the pavement towards the house and paused at the foot of the steps. No sign of her. Eric James cursed the traffic as he fiddled the rusting key in the lock. He was twenty minutes late. She had sounded classy on the phone, not someone to keep waiting, and this house was proving the very devil to sell.

Always a chance she'd been delayed, too. He groped for the light switches. Still no electricity, but there was some sort of life in what he liked to call the ballroom.

He stopped halfway across the parquet floor. Garish lamplight from the street clamoured at the curtainless windows and fell in rectangles across the room. Someone was lying in one of these rectangles, stretched in front of the empty fireplace. Not only lying there, he now saw, but writhing about and moaning, as if in pain. Eric James used to be in the army and he knew about first aid, but he didn't fancy being responsible for some kind of accident in one of his properties.

The person moaned, and he stepped forwards. It was a woman. How could he have failed to notice? She was all curves, all breasts and hips and knees, and she was arching her back, the sinews in her throat straining as she threw her head back and a pair of huge pale breasts rose invitingly in the moonlight, nipples jutting like acorns. Her legs were splayed wide on the floor, white thigh flesh above white stockings, and her ripped dress was rucked up round her waist. She looked as if she were possessed in some kind of ecstatic trance but how she was turning herself on like that he couldn't tell. There was only her and the hard floor.

He peered to see if she was fingering herself, sticking her hands up into her cunt. He loved to see women masturbating, those thin fingers shyly exploring through their soft beavers towards their own sex when he asked them to, embarrassed at first, but when their necks started to loosen, heads falling back, hair swishing as they pressed the button and startled themselves, then he knew he was on to a winner. They'd reduce themselves to jelly, squealing and gasping, and they'd be putty in his hands. He could take the rod of iron that quivered impatiently in front of him, rising at right angles out of his loins as he watched them, and he could replace their fiddling fingers with his own hard cock.

This girl's buttocks bounced off the floor as her legs opened wide and closed, drawing his eyes to the shadow of her bush, but her arms were flung behind her head. Blood rushed into his head and swelled into his balls. The whole house was deserted but still he glanced round to make sure they were alone. Hope to God no one at the office had double-booked this viewing...

'Did you come to see the house?' he blurted out, banging his knees down on to the floor beside her. She just swung her head from side to side, curious ringlets of hair unravelling around her ears. She bent her knees up and crossed her ankles, as if trying to grasp something between her naked thighs.

'Don't dare stop now,' she groaned, arching her back to offer those glorious tits upwards. The nipples were dark red, like raspberries, pointing straight at him. The white material of her dress lay in tatters over her heaving ribcage, and she had bitten her lip, dribbled something red, like blood, down her chin on to her throat. Her mouth and legs were open, wet, vacant, unoccupied, available, immediate possession, under offer, local search, quick sale, all the crude office puns jostling in, flitting off, and his penis unfurled, growing stiff and long and pushing against the good tweed of his suit.

'Do it, just do it to me,' she urged, offering her breasts feverishly towards him, and Eric James didn't need telling twice.

So he was changing his mind. After all, what red-blooded man would shrink away from a spread-eagled woman who was begging him to fuck her? At last Fran could feel some real masculine weight bearing down on her, blocking out some of the cold air, solid muscle and heavy bone as he positioned himself between her legs, half leaning over her torso so that she could lock her ankles round his back and yank Marcus towards her. His ruffled shirt felt rough, though, like tweed, and she heard the scrape of a zip instead of the flipping of buttons as he fiddled to undo his trousers.

Fran tried to open her eyes as the rounded end of his knob thumped on to her stomach and slid down to nudge against her sopping labia like a blind animal snuffling along to its hole. Her eyelids felt sticky as if she'd been sleeping, but she forced them open to stare again at the haunted face of her ghostly lover.

The man looming above her and edging his cock into her waiting cunt had a square chin and broad shoulders, and instead of a white ruffled shirt he wore some kind of thick jacket and a neat tie. His hair was cut short and his mouth was closed in a solemn pout as he studied her with clear blue eyes. It wasn't Marcus.

Fran struggled on to her elbows, but the newcomer shook his head with a slight smile and shoved her down again. His manner was different. Though bigger built than the spindly Marcus, this man seemed surprised to find himself poised between her open thighs. He'd simply materialised in this room and couldn't believe his luck, and wasn't letting her get away.

'Where's Marcus?'

The man shrugged. 'I know no Marcus,' he murmured slowly, licking his lips as if he were studying a luscious pudding. 'I'm the only one with keys.'

It made no sense at that moment, but then nothing in the old house made any sense. Any question forming on her lips was silenced by the feel of his big hands smoothing over her thighs, cupping her butt cheeks and easing them apart so that his fingers slid through the damp crack dividing her body in two. Her nipples were still tingling, hard and cold, but he didn't touch them, focused as he was on treading his fingers round to her bush, keeping her spread open, burrowing into the curling hair, keeping his eyes on her while he spread her sex lips to reveal the pulsating cone of her clit radiating heat to the edges and into her vagina. His fingers were everywhere, crawling into her anus, along the cleft, tickling the soft folds of hairless skin, rubbing the head of her clit, diving two or three at a time into her restless pussy ...

Seeing her eyelids fluttering closed again, he pushed his thick cock inch by inch inside. This was what Marcus had prepared her for, and his friend was carrying on where he left off. Fran couldn't, wouldn't, stem the flow of it by asking questions. She pulled his shoulders towards her so that he was stretched above her and his groin ground against hers. He pushed his swollen length up through her gripping muscles, bumping over the ridges of tight flesh as if his penis were a train travelling up a jointed track, and kept on pushing so that the two of them slid as one tentacled object across the shiny floor.

Fran flicked his shirt tails up and pinched at his braced back and his buttocks, glad of something to grab as his breath rushed in her ear and his buttocks reared back, dragging his cock out nearly all the way so that violent spasms rippled up towards her navel as every fibre tried to grip the welcome shaft of muscle, but he teased them both, throwing his head back for a moment, biting his lip as the tip of his cock hovered at her entrance; then he slammed it back in, shoving them both towards the windows with the force of it; then he was off, banging it into her, and Fran greedily crushed her groin against his in rhythm. His rock-hard cock filled her to the top, thrusting in and in until the contracting of her muscles started to become fluid, sensations swirling in circles and sharpening as the wave of orgasm approached the shore, and she shouted out with exasperation that it was coming too quickly and screeched with helpless pleasure though she couldn't halt it.

Fran wrapped her arms and legs around him like a cat holding a branch. He paused, silent while she whimpered into his chest. He towered above her, mouth an open gash now, teeth biting at his lips as he stared, one lick of hair dropping over his forehead as he strained against the desire to fuck her. Then he kicked two mighty thrusts into her and shuddered, the arrow of his prick lodged deep inside as if he'd knocked through a wall. The aftershocks of his climax crashed towards her head as the electric circles bunched and exploded all through her, and they fell in a gasping heap just by the tall bare window.

There was nothing for a long time except traffic passing outside the window and their receding breaths.

'I'm Eric James, from the estate agents,' he said at last, face hidden in her hair. 'I only wanted to finish what you'd apparently started.'

'What happened?' Fran asked stupidly, lying beneath one heavy arm, her legs splayed on either side of his half-pulled trousers. 'You weren't here before. Someone else was here –'

'I'm sorry I'm so late. The traffic –'

'He was biting me. I thought he was going to screw me. I wanted him to screw me. I couldn't really feel him, but he was biting my neck.'

'So it *is* blood,' Eric James breathed, sniffing below her ear. 'That's priceless! The story goes that a vampire used to live here, way back, two hundred years or so. I think his name was Marcus –'

Fran twisted upright then, forcing herself out of his

grasp. Her frozen skin crawled. She shook her head to get rid of the horrible notion that she'd nearly been fucked by a ghost. Eric James watched, shirt still buttoned and tie still tied, while she rocked slowly on her hands and knees. Her breasts were bare in the lamplight and her borrowed dress lay torn into shreds. A taxi hooted outside and was answered by another car. The modern sounds elbowed the sinister history of the house, and Fran forced herself to calm down.

'He wasn't showing you round, was he?' Eric James laughed. 'That's my job.'

'I should get back into the real world,' she jittered, looking round for her coat. 'I've a party to get to.'

'You can't go out into the street naked like that. Your clothes are in shreds.'

'My coat's all right. I'll just wear my coat.'

'Too juicy to go out like that.'

He looked down at her breasts, whistled between his teeth, and fanned his fingers out to take hold of them. Fresh excitement yawned and awakened in her stomach. His fingers held, and tightened, digging into the soft globes, pushing them together like sponges. He pulled them, extending them, dragging her after them, pressing them into his chest.

Her arms came up round his neck and she knelt up so that he could reach the frustrated nipples, nibble and suck them as all men wanted to when she dangled her delicious tits in front of them. But he gripped harder so that it started to hurt. The excited-schoolboy act had disappeared. Fran wanted to wrench his head round to look at him, but he was lowering his chin towards her shoulders. She hitched her breast towards his face, desperate for him now to suck it, but he flattened her torso against him so that the only place her head could go was backwards.

Cold air crept across her exposed throat and the street light clearly illuminated his profile. Mr James grinned again, and Fran started to smile too, relaxing into his grasp, tensing her thighs to wrap them round his waist, but his mouth went on stretching until his teeth were bared, square front teeth at first, neat row of gnashers at the bottom. The ridiculous thought nagged at her that he probably had a metal brace when he was young, his teeth were so straight.

Behind his head, a slim figure crossed in front of the fireplace, and spidery shadows leaped across the walls as a man moved towards the place where Eric and Fran were sprawled on his floor, in his house. His hair was wilder, his white shirt open over the tight breeches, and he too was grinning.

And, when Marcus crouched down to join them, Eric James lowered his face once more, arrowing into Fran's neck two perfect, pointed fangs.

# Bare Fantasy Lucy Ferdinand

It started as a dare, between my lover and me: 'You tell me your fantasy and I'll tell you mine.'

A game in the dark, in the warmth of our bed. Whispered confessions, explicit and arousing. Of what I'd dreamed about in the recesses of my mind, the most private of my thoughts.

It started off as nothing unusual in the requests and dreams. It being the first time we had dared to confess such intimacies to one another, the more mundane, or at least the least shocking, came first.

Sex outside, with me against a tree, my skirt around my waist with my lover fucking me from behind. That was his.

Being watched while we screwed, by another man who was desperate to join in – who demonstrated his desperation by wanking his cock furiously at the show we would put on for him. That was mine.

It was good to know that my lover wasn't shocked by my unveiling that, deep down, I was nothing but a slut, wanting men to want me, wanting to see them grow hard and desperate to have my lips or my pussy around their aching cocks. He wasn't shocked: he grew harder at the explicit words that spewed from my lips. He loved hearing me talking about doing things he had only watched in videos. Videos that, when he was a teenager, had made his balls ache and his prick rock-hard from wanting a woman who had the same dirty thoughts and desire for sex. And there I was in his bed.

As I grew more confident that I wasn't going to shock him, that he was as excited by situations and games as I was, I grew more daring. And so did he. We opened up more and more, getting deeper and deeper into each other's mind.

To see me being fucked by another man, while he watched. His.

To strip for him and his friends, without their knowing who I was. Mine.

To send pictures of me to a 'Readers' Wives' section of a porno mag. His.

To have me dress like a nurse, and give him a bed bath. His.

To be filmed while we fucked, so I could see what he saw. Mine.

To be totally filled with cock, in my pussy, my mouth, my arse. Mine again.

The next came from him, shaped by countless girlie mags, images of girls with perfect tits and hairless pussies that he had pumped his cock to until he covered their images in his sticky hot come. Images where nothing was hidden, every detail of their shining pink slits visible.

He wanted to see my pussy naked, denuded of every hair. He wanted to do it himself, right there on our bed.

I was already wet after listening to and talking about things other people might be shocked by and find depraved. That just excited me more. I smiled softly and slipped off the bed, leaving the room, motioning to my lover to stay where he was.

Minutes later I was back and burning with excitement. Back with towels, water – the things you need to shave. His shaving gel, his razor. I wanted him to shave me now. I wanted him to use his razor so the smell of my pussy would be there the next time he used it. I wanted him to remember the sight of my pussy spread for him, bare and soaking wet. I was ready.

The look of desire on his face was unmistakable as he laid the towels over the bed and gently pushed me down. He parted my legs with his hands and took a moment to admire the sight spread before him – the shining pink of my wet hole, surrounded by the dark fur on my mound. He ran a finger lightly across my pussy, releasing an involuntary moan from my lips. I wanted to feel his hands upon me.

I closed my eyes, and waited.

Water touched me, dripped on to me slowly to lubricate my skin. My pussy was doing well enough lubricating itself; the anticipation almost too much to bear.

A trickle of hot water slid from my pussy lips and ran across me, over my wide-open sex and finally coming to rest after dribbling over my arse. The water cooled as it went, from hot to tepid, but feeling just as good. My lover saw the drop and touched it with his finger. My pussy responded with a fresh rush of wetness and I responded with a sigh.

Encouraged, he leaned his face into me and licked the drop of water from my anus, cupping me to his face with a hand on each buttock, his face buried between my legs. It felt so good, his wriggling tongue flicking over me. As I began to move slightly, in time to his ministrations, he stopped. 'Patience' was his only word.

I heard the hiss of the foam as he squirted a generous amount into his hand. I smelled the fresh lime fragrance, and I smelled myself, the scent of my arousal, musky and pungent.

The foam was soft and cool, creamy, making my clit tingle. My pussy was gushing with hot juices, desperate to coat a thick hard cock being rammed into me. I felt so frustrated. I just wanted something inside me, anything.

I wanted to be fucked, hard and fast. I felt sure I would come the minute I was entered: by finger, cock or whatever. My juices were beginning to escape the confines of my cunt and mingle with the shaving foam, making little streams in it.

Sensing my urgency, the lightest touch of his finger stroked my clit. Both my vagina and my arse contracted together, desperate now for stimulation. Gently, my clit was being rubbed, making me squirm with longing. Harder now, his fingers were working me, sliding over the whole of my sex now, but still stopping short of the mouth of my cunt. I pleaded for him to push his fingers deep inside me, to bring me off, to give me the orgasm I was craving.

He knelt above me, smiling. Dropping over for his mouth to take its place on my tits, he took a swollen nipple between his lips. His fingers continued their probing and rubbing on my pussy. Teeth clamped around my nipple, biting, nibbling. Sucking, licking. My other breast, aching for the same attention, felt bare and lonely. I grasped it with my hand, rolling the nipple between my fingers, kneading and pulling.

Feeling the tugging on my nipples connecting with the throbbing in my groin, I was breathing hard now, in short gasping breaths. But I still didn't have anything inside me. Just one hard thrust was all it would take. I was denied it. As I moved closer to my climax, the rubbing and nibbling suddenly stopped. 'Bastard,' I hissed.

Again: 'Patience.'

The contrast of the hot water and the cold steel of the razor blade felt delicious on my skin. My pussy contracted as the blade touched my skin. It felt decadent and dangerous at the same time, so intimate and daring, at least for me. I lay in the candlelight, imagining how it must all look from my lover's perspective, what a view he must be getting tonight!

The blade began to shave my hair, gently, carefully. My pussy lips were being held open by my lover with one hand as he guided the razor with the other. His breathing was changing, as the more bare pussy he revealed, the more turned on he got. I reached between my legs with both hands, parting my fanny wider, both for ease of shaving and so that my lover could see right into my cunt now. He couldn't miss the slick river of wetness that lay there, shining, waiting for him.

'Fuck, you're so wet,' he hissed, teeth clenched. As he moved, his cock touched me. Rock-hard and bigger than I had ever felt it, it seemed as impatient as I was. He groaned, as he shaved off the last small patch of fur.

More water now, cooler than before, running down my legs, across my skin, into the folds of my pussy. Then the roughness of the towel against me, as he gently dried every nook and cranny, every fold of my most intimate places.

Then it was done. He stood back to admire his handi-work, to see my pussy totally bare for the first time. It reflected in his eyes that he liked what he saw. His eyes shone as he gasped his admiration.

'That looks so beautiful – it's so soft and shiny, so innocent.'

I swung my legs around, sitting up. Still seriously aroused by the whole thing, I moved to the mirror to take a look.

Standing in front of the full-length mirror, I observed how like a schoolgirl's my pussy looked. How bare and strange it was to look like this again, the way it had looked twenty years ago. It was strangely erotic, tantalising.

My lover stood behind me, his hardness pressed into

me as I stared into the mirror. My hand curved around and dipped between my legs. My eyes never left his, through the mirror. He watched as I sank to my knees, all the time watching. I spread my lips with one hand and sank the fingers of the other into myself. I groaned, as did my lover. Rubbing and tapping my clitoris, probing my pussy.

Withdrawing my fingers, I offered them to his lips. He took them greedily, sucking and licking. 'Your pussy tastes fucking gorgeous.' I put my fingers back for another helping of the creamy juices and tasted for myself. He was right.

I continued to move my fingers across and inside my pussy, revelling in the bawdy picture in the mirror, watching me touch myself, my lover behind me watching me masturbate. It felt naughty, like something in a porno video. I liked the feeling. It made me feel powerful, as if I could do anything I wanted to my lover. But I wanted to have him dominate me, to be so overcome that he could hold back no longer. To be desperate to fuck me. Wild for my pussy.

I turned and reached for his cock. I had always enjoyed my lover's cock, so wide and long that it stretched my slit to capacity. But tonight it was bigger and harder than usual. As we both knelt, I bent my head to take his prick head in my mouth, delighting in the salty teardrop on the end. He groaned: cursing, telling me he was dying to shoot his load into my mouth right then. As I took him further into my lips, his breathing grew shallow and his hips began to move in time to my suckling, fucking my mouth, rubbing his cock against my tongue, the roof of my mouth. As it began to throb, I could feel the spunk moving up his cock, about to shoot within seconds. I withdrew my mouth, eager to get revenge for earlier and to tease him to despair. It worked.

'You bitch!' he howled. But he smiled at me with a glint in his eye as he caught my wrists. 'I'm going to have to teach you a lesson.' He grinned as he pushed me on to the bed. Climbing on top of me, he slid his cock into me in one urgent thrust. It was like coming home.

After being teased for so long by each other, we were both gagging for a shag. But he meant what he said, and withdrew.

'Do you want more?'

'Oh God, yeah.'

He edged the head of his prick into me and held still.

'Is this enough?'

'No,' I replied. 'I want more.'

An inch or so more of his dick slid into my wetness.

'How about that – is that enough?'

'No!' I gasped and grabbed at his hips, trying wildly to pull him right into me. I failed and it was driving me crazy. 'I need all of your cock in me, filling me up.'

'Patience!' he said again. 'I think you've had enough cock for now. Turn on to your hands and knees – I want to look at your pussy from behind.' His tone of voice told me not to argue, not that I would have. I loved to be dominated as much as I loved to dominate him.

A favourite position of mine, it made me feel totally wanton, like a dirty little tart in a magazine. I could imagine men looking at me, wanking themselves off, dreaming about being inside me, sliding their pricks into my pink hole. I longed to be able to see what my lover saw, to be able to see everything. Positioning himself behind me, on his knees, he pushed my legs further apart. Lightly running fingers across me, or gently rubbing at me with his cock, he teased me, nudging against my hole and no more. I was begging for him to fuck me.

Suddenly, my pussy was full. But it was fingers, not cock that were stretching, fucking, probing inside me. It was the most intense feeling I had ever had, and, as his fingers managed to fill me, slide across me twisting and turning, and rub my clit, all at the same time, I felt my pussy tying itself into the knot that was my orgasm. I came, shouting and gasping, gushing even more wetness over his fingers, not caring how loud I was, not caring that the neighbours probably thought I was being murdered.

Feeling me come on his fingers was enough. He pulled them out, licking them as he did so, and buried his face between my legs for a minute or two, sucking at the juices that he found so delicious. Then he was inside me, ramming his huge prick into me, pounding me. I felt my orgasm building again, as he slid in and out of my pussy, feeling his balls slapping against my arse.

'I'm watching my cock while I'm fucking you.'

'Can you see everything?' I asked, eager for him to describe it to me.

'I can see my cock, surrounded by your tight pink hole. I can see how wet you are; my cock is shiny from you and it's wetter every time I come out.'

I was so jealous – I wanted to see too. I would have to get him to take photos next time. But now I was eager to be in control again.

'I want to be on top.'

This was one of his favourites: he loved to watch my ample tits bouncing up and down in front of his face as I moved on his prick, and to watch my face as I came.

His dick slid out of my slit, leaving it empty. I wanted it back. I needed it back. As we moved, his mouth found mine. His tongue snaked between my lips, probing my mouth, dancing with mine. As we kissed, I became aware that my pussy was dripping with wetness and slid my hand back between my legs, filling the emptiness.

He was lying on his back. I wanted to ride on his cock,

to take my orgasm, to feel him shooting inside me. I knew it would be quick – he couldn't take much more, and neither could I.

I climbed on to his cock, crying out loud, and rode it, sliding relentlessly up and down its length. The throbbing started again in his dick, and I was rubbing harder and harder against him, desperate for release. I sat bolt upright, so I could feel his warm balls against me and he could feel my smooth, hairless mound against him. I felt him reaching for my tits, my nipple in his mouth, being suckled as if he were a small child, gulping and kneading at me. Then they were both in his hands, as he pushed them together, enjoying the sight of a pair of tits to rival any 'Page Three stunna'. Then he was coming, crying my name as he shot his hot wet come into my thirsty pussy, eager for his load. As it hit my cunt insides, I felt myself tip over the edge, gripping his prick and milking it with my hole. Searing white heat shot through me, pulsing with waves of desire. I was aware of every inch of his cock inside me, yet, at the same time, I was aware of nothing but the fucking wonderful feelings deep in my cunt.

Satisfied at last, we lay back, exhausted. As we got our breath back, I replayed what we had just done in my head. My hand went to my mound, and I idly stroked my smooth fanny. It was dripping wetness, his come and my juices mingling together.

He slid his head under the sheets, and buried his face in my muff once again, licking the juices, drinking in the taste and smell of sex. Then he kissed me, so I could taste it too. Bittersweet, it made my head spin and gave me the beginnings of desire again.

I had decided I enjoyed being dirty, being a slut. I wanted more, wanted to do more. I needed to fulfil my horniest desires and needs, but how would I pluck up the courage to broach the subject? There was one particular fantasy that I had that I longed to act out, but how could I ask for that, when it made me sound such a slut? But I needed to start somewhere.

'That was some fantasy.'

'I didn't think you would do it,' my lover confessed. 'But it lived up to every expectation. Since we've made a fantasy of mine come true, it's only fair we should try one of yours soon. Your choice, whatever you want. Any ideas which one?'

'I'll have to think about that one,' I said lightly. But in my head, I was already picking out the two other men that I would need ...

# Liar, Liar Tina Glynn

'And now,' slurred Janie, swaying drunkenly in her little yellow pyjamas and using the bourbon bottle as a microphone, 'the highlight of the evening – *hic* – I give you Miss Celeste O'Rourke!'

Me and Sylvie, cross-legged on the bedroom carpet, clapped and jeered as Celeste rose unsteadily in her candy-pink baby-doll ensemble and gave us a curtsy. It was her turn to give us her latest 'going all the way' story – something that had become as regular a feature of our weekend sleepovers as the smuggled-in booze, the atmosphere thick with cigarette smoke and nail-polish fumes and Elvis LPs playing in the background.

Tonight, as Celeste took a pre-story slug of bourbon and Canada Dry from her tooth mug, it was 'Love Me Tender' that the King crooned from Janie's Motorola record player. Kind of ironic, really, seeing that love and tenderness and all that goo were strictly prohibited. What we wanted was juicy sexual detail that would make our pyjama bottoms damp at the crotch and Celeste, with her talent for wild exaggeration and her phoney, breathless Monroe voice, had turned the telling of these tales into an art form.

'Well, we'd climbed into the back of his Daddy's Bel-Air convertible,' she began, settling herself on the edge of the bed, 'and I was just panting for him after all that necking. I pulled my sweater up over my head, figuring he'd unclasp my Playtex and fool around with my tits a little, suck on my nipples and stuff. But you know what guys are like.'

I joined in the slow world-weary nods of agreement.

'Yeah,' she went on, encouraged by the spirit of girlie camaraderie, 'he'd decided to cut out the preliminaries and concentrate on getting his hand straight into my panties, so's he could stick a finger inside me to check the wetness levels.'

'Like when Mom puts her glass thermometer in her sponge cakes to see if they're done,' added Sylvie, helpfully.

'Hey, whose story is this?' Celeste snapped, her sex-kitten voice momentarily turning into an unladylike bark. 'Anyhow –' she shot Sylvie a warning glance '– getting his hand in shouldn't have been a problem since I was wearing a dirndl skirt and we all know how the slightest breeze can lift one of those darn things right up over your head like an inside-out umbrella – but what does he go and do?'

We looked blank.

'Only tries to squeeze his hand into my waistband!'

She paused until the shrieks of laughter had subsided.

'Can you believe it? I mean how dumb *are* guys? Naturally the great ape goes and breaks the zipper and we have the biggest argument, but eventually we get to kissing again – real deep-tongue stuff. The windows are soooo steamed and I'm horny as hell. Then I undo his jeans and I roll a rubber on to the biggest, hardest stiffy you ever saw and he starts fucking me from behind –'

'But you don't like it from behind, Celeste,' said Janie, perplexed.

'True, Janie.' She nodded sagely. 'But it's the most comfortable way in a Bel-Air on account of the width of the back seat. Different story in a Ford Fairlane or a '57 Chevrolet, where on your back is best. Now where was I?

Oh, yeah, he's really bouncing off my ass and my tits are jumping with every hard thrust and – get a load of this – it's all taking place right there on his parents' drive. Can you imagine? There we were fucking in his dad's car in broad daylight.'

Sylvie and Janie were shrieking like a couple of banshees on a roller coaster, their bouffant hairdos wobbling, their cheeks red hot from the liquor and the laughter.

'Jeez, that is so audacious,' marvelled Sylvie. 'What if his mom had decided to go to the store or something?'

'Oh, my God,' squealed Janie between hiccups, 'you are the worst, Celeste. Just outrageous!'

But I could only force a weak smile. While Celeste was certainly the best storyteller in the room, for me she always left one question unanswered.

'And did you get to come?' The words left my lips before I could stop them.

She hesitated for a moment, screwing up her face at me as if I were some kind of strange insect. 'Don't be an asshole, Valerie. Sure I did.'

'How did you get to come? Did he finger your clit as he fucked you?'

'No.'

'Did he go down on you?'

'No. Yes. I don't remember. Christ, Valerie, you ask some dumb questions. How could I not come. Brad has *the* biggest cock, and he's really good-looking just in case you hadn't noticed.'

I raised my eyebrows cynically. Janie and Sylvie never questioned the truth of Celeste's confessions. They idolised her because she was the oldest girl in class, not caring that the reason for this was that she'd flunked first grade and had had to repeat the year. The two girls were her own personal handmaidens, taking turns to carry her cardigan when she got hot; fetching her a soda when she got thirsty; lighting her cigarettes; and never tiring of telling her (though she was way too chubby for it to be true) that she was heaps prettier than most of the leading ladies in Hollywood.

But she was a liar. I knew she was.

I'd been out with enough Brads to know that the only things these guys were any good at oiling up were (a) their stupid cars and (b) their stupid hair. Always in a rush, they bit your nipples before you were ready to have them bitten; if you were lucky they fumbled for your clit, but then they were too rough to give any pleasure. For them sex was all about getting their prick inside of you so's they could boast to their slack-jawed friends that they'd fucked you till you walked to your front porch with the gait of Calamity Jane. The reality was that they'd spurt all over the leatherette seats of Daddy's car the minute you licked their earlobe.

I would've put down my last dollar that Celeste never came with Brad or any other of her Juvenile-Hall dodging boyfriends. I sure as hell never had with mine.

In fact, the best orgasm I ever had was courtesy of *the* most unlikely person you could imagine, but I couldn't tell them about that, could I?

'So, Miss Sex Expert,' said Celeste, leaning across to stub out her cigarette irritably on the bedside locker, 'it's your turn to impress us all.'

Perhaps it was the challenge in her voice, or maybe it was the liquor, but at that moment a wild impulse took a hold of me. Looking straight into their dumb, expectant faces I decided to tell them every sordid detail of my most spectacular orgasm and be damned! At least it was true.

I wiped the top of the bourbon bottle that Sylvie handed to me, took a man-sized gulp and, once it had lit up my insides like kerosene, I began.

'It happened last fall. I'd bunked off school to go to the afternoon matinée at the movie house on Stanley Street. They were showing a rerun of that old Errol Flynn film, the one about Robin Hood.'

As I told my story I was transported back there. I was in total darkness except for the magical beam of projected light. I was breathing in that heady mixture of velveteen upholstery and sweet popcorn. My hands were clammy with fear that an off-duty teacher might catch me playing hooky.

'Anyway,' I continued, 'in the film Errol wears these dinky little tights that really show off his enormous bulge and I kind of got to wondering what his cock'd look like if it got hard in them.'

'Yeah, lucky old Maid Marion,' giggled Sylvie.

'The more I thought about Errol's dick the more worked up I was getting. So worked up that when the trilby-hatted old guy in the seat next to mine put his hand inside my coat flap and brought it to rest on my knee, I . . . I kind of liked how it felt.'

'And that was it?' Celeste wrinkled her cute nose. 'You got your knee felt by someone's grandpa?'

'No,' I replied haughtily, 'that wasn't it at all. The guy left his hand there for a few moments and then, when he was satisfied that I wasn't gonna scream or anything, he started moving it toward my stocking top and then across to my inner thigh. I held my breath, my eyes fixed firmly on the screen as his fingers reached the bare skin above my nylons and started to make these small, tingling circles. God, I was so turned on I actually started to open my legs, knowing I shouldn't, but by then I was totally out of control. I felt his finger running slowly along the edge of my French knickers and then *wham!* His hand slid straight inside the crotch. I'm telling you, this guy might've been old, but did he ever know how to bring a girl off! He had one finger on my clit and around three shoved inside my pussy. He slid his creamy fingers in and out and rubbed the very tip of the little bud until I couldn't stand another second and I came like crazy just as Errol Flynn was kissing Olivia de Haviland, my pussy muscles spasming round the hot wet fingers of this total stranger. It was the best orgasm I ever, ever had.'

'So what happened then?' Sylvie asked eagerly.

This was a question I hadn't anticipated.

I bought myself some thinking time by taking another few sips from the bottle. The dull reality was that nothing had happened then. I'd lain back in the plush seat, my breathing heavy, my eyes closed against the flickering half-light. Once the guy had brought me off he'd hurried out, probably straight to the john. I suppose I should have just told them that, but as I looked at their scandalised faces, their shining eyes, I realised that for once it was me, not Celeste, but boring old Valerie Nesbit, who was the centre of attention. I took a deep breath and, putting all my faith in my dirty imagination, I ploughed ahead.

'Well, figuring I ought to reciprocate, I snaked my hand under the raincoat he had folded across his lap,' I lied shamelessly. 'His cock was hard, and big, real big. I could feel it through the itchy wool of his trousers. I rubbed it a few times and it kind of twitched under my hand. He had buttons on his flies, little plastic buttons. He lifted himself up slightly to help me undo them, one by one, and then I edged down his shorts. He caught his breath as my cool hand made contact with the wet tip of his cock. I ran my hand along the stem. It felt silky and warm – pretty much like a young guy's really. I closed my fingers around it and he let out this moan, which he disguised with this real polite little cough.

I started to really pump him then.

He pushed his pelvis upwards to meet my strokes and I increased the tempo, jerking his big cock faster and faster until his body seemed to kind of freeze and, hiding his final groan behind the weirdest cough you ever heard, he spurted up my arm and all over his raincoat.'

I sat still for a few moments and then, snapping out of my semi-trance, I looked around me.

Janie's hiccups had stopped.

Elvis had done crooning.

There was total silence except for the sudden, intermittent bursts of tinny laughter that drifted up through the floorboards as Janie's mom watched *I Love Lucy* on TV.

The first to speak was Celeste.

'Jesus Valerie, are you saying you jerked off an old guy? If that were true it'd be just ... grotesque.'

'He was only around fifty,' I protested.

'"Only around fifty",' echoed Sylvie, her face contorted with revulsion. 'That is the absolute pits.'

Janie was busy sticking her finger into her open mouth, pretending to gag at the very idea. Pretty damn rich, I thought, for a girl who an hour ago had confessed to sucking off a pimply sales assistant in the parking lot behind the Piggly-Wiggly store while her mom shopped for groceries.

And Sylvie – sitting there primly shaking her head – was this the same girl who'd told us that she's only taking it up the ass lately because her new guy has such a narrow prick?

Then there was Celeste. Hadn't she just kind of admitted that guys of our age just haven't got a clue?

'If I really believed you,' she said, buffing her nails, 'I'd think you were crazy. But c'mon, Valerie, it's a joke, right?'

I shook my head. OK I'd exaggerated a little, but no more than she always did. I could've even gone on to say how the memory of that afternoon plus my own fingers had made me come more times than any downy-faced, soap-scented, rebel-without-a-brain ever would, but I figured I'd probably said enough already.

She stared at me for a few moments, weighing me up the way animals do when they're trying to work out who'd come out best in a fight. 'OK,' she said eventually, folding her arms across her chest, 'so you won't mind proving it, then?'

The smile she shared with the others was kind of dangerous.

'No,' I said, heart pounding, 'though I don't see how –'

'Just meet me in town on Monday at around seven. Oh, and you'll need to dress old.'

'What d'you mean, "dress old"?'

'Well, I don't mean fifty years old like your "*boy-friend*",' she mocked. 'Just try to look twenty-one, you know. Leave off the bobby socks, ditch the poodle skirt, borrow your mom's heeled pumps. I figured we'd go buy some booze at Latimer's liquor store ready for my party next weekend.'

I wanted to ask her how buying booze at Latimer's would prove I'd told the truth about the guy in the movie house, but she changed the subject before I could open my mouth by demanding to know which of us schmucks had plunked down their tooth mug on her new Pat Boone LP.

Fortunately, Mom wasn't in when I got home from school on Monday. A note next to my cold snack told me she'd gone bowling with Arnold, a guy with synthetic-looking hair who I'd seen creeping round the house the last few mornings.

Her absence left me free to set to work on my new, 'mature' appearance. I slapped on a coat of her Tru-glo face make-up, which made me look kind of orange, but, with the addition of black eyeliner, mascara and thickly applied Max Factor carmine-red lipstick, I felt that I looked 'exotic', in a Latino hooker sort of way.

My face fixed, I turned to Mom's wardrobe, finally deciding on her new rayon sundress. It was a deep scarlet, with giant, Hawaiian-looking blooms, and the strappy shoulders meant I couldn't wear a bra. I smiled to myself. No bra! How mature was that?

To complete my new, sophisticated look I yanked off my Alice band and vigorously back-combed my mousy hair into a medium beehive. Hmm, I thought to myself as I quickly dabbed some dime store Moonlight In Sienna perfume between the cleft of my cleavage, I'd never make a prom queen, but I didn't look at all bad.

Latimer's liquor store was around ten minutes on foot from my house, a short walk in sneakers, but a total marathon in Mom's black suede high heels.

It was a green-painted clapboard building sandwiched between Rosselli's ice-cream parlour and the hardware store. Celeste was waiting outside when I arrived. She was wearing a tight yellow dress and her platinum-blonde, Lana Turner-style hair had been brushed until it gleamed.

'Just let me do the talking, OK?' she whispered urgently, grabbing my arm as she pushed open the door.

Hearing the shop doorbell, Mr Latimer turned from the shelves he was restocking with gin. He was a hand-some guy of around forty-five, though he could've passed for younger if it hadn't been for the silver flecks in his neatly cut hair and the 'V' of hair visible at the neck of his chequered shirt. He was wearing faded denims and his weather-beaten face was set with the most honest-looking, pale, pale-blue eyes I ever saw.

'Hope it's only gum you're looking for, Celeste,' he said, climbing off his stepladder, ''cos I know damned well you and your friend ain't old enough for anything else.'

'You'd be surprised how much we're old enough for, Al,' she said sassily. 'Just sell us some beers and a couple of pints of bourbon and my friend Valerie here'll show you.'

He acted cool but couldn't hide the tremor in his voice as he replied, 'Sorry, Celeste. I'd lose my licence. Now be a good girl and go on home.'

'Oh, Al,' she simpered, punching the air with her hips as she moved towards him. 'Can't we just go out back and discuss this?'

Al shook his head, but try as he might his eyes seemed magnetically drawn to Celeste's milky, powdered cleavage, which was now just inches away from his hungry gaze. Sensing that his resolve was wavering, she worked her full lips into a playful pout. 'Well, we won't leave until you do,' she said, her girlie voice barbed with an edge of menace.

He looked from Celeste to me and back again, then walked across to the counter, lifted the wooden flap and beckoned us in. 'OK,' he said, his voice cracking slightly. 'Anything if gets rid of you faster.'

The back room was small and mostly filled by a big old mahogany desk covered in neat piles of paper plus an adding machine and a photograph of two boys, both miniature Als, dressed in cowboy costumes. The only other 'furniture' was two beer crates that were pushed against the wall and turned into makeshift seats by the addition of some blue plaid cushions.

Celeste made straight for the desk and put down her purse and cardigan. 'I'll get right to the point Al,' she said, comically businesslike. 'I've seen the way you look at me when I pass the store. You can't take your eyes off my ass, can you?'

Al's face coloured slightly.

'Not that I'm complaining,' she continued. 'I mean, it must be real lonely for you since Ellen took off like that. How long ago now, Al? Six months?'

'What exactly are you getting at?' he snapped, clearly starting to get pissed that this uppity little bitch had taken to speculating about his frustration.

'Oh, I think you know what's on offer here.' She licked her lower lip with the pink tip of her tongue. But not from me,' she added quickly. 'My friend Valerie here's got this thing for older guys.'

I smiled tightly, clutching my cardigan so hard my knuckles hurt. She thought I'd turn and run out the door, but the strange thing was, while I was scared stiff, I was also really attracted to Al. The lustful stare he'd fixed on me since Celeste had so generously offered him *my* body was making me hot and my clit had begun to tingle almost uncomfortably.

I wanted him, a fact made all too obvious by the way my tight, hard nipples made sharp peaks in the sheer fabric of Mom's dress. I wanted his experienced, work-calloused hands on my body and wanted to feel the cock that was visibly trying to burst out of his denims deep, deep inside me.

Heart pounding, I moved towards him and raised a hand to stroke his slightly whiskered cheek. It felt feverish – it really had been a long time. I placed his face in my hands and guided it until our lips met. My kiss was gentle, tentative at first. But, when I closed my eyes and I imagined Celeste's shocked, 'well, I'll be damned' face, I kissed him harder, wrapping my arms tight around his broad shoulders, pushing my tongue into his willing mouth.

As we kissed, he began to grind himself against my dress so's I could feel his stiff cock pressing into my stomach. Taking encourgement from my gasps, he pulled down my two loose shoulder straps, exposing my naked breasts to the air and, lowering his head, teased my nipples with his tongue, rolling it around the granite, deep-coral-pink buds till the blissful sensation made my cunt feel too heavy to bear.

While his mouth pleasured my breasts his hand slid under my skirt and up my thighs till they reached my panties. He began to tease my swollen clit through the sopping crotch – just the slightest, feather-light skimming, but it was enough to make my juices flood into the thick cotton. I let out a yelp of pleasure as one of his fingers strayed inside my panty elastic and slid between my burning pussy lips. My God, I thought, biting my lower lip to stop myself crying out. Whoever this Ellen was, she must've been crazy to have left a guy like this!

It was then that I heard the sound of Celeste's footsteps beating a quiet retreat across the wooden floor. She was opening the door.

'No, Celeste!' I turned to face her. 'You have to stay.'

Damn right she had to stay. She had to stay and she had to watch. I wanted her to suffer *the* most maddening ache in her pussy as she witnessed what I was about to do.

Only when I was sure she'd closed the door did I carry on.

Kneeling down, I unbuttoned Al's jeans and slid them

down along with his underpants. His cock sprang instantly towards my face. I kissed and nuzzled the fat, slippery head, drinking in the musky scent and thinking with each flick of my tongue, How's this for 'audacious', Celeste?

As I fed his cock into my mouth he groaned and started to buck, burying it deeper and deeper into my throat, using it, grunting with pleasure yet still so, so in control. In fact, it was only my impatience to have him inside me that brought the cocksucking to an end. Then, positioning myself so's my ass was on the hard edge of the desk, I watched over my shoulder as he bent his legs slightly and then fed his deliciously rigid, saliva-glazed length right into me.

He fucked me slowly at first, slamming his cock into me and then teasingly withdrawing all but the head, before sliding it back in again. The whole time he thrust into me he kept an expert finger on my clit and rocked it back and forth, setting its sensitive membranes on fire, making the room spin fuzzily around me. I came first, my pussy muscles contracting violently, milking his cock, as I cried and shuddered my orgasm. He hurriedly withdrew. 'Take it in your mouth,' he rasped, his entire body trembling with anticipation. I fell to my knees again and, the moment my lips closed around the throbbing girth, I felt it spasm and rhythmically spurt.

How's this, Celeste? I wanted to shout as I proudly swallowed every last drop of his salty come. 'Just how *outrageous* is this?'

I wanted to see her face, wanted her to see the glow of triumph on mine. But when I looked around she wasn't looking at me. She was sitting on the crates with her head tipped back against he wall. Her peach-coloured panties lay on the ground beside her, opaque and shiny at the crotch. Her legs were splayed wide and I could see her swollen, dark-haired pussy lips and the brisk movement of the jagged pink flesh in between as she wildly fingered her clit.

Al, his breathing still ragged, his cock flaccid, was watching her, too.

He shot me a smile and then moved across to her and knelt between her legs, hooking them over his shoulders.

She whimpered her gratitude as he opened her slippery lips and started to lick her luscious pussy. As his head bobbed faster, hers thrashed uncontrollably from side to side. She wriggled herself against his face until her moans became a broken scream and she arched her back, her body convulsed with orgasm.

It was dark when we left Al's; the only sounds were the chirrup of crickets and the repetitive clanking of the bottles in the brown paper bag I was carrying. The night air felt soft and delicious on the tingling skin of my bare shoulders. My pussy was still tender, my head still full of exploding stars. Celeste was a few steps behind me on the sidewalk. I paused for a moment to look back at her. She was in a world all of her own, her smile dreamy, her eyes glittering, my cardigan folded neatly over her arm.

# Virgin Bride Francesca Brouillard

His is not a lover's kiss, exploring and tasting; rather, his tongue bullies my mouth, asserting rights and demanding submission. Likewise his hands on my shoulders do not caress in a lover's embrace but push me insistently to my knees in front of him. I am naked, as instructed, and ready to please my husband. And this is how he chooses to be pleased right now – by an obedient woman kneeling at his feet, willing to fulfil all his sexual demands.

I am always totally submissive when we play this particular fantasy. It heightens the excitement to an almost excruciating pitch.

The familiar roughness of the rug under my knees, and the coarse jeans grazing my nipples as he forces me down, set marbles rolling in my belly. My body tenses and a flutter like a nervous tic starts up behind my pubic bone. I wonder how he will use me today? The intimate smell of his body, so close I can feel the heat emanating from his groin, makes my mouth go dry and, despite myself, my body starts trembling.

Sometimes he commands me to unbutton his jeans but today he wants to assert his control by different means; I can tell by the rough way he intertwines his fingers in my hair. He undoes the buttons with a deliberation calculated to heighten my apprehension. My breath comes fast and tight now as I anticipate his next move. He pulls out his cock, swollen and rubbery, and holds it up in front of me, then slowly he starts rubbing the glistening end round my face, tracing my brow, my cheekbone, my jaw, painting me with his juices. I can feel my skin tighten as the pre-come dries.

Then, with a clumsy brusqueness, he grabs my hair and yanks my head forward, shoving his cock between my lips. As my mouth is forced open a cold wave sweeps up my body from my knees, twisting my nipples and putting goosebumps on my arms. Then it flows hotly back down, leaving my face burning against his groin and a sensation like molten lava between my legs.

Our relationship has not always been like this. Before we were married it was what would probably be considered far more 'normal'. It was my first proper full-blown sexual affair and he tended to take the initiative. Which was fine with me. I'm not really one of those women who want to be in charge of the sexual side of things; I'm more comfortable leaving it up to the man.

Being inhibited by my lack of experience I generally relied on him to lead and show me what to do and how to pleasure him. I suspect now that he couldn't have found me a very stimulating lover. Though I found the relationship satisfactory, I think it lacked that sharp edge of excitement that keeps you hungry for more.

He grasps my head with both his hands and presses me hard against his groin. When I feel the swelling of his cock straining against my mouth, something is released in me. I relax, knowing I must accept whatever he does to me. There is no need to look for ways of pleasing him for it's not my participation he wants but my passivity; he will use me to feed his fantasies and I must just be obedient and compliant. It is all part of the game.

A low, bass throbbing starts up in my womb and a deep sexual yearning wells up inside me. Excited by the thought of total submission, I grant my husband absolute control over me. He allows me no rights or expectations in our game; I must hand my body over to him for his pleasure alone.

This powerlessness arouses me and the awareness of my willing subjugation fills him with desire. Yet any sign of resistance will be a signal for him to be forceful. He tells me it is unseemly for a wife to be seen to enjoy sex so I have learned to be secretive and suppress all outward signs of my passion on these occasions. As I burn and boil inside from his crude attentions and struggle to hide my rising lust when he forces his way into me, I endeavour to maintain an outward appearance of complete indifference.

His nails dig hungrily into my scalp as he pulls me further and further onto his cock. I force my mouth to relax and overcome the gagging reflex as he pushes further into my mouth. With one hand he grabs my chin and pulls my jaw wide open so he can feel the tip of his cock against the constriction of my throat. I am aware of the rubbery slipperiness probing the roof of my mouth and straining to reach to the back and down my throat.

My hands are squeezing his buttocks convulsively as I struggle to keep my balance and not choke. This gets him buzzing. Now both hands grip my head again and move me to a silent rhythm governed by his own passions.

Our relationship changed abruptly on the night of our wedding. I remember how he carried me, laughing and giddy, up the creaking stairs of the cottage we had taken for our honeymoon in Provence. It was miles from anywhere, and though it had charm, it felt rather plain and simple after the froth and extravagance of our wedding. Still, I was crazily in love and felt secretly excited at being a 'wife' and being carried over the threshold by my new husband. We were now one, to love and cherish and all that; everything I'd always thought rather corny until he actually asked me to marry him.

The bedroom door shut and his role of loving boy-friend – now husband – turned into the role of a master. Later I realised it was only due to this transformation in him that I discovered a new and unsuspected side of my own sexuality. It was a discovery that altered the whole nature of our relationship and introduced a dark and thrilling element in which pain, dominance and sub-mission became inextricably bound up with lust, desire and passion.

My nose is crushed in the wiry coils of his pubic hair and my lips chafe as he grinds me into his pelvis. I am asphyxiating in his lust and crying. Partly it's caused by my eyes watering as I choke on him but also I am moved by an overwhelming desire to yield myself completely. I clutch at his jeans as I struggle to let him drive his cock right down my throat. Saliva fills my mouth and trickles down my chin. Down the soft insides of my legs other juices trickle, as though he has already filled me and seeped right through my body, possessing it completely.

A hot ball grows inside me as his thrusts increase in urgency and take on a new tempo. Although I have no stimulation other than the swollen pumping of his cock in my mouth, my body responds to his movements and a burning sensation suffuses my cunt. If I put my hand down there I know my clitoris will be hard and slippery. But that is not allowed.

Any minute he will explode in my mouth, flooding me and scorching my throat with juices which I will swallow greedily. I am desperate to feel him pouring his lust into me and already I imagine his balls clenching in spasms as he empties himself in my mouth. My lips close elastic tight on the base of his shaft in my excitement, and my tongue presses hard against his cock. Despite his apparent abandonment he detects my rising desire. I have broken the rules. When we are in dominant/submissive mode I must not display any sign of arousal.

Grabbing a fistful of hair he yanks me off his cock. Briefly he holds it wet and rigid right up against my face as if threatening to slap me with it, then he drags me to my feet. I am trembling already, anticipating what will come next. The hot ball of lust in my womb revolves and a cold sweat of apprehension sweeps over me. Adrenaline sends my blood racing and my nerve endings jangling. My nipples tighten with a sweet pain and my cunt contracts.

A moment later he has thrown me onto the bed and rolled me onto my stomach. There is no point resisting; he will take me anyway, just like that first time on our wedding night. My bottom is roughly tugged up in the air. I blush in humiliation at being so exposed to him and I know this adds to his satisfaction. Even at my most uninhibited I have hated displaying my open cunt and arse; it has always been one of those deep-felt embarrassments with me. He pulls at my hair, this time to force me to kneel up on my hands and knees with my breasts hanging free. He knows I am sensitive about the size of my breasts and is excited at the thought of making them swing pendulously with every thrust of his cock. I feel the bed sag as he mounts me.

Whenever I smell dark old timber churches, that room in Provence comes rushing back to me with its rich smell of wooden stairs and floors polished by generations of feet. My nose fills with the scent of dry lavender that rose from the bed where he tossed me after carrying me over the threshold. The antique bedspread was embroidered with tiny pink and lilac flowers that I recall finding very pretty at the time. Later, in the private shame of the bathroom I noticed my breasts were patterned with the embossed flowers; it was a shocking reminder of what had passed and, worse, what lay ahead. That was how it felt at the time, anyway.

He fell on top of me, tugging eagerly at the neckline of my wedding dress with clawing hands. I felt a pang of regret as I heard the ripping of the delicate lace. I'd held a romantic vision of keeping it wrapped in tissue for a future daughter. But my regret was soon lost in the thrill of his animal lust. Never had I seen him so desperate for me. He tore the bodice open savagely and pulled my breasts free, squeezing them hard together so he could get his mouth round both nipples. He tugged with his teeth, pulling upwards so the soft nipples became long and extended. I gasped in pain at first then, when he bit harder, an exquisite sensation soared right through my body from the excruciatingly drawn-out tips of my nipples straight down to my cunt, where I felt the fleshy folds of my labia swell with arousal.

When he raised his head, and I saw the indentations of his teeth on my breasts, another wave of desire flooded me. That uneven purple ring round my nipples was like a sign of ownership: a brand, marking his possession of me and cementing the physical bond of our marriage. Perhaps that was the first inkling I had of another side to my sexual nature, one that thrilled at the prospect of being dominated and used.

Rolling off me he reached over to a bag he'd put by the bed and pulled out a bottle of virgin olive oil. He held it up to show me and smiled. 'For a virgin bride!'

I laughed, 'Hardly!'

'It'll make the loss of your virginity less painful.'

It seemed an odd thing to say, considering how long we'd been having sex together, but I assumed he wanted to play make-believe.

He grabbed me by the hips and pulled me off the edge of the bed so I was kneeling on the floor with my arms and upper body lying across the bed.

Rustling layers of satin and lace were unceremoniously raised and the voluminous skirt of my dress thrown back, tickling my neck and bare shoulders as he exposed my behind. There was a pause, then I felt cold metal on the inside of my thigh. I shuddered. A sudden snipping sound was accompanied by a sense of release and I realised with shock he'd used a knife or scissors to cut through the crotch of my pants. He was now pushing the severed silk up my hips, out of his way. I was scared. Maybe it was the thought of having a sharp blade so close to my intimate parts. Maybe I had a premonition of what he had planned.

I was soon distracted by the cold drizzle of olive oil being trickled down the crack between my buttocks. I felt it running down towards my cunt then being scooped up in his fingers and rubbed into the smoothness of my behind. With slow circular movements he massaged the oil into my skin, gradually moving down to my thighs, then up into the crease of my groin and finally into the wetness I knew was already there. Greasy fingers probed my labia and sought out the nub of my clitoris. Gently he rubbed it, squeezing it between his fingers and tugging it lightly. A shudder went through my legs and a groan crept out from deep in my throat. The fingers began to explore the intimate folds and buried themselves deep in the slit that led back towards my anus. I tensed as he neared this no-go zone and clenched my buttocks, but his hands slid swiftly on and started kneading my behind.

Soon the head of his cock was pushing at the opening of my vagina. I tilted my hips to give ease to his access. He needed no assistance; with the olive oil and my own abundant lubrication, his shaft slid in like a well-oiled component.

With a sigh of relief I leaned back against him, wanting to feel his thrusts reach deep inside me, pushing up towards my womb. Despite his unhurried movements I was close to the edge of orgasm and could feel my vagina contracting in spasms. My hips began moving to their own music and my breath started coming in short gasps. Suddenly he pulled his cock out of me with a wet slurping sound, leaving me suspended on the brink. He must be teasing me, tormenting me with my own desire! Sure enough I felt the exploring fingers reaching into the wetness and dabbling in the juices. There was a rhythmic squelching as his hand slid in and out, rubbing my lubrication into the cleft of my behind. Almost accidentally it seemed his hand slid closer and closer to my arsehole.

Horror filled me as he poked a tentative fingertip into my anus. I went rigid. He'd done the forbidden. I contracted my muscles trying to push him out and pulled my hips away but he pushed his finger further inside me. I felt his knuckles press against my buttocks as he shoved his whole finger up, forcing it through the tight ring of my sphincter.

'Don't! Please!' I blushed with embarrassment, grateful for the layers of skirt covering my head. I was mortified. He knew that 'that' was taboo for me. We'd discussed our fantasies and fears on numerous occasions saying what we'd like to do or have done to us and what things we found distasteful. He knew!

He pulled the finger out with a short laugh that I took to be embarrassment at having gone too far. After all, it was our wedding night; maybe he thought he should try something new.

There was the cold trickle of more olive oil on my backside followed by a sudden terrible burning as he shoved two fingers roughly up my arse. I tried to push him off but he grabbed my wrist and pinned it down to the back of my neck, preventing me from moving. The fingers inside me wriggled against my efforts to squeeze them out and seemed intent on trying to open me up. They stretched the closed ring apart in a scissor action. I started feeling angry. My wedding night was turning into a humiliation at my expense!

I felt the fingers withdraw and a brief wave of relief washed over me but, the next moment, his knuckles brushed hard against my buttocks and I could sense the end of his cock being pressed against my tightness. I began protesting as the pressure increased. The hand on the back of my neck pushed down to subdue me. Now he was rubbing the tip of his cock up and down my cleft, sliding it in the greasy juices. Maybe he would just slip it back in my pussy and everything would be all right. I felt it locate my anus again and test the resistance. I tensed. There seemed to be a long reprieve and I had just begun to relax, when with a sudden lunge, he pushed his cock through the muscle ring and slid into me. An unnerving discomfort shot through my insides as he pushed rudely up my most private and intimate orifice. I realised I was totally helpless to keep him out. I wanted to die of humiliation and shame.

At first I thought I was going to split apart. I was too tight for him, couldn't he tell? He'd burst through the walls and damage me. Surely he'd stop if he knew? He wouldn't want to hurt me. Maybe other women he'd been with were bigger. But, even in the midst of my pain and terror, I knew he wouldn't pull out of me till he was done. He wouldn't be satisfied till he'd broken down all resistance.

For a while he just kept still inside me as if letting me get used to his size and the feeling of being stretched apart. Then he leant over me, resting his body on mine and crushing my breasts into the bedspread. Very slowly he began to move his cock in and out, and as he did so, he started whispering in my ear and nibbling tenderly at my earlobe.

'Relax, baby. Relax and make it easier on yourself ... I'm your husband ... it's okay to do this to you ... "to love and obey", remember? I want to possess you completely, love; to take your whole body. I want to fill you with my juices. You're my wife. I want you to enjoy giving yourself to me. You're mine now.'

Even in the horror of those degrading moments hearing him call me his wife sent a thrill through me. Was I his possession as a wife? Surely not? But something inside me, instead of revolting against the idea, was excited. Some secret part of me wanted to lose control and be 'taken' by him.

The whispering continued. I can't remember the exact content anymore but I was aware of the blood pumping through my cunt as he talked of his desire to dominate me. Despite the stabbing pain of his penetration I felt aroused. His thrusting increased and there was a new excitement about him I'd never witnessed before. Inside me his cock felt as if it was swollen to twice its usual size and I cried and screamed as he fucked me, sure that I should be ripped open when he finally exploded inside me.

If I'd hoped he would be in some way repentant or tender when he'd burnt out his lust I was wrong. Once he'd come he slid off me and slumped onto the bed exhausted. I just wanted to go and clean myself up. I'd been soiled. It was difficult to walk and I felt like I still had his organ rammed up me, keeping my buttocks apart and forcing my sphincter open. I was raw and sore inside and my knees were stiff from kneeling.

I stood under the shower for an eternity trying to wash my shame away with the sticky mess that ran down the back of my legs. Afterwards I put the defiled wedding dress back on. For some reason I didn't want to be naked in front of him. Despite the intimate way I'd been exposed to him, I felt suddenly painfully shy. When I went back in the bedroom he pointed out flecks of blood on the back of the dress. Proof of my virginity he said, grinning. He took me in his arms and kissed me gently, telling me I was now properly his wife.

My hanging breasts wobble slightly as he gets onto the bed to mount me. This position, with me on all-fours, my rump open to him, is his favourite. He leans over me and, reaching round, pinches my nipples hard and tugs down on them alternately as if he is milking me. The sharp pain as he squeezes and nips me with his nails immediately floods my cunt and I feel my clitoris prick up inside the swelling arousal of my labia. His cock dips into the wetness then reaches up for the tight resistance of my anus. At the insistent pressure of its head I relax my muscle ring and he pushes into me. Constant use has stretched me so it is no longer painful to have him enter me but, if we are playing our dominant/submissive roles, then I still pretend to be reluctant and embarrassed.

It is hard to describe the exquisiteness of the surge of excitement that overtakes me when I feel him force his cock into my arse or that wave of pleasure that suffuses my whole being when his final swelling and hardening stretches me wide, ready me for the hot explosion. I want to just melt and be absorbed into him as our juices intermingle in this most intimate union.

I quickly learned on my wedding night that ours was to be a marriage where experimentation would play a big part. Despite being inexperienced, I soon came to relish being submissive on those occasions when my husband wanted to dominate me. Some women might have walked out then, seeing his demands as outrageous, but I didn't. His desire to dominate had aroused a strange and powerful response. I realised it was matched by a deep yearning in me to be controlled and overpowered which, once triggered, exploded into an insatiable craving.

Before the sperm had even dried on my skin after the passionate consummation of our marriage, I had understood that my new husband held the key to unlock a fierce and depraved passion trapped inside me. A passion I was not going to waste.

# Carnival Lights Michelle Scalise

Black velvet-lined walls of the box closed in on me like a bad dream and I couldn't breathe. An uncomfortable heat burned into my cheeks from the stage lights. Clarissa, the magician's assistant, smiled at me, appearing even sexier than she had from my seat in the audience. She wore a red one-piece outfit so snug it seemed like a second skin. I leaned a little to the side and observed Kelly's face beaming in the front row like a proud parent. I wondered if they'd let me out of the magic trick just long enough to slap her.

'Don't be frightened,' Clarissa said, reaching in to harness me to the back wall as if I were a human target. The musky scent of her perfume filled the small space and for a moment I considered pulling her in with me. 'Stand very still and we'll take care of everything.' Her lips brushed my ear as she whispered, 'It'll be like dropping through clouds. Just close your eyes.' I felt a shiver run down my spine as her warm breath eddied against my neck.

The audience roared their approval as she spun round and I was looking into the face of the magician. His smoky black eyes drilled into me as he closed the door. Kelly was right: he did have the kind of eyes that would make a woman come in the dark.

I realised the floor directly beneath my feet was hollow a second before it opened up like a black mouth and swallowed me.

* * *

Kelly had insisted we go check out the sideshow before it closed. 'Amy, how can you turn this down?' she asked, waving the flyer and a half-eaten stick of cotton candy in my face. 'Twelve acts on one stage. And Christian and Clarissa, the world's only conjoined-twins magic act. Look, there's even a picture. They're attached at the lower spine.'

I pushed the paper away, laughing. 'I know you're not that naïve. They've probably just sewn their costumes together.' Pulling out my travel guide, I flipped it to a dog-eared page. Coloured lights from the carnival rides bled shades of red, blue and gold across the paper. 'You promised we'd visit other tourist spots in the city and it's my choice. I want to see the modern art museum before they close.'

'Not a chance,' she said, pulling me down the midway. 'My turn's not over until we've seen all the attractions here and I'm not about to miss something this weird.'

Outside the old brick theatre in the centre of the fairground, a barker stood in a frayed black tux and top hat tilted back from his forehead, shouting to the crowd that was slowly gathering. 'He swallows swords, fire, glass, razor blades – anything you dare him to eat.' The man's arms waved wildly like a preacher caught up in scripture. 'Is it magic you want? Then how about conjoined twins performing feats never before attempted. Come on, folks! Get your tickets right here.'

I wanted to sit in the back row so we'd be able to sneak out later, but Kelly insisted we take our place right up front where flames from the fire-eater seemed almost inches from my face at times.

Christian and Clarissa were the second act. I was busy trying to work a cramp out of my leg while Kelly gazed at the twins' picture, going on about the magician's come-fuck-me eyes. Only the surging sounds of an electric guitar from overhead speakers silenced her. With a single pale light haloing them, the brother and sister walked gracefully out on stage. Tall and slightly muscular, the magician faced us dressed in tight black pants, red shirt and a velvet cloak draped across his shoulders. Short dark curls framed the sharp lines of his face. Looking out at the audience with a satisfied grin, he bowed slightly, then spun around.

The crowd cheered as Clarissa, wearing the same cape, now stood in her brother's place. She was smaller than Christian but with a similar piercing gaze and black curls that hung down to her waist. Her pouty smile, painted a rose-petal red, was more sexual, though, as if she knew everyone was suddenly aroused.

She blew a kiss to us before pirouetting again and again. The velvet wrap fell from her shoulders and puddled on the floor. For a brief moment lights flashed in brilliant clarity on the stage, then quickly dimmed to a whorehouse shade of scarlet. At that instant we were given enough time to discern a spot at their lower backs where the twins were fused. Her costume and his pants stretched out, joining in the middle of a six-inch section that seemed to bridge them.

Kelly grabbed my arm, screaming, 'Oh my God, they're so beautiful.'

I rolled my eyes and considered the valuable vacation time I was wasting on a silly carny show. Flipping through the guidebook, I searched out other tourist sights that might entice my friend away from the carnival. The sting of Kelly's fingernails in my wrist made me glance up. On stage Clarissa was facing forward; the back of her twin's head had risen about a foot above his sister. She swayed slowly in the red glow to a screaming guitar as Christian's hands coiled around her waist, kneading her skin as he crept up to her small breast. His fingertips pulled at one and then the other nipple until they grew hard under his touch.

Heavy sighs and gasps escaped from the darkness as couples sank deeper in their seats. I dropped my guidebook on the floor. Kelly leaned over, whispering in my ear, 'Can we take them home with us?'

I stifled a laugh and tried to shush her.

'I promise to feed and water them religiously,' she continued.

Christian spun to the front, staring down at me as his twin's small fingers ran up and down his thighs. I squirmed nervously in my chair, unable to look anywhere but at those tiny hands working his body. Even in the soft lighting I could plainly see the bulge in his pants. He raised his arms and the stage lit up. 'Before we go on, I think we need someone from the audience to verify that we are actually conjoined twins. Who'd like to be a star for the night?'

Kelly, like everyone else around us, jumped up, waving her arms in the air as if she were drowning. I looked at the stage and saw the magician's hand stretched out to me, a mischievous grin on his face as if he sensed I were the last person on earth who'd want to be there.

I could hear Kelly through the din as she pushed me forward, saying she'd gladly take my place if I couldn't handle it.

I was led to centre stage, where hundreds of eyes could plainly see the look of terror I knew wasn't hidden on my face. The music started up again and the twins circled me as if I were suddenly part of a strange ritual I didn't understand. Lights flashed on and off over my head in a strobe effect. I felt as if I might fall over, growing dizzy in the blur of their bizarre figure appearing and disappearing beside me.

First his face, then hers, until they seemed to transfigure into one being. I wanted to run for the door but I knew Kelly would never let me hear the end of it. Hands grazed my breasts but I couldn't be sure if it was his or hers or both of theirs. Far away the audience's applause melded with the pounding music. My legs were starting to give. I grabbed hold of shoulders, not knowing which pair they were. Clarissa took my hand in hers, placing it on their conjoining muscle and squeezing. I stumbled back as she laughed.

The lights went up again.

Christian held my arms to keep me from collapsing or making a quick exit. 'Tell them what you felt,' he said.

I mumbled something about joined skin. Behind me, the man who'd sold us tickets wheeled out a case of knives, saws and two large glittery gold boxes. One stood upright, the size of a small closet. The other one looked more like a coffin at a Vegas funeral.

Christian asked my name as Clarissa opened the latches on the tall case. The two of them guided me towards it as if I were being dismissed. I stepped in, knowing it was a huge mistake. I hate small spaces – I can't even ride elevators without going into a panic – and the black interior made it seem even narrower inside.

I shook my head at Clarissa, hoping she'd understand and set me free. She just smiled.

Instantly I was falling through darkness. I slid feet first until I reached the ground, landing with a soft thud against foam matting. I was in an unlit dressing room. A window set high above me sent waves of garish lights flashing across a pillow-covered bed, a dressing table with two chairs, a stereo and a tumbled stack of CDs.

The walls, plastered in scarves and postcards, gave the room a gypsy-caravan atmosphere. The box I'd fallen out of was slowly making its way back up into the ceiling, its small frame banging softly.

I scurried to my feet and tried the door. It was locked. 'Shit,' I muttered, looking up into the black hole above me and wondering what the magician would think when I didn't reappear. I could hear more applause, so I figured they'd talked their way out of it somehow. Or else they were just busy feeling each other up again.

With nothing better to do, I spent the next twenty minutes studying a stack of photographs on the floor. From the pictures it seemed as if Christian and Clarissa had travelled the world. And in every shot they were joined, each of them faced slightly towards the camera.

A key in the lock turned and I quickly stood, straightening my dress. Christian entered first, black eyes searching, 'Did you get lost, sweetheart?'

I wanted to say something about their crappy disappearing box but all I managed was a weak apology. Up close without the theatrical lighting they were still a strange sight.

Clarissa spoke. 'I told you the latch on the box wasn't closing properly!' And she hit his arm playfully, spinning around to face me. 'It's all right. We just need you to stay in here until the show's over. We told your friend you'd reappear across the midway at the Ferris wheel when the other acts are through. If we'd told her you were there now the crowd they would have cleared out. Christ, the other performers would have killed us. And, trust me, you don't want to piss off the Amazing Pinhead.'

They walked to their dressing table and I sat on the edge of the bed, watching Christian as he pulled a joint out of a small box and light it. He took a hit then placed it between his sister's crimson lips. Smoke curled up past her head and into the shadows.

'What did you think of the sideshow?' he asked. 'I mean, what little you saw of it.'

Clarissa held the joint out to me and I shook my head.

'I enjoyed your performance,' I said. 'Your dancing was ... really amazing.'

Clarissa laughed. 'That's the best part.' She licked Christian's neck, her tongue darting in and out of her mouth. 'I love to look out and see their startled faces. I mean, a few of them are obviously appalled but most of them can't get enough.' She patted his thigh and the two stood as if on cue, reseating themselves beside me.

'So, how long have you two been doing this?' I asked. 'I mean, the magic.'

Clarissa, who was watching me, giggled, running her fingers down my leg until she reached my knee. 'Did you like watching us, Amy?' The smell of pot, like an exotic incense, filled the room.

I nodded, searching for something to say.

They should have picked Kelly, I thought. She would have loved this.

'Did it get you wet?' she asked. I looked back and all I could see was that red, red mouth. She got on her knees and spun. Christian's eyes were before me now. 'You dropped your book when I felt her up.'

Clarissa was in front again, smiling. 'Would you like to dance with us?' Her hands were on my shoulders, pushing me on to my back, her lips luring and catching mine as I sank into a sea of pillows. Hands tore at the buttons of my dress but I was too lost in the earthy taste of her mouth to question who was doing it. And too stunned to think about what was happening. She stopped to take another hit from the joint, then quickly locked her mouth to mine again. I took in the smoke and her wet tongue again and again until I felt the bed tilting and spinning. Carnival lights outside played across her face like a mask as they mounted me. I could feel Christian's cock growing hard against my stomach, rubbing back and forth. Clarissa drew my breasts out, sucking each one between her lips. Christian's hands gripped my knees, raising them up. His fingers slowly moved between my thighs, forcing me open until I obeyed. Clarissa pulled at a row of snaps that ran up the insides of her red costume, crawling further up me until her cunt was at my mouth.

'Christian,' she said. 'Slow down. Don't make her come yet.'

Clarissa's legs tightened, her back arching, when I suddenly pushed a finger up into her.

'Dance for me,' I whispered, feeling her move up and down. Christian's hand reached around to grab one of her breasts, squeezing it with each push. I chewed at the inside of her thigh, pressing my cheek to her pubic hair and letting it scratch my chin. I breathed her musk in deeply, my tongue tracing down near her clit but not touching it, working around her pubis, and I giggled as I did it. She began to flail, her leg muscles locking and loosening and tightening again. I hung on, moving my tongue to dip against the folds of her cunt. Easing two fingers into her, I licked my thumb to press into her ass. She cried out, coming in my mouth.

Christian drew the two of them down off the bed before Clarissa could catch her breath. He grabbed pillows from behind my head, shoving them under me, then unzipped his pants. With both my calves locked in his hands, he drove his cock into me. His eyes, black as the disappearing box, watched me in the dark. Clarissa's fingers played with his balls as he pressed deeper, squeezing them gently, then harder, as he grunted. I wrapped my hands around his hips, urging him as deep as he could possibly go. I couldn't get him close enough. I wanted to keep pushing up against their contorted flesh until I reached the other side and Clarissa's mouth. I wanted to feel them both inside me at once. Crying out, I came in waves of coloured lights.

A hand shook my shoulder, tugging me out of the shadows of a dreamless sleep. 'Amy, wake up,' Christian said. 'The last act is almost finished. We have to get you to the Ferris wheel to meet your friend.'

I stood and reached out for the bedpost, my head reeling. 'I don't remember the way back.'

Christian chuckled, stretching his legs. Clarissa seemed to be sound asleep at his side bundled under the blankets. 'Don't worry. I've got someone who's going to take you there.' He pointed to a grey-haired woman standing in the open doorway tapping her foot.

I buttoned my dress as quickly as I could and grabbed my shoes.

'Goodnight, sweetheart,' Christian said with a smile. 'I'll give Clarissa your best. You seem to have worn her out.'

I had an uncontrollable urge to giggle but it was quickly silenced by the woman's gruff voice behind me. 'Come on, honey. If I leave my old man to run the ride by himself he'll be givin' out free passes to all the pretty girls.'

Christian waved as I closed the door behind me.

The carnival lights and sickeningly sweet scent of cotton candy made me feel as if I were still spinning, and I stumbled a few times running to keep up with the woman. I watched her back as she darted in and out between people until the shadow of the Ferris wheel loomed above my head like a giant spaceship. I stood for a moment staring up into its metal insides until I heard Kelly yelling my name. A crowd followed behind her, applauding.

'How did they do it?' she asked. 'You gotta tell me.'

I looked around at all the faces and smiled. 'I don't know,' I said. 'One second I was on the stage in that box and then I was here.'

Kelly rolled her eyes. 'Come on, you can tell me. The box had a back exit and they snuck you behind the curtain, right?'

I said I didn't have a clue.

At the entrance gates I felt someone shove against me. The old woman bustled past me, speaking in a clear soft voice, 'Thanks for the dance.' Her blood-red lips parting in a smile as she tucked a loose curl under her wig and hurried away.

'Oh, you must know,' Kelly demanded. 'Or else you wouldn't be laughing.'

'It was magic,' I said, looking back at the lights.

# **Padraig** Emma Wallace

He was crossing from the other side of the street, walking straight towards me. There was something about the way he moved, like a predatory beast, that drew me to him, forcing me to take notice of him.

I couldn't take my eyes off him.

He chose that very same instant to look at me, green eyes locked with mine. I felt a bizarre sensation, my mouth tingled, and my whole body was gripped by a fierce ache. I was shaking. I couldn't move. I didn't want to.

Regaining some composure, I began to cross the street. His stare penetrated. God. Those eyes. They were the kind that drew you in, but at the same time made you want to run like hell. Unable to sustain the piercing contact, I was the first to avert my gaze.

I was intensely aware of myself, of how I must look – my flushed cheeks, my breath coming in short uneven rasps forcing my breasts to swell and struggle, threatening the fabric of my shirt.

He was still watching me – I could feel him. Compelled, I returned his gaze, reaching up to smooth back the curls from my brow so I could get a better look at him. Satisfaction shivered through my body. He was perfect. Dangerous-looking. But *sexy* dangerous.

I guessed he was probably in his early thirties. His black hair was cropped short, his Roman nose was framed by high cheekbones and those beautiful green eyes betrayed little. A jagged scar was carved high on his right cheekbone and ended just beneath his eye. Absently, I wondered how it had got there. His mouth was full and red – truly kissable lips. His skin was tanned and ruddy, as though he were used to spending a lot of time outdoors – stark contrast to the smart suit.

We were now only inches apart.

He continued to stare coolly back at me, causing my blush to spread lower and quicken to an almost painful beat between my legs.

The corner of his full mouth quirked in what was surely a knowing half-smile before finally, as we passed, eye contact was broken. We did not touch, but I felt him.

Unable to stop myself, I inhaled the fresh smell of him as I turned to watch him walk away. It was an effort to break the contact entirely, so as I turned the corner I took a final glance back.

He was gone.

The lights were dimmed but it was not dark. My uneven breathing was the only sound filling the hotel room. I stood close to the bed, wearing only high heels – he hadn't asked me to remove them. His suit jacket grazed my bare back, tickling my skin, as he gently kissed and nuzzled my neck, feathering his lips over the gentle curve between shoulder and ear, then softly biting down. It was slow and delicious.

Promising so much.

My nipples ached. I desperately wanted him to touch them. Instead, his tongue slid up to my ear and bit down a little harder. My pussy twitched at the thrill of what was to come. My clit swelled in anticipation. I could feel his cock through his trousers, huge and stiff as it strained towards my back, the heat of it blazing through the expensive material of his trousers, scorching me, making my flesh burn.

'Spread your legs.' It was a command. His voice was low and firm. I obeyed. My cunt dripped.

His knee nudged my legs further apart as, at last, his big anonymous hands brushed my tits. I couldn't help myself: I lowered my eyes so I could watch what he was doing. Ringless hands roughly cupped my breasts, feeling the weight of them, expressing his appreciation, his thumb and forefinger pinching and kneading my hard nipples in a circular motion. Squeezing and releasing, squeezing and releasing. Hard. Always releasing them with a turn of his wrist, the motion causing my grateful tits to sway.

'Ah, you like it like that?' he whispered.

I nodded. I couldn't speak. I couldn't tear my eyes away. I didn't want to. I watched my flesh grow pink where he'd pinched, my nipples turning to hard red peaks. I was unable to stop a moan escaping my parted lips, and that was all the encouragement he needed: he pinched harder, increasing the pressure as he bit sharply into my shoulder. I watched as his hand left my breast and worked down my body before gripping my hip and pulling me more tightly against his burning cock.

'And this. Do you want this?'

'Oh, God, yes.'

Instinctively, I pushed back. I was ready. I opened my legs a little further. At that moment, I would have done anything he asked of me.

His fingers strummed against my slippery bud, making my breath catch in my throat. He explored further, his probing fingers rubbing my fragrant cream around my swollen lips. Oh, how I loved that smell! He wallowed in my wetness, stroking my pussy before two skilful fingers plunged deep inside me.

Thrusting.

My cunt eating greedily at those fingers.

I wanted them so badly I thought my legs would buckle, but he steadied me with his free hand, his arm banding my trembling belly, his fingers biting into the flesh of my hip.

'Not yet, baby. Not yet,' he said.

Just as abruptly, his seductive fingers were gone, leaving me feeling bereft. A little whimper escaped me. Deliberately, he held his shiny fingers before my eyes. My cream oozed down them. Then I could hear him behind me, sucking them clean, savouring my taste.

I closed my eyes as my head lolled back against his shoulder. I wanted him to fuck me. Hard! Right now!

Reading my mind, he brought his lips once again to my ear.

'It's all right, it's only the beginning. This night is all for you. But be sure of one thing. Before it's over I'm gonna fuck you every which way. I'm gonna fuck you so hard you're gonna scream for me. I'm gonna fill you up with my hot come and you're not gonna be able to get enough of my fucking.' I didn't think it possible, but those words combined with his rasping Irish accent turned me on even more. I had a feeling I'd never get enough of this man.

He loosened his tie. There was a slithering sound as he removed it.

He covered my eyes with it, careful to check that I was comfortable, and knotted it securely in place. I was trembling; no one had ever done this to me before. I could smell my fragrance on his fingers as they trailed over my parted lips.

'You've been a good girl. Now, I need you to do as I say.' I couldn't disobey him even if I wanted to: my body wouldn't allow it. I needed to feel his cock sheathed deep and hard inside, and I would have done almost anything to feel it there.

He whispered another order in my ear.

I crawled on to the bed on all fours so that I was exposed and open to him, feeling wickedly decadent knowing his eyes would be fixed on my swaying breasts and sex-soaked cunt.

Still he didn't touch me, but I was aware of his eyes enjoying the sight of my arse high in the air, my pussy splayed wide, my clit peeking out at him, eagerly waiting for him.

Glistening. Inviting.

The knowledge that I was at his mercy and that he was watching me made me all the hornier. I wondered how long he would leave me like this, open and waiting. I admired his control.

The midnight darkness was heightening my senses, spiralling me into a world where only his touch mattered, just as he'd promised.

I didn't have to wait for long. I felt the bed give a little. I thought he was getting on beside me but he was only leaning on it, reaching out to me, his hands fastening on each of my hips before dragging me back towards him, still on my hands and knees, and repositioning me a little closer to the edge.

He was still fully clothed.

His hand stroked the length of my back and over my cheek. Instinctively I rose to meet it.

Then without warning he slapped me, fast and hard. Once, twice, the stinging pain slicing through my buttock and taking me by surprise. It hurt like hell. My poor wounded arse.

I screamed. What the hell did he think he was doing? My eyes stung with unshed tears. Nobody had ever done anything like this to me before.

I was shocked – shocked that he would dare. And then, as the pain began to fade, I felt the afterglow, the rush. I was shocked that I was actually starting to enjoy it. What was wrong with me? Surely this wasn't right? But for now I didn't care about that. I wanted more. I wiggled my arse provocatively. Pushing it out at him, inviting him to do it again.

He did. Harder than before. The crack of it loud in my ears. *Oh, damn, it was good!* I groaned loudly, the heat suffusing my cheeks. My backside and thighs burned as he spanked me again and again. The pain built, spiralling through me with every thwack of his hand. 'Are you enjoying this, my sweet?' Listening to his honey voice, I didn't know who was taking more pleasure from this. Did he really have to ask? My body was on fire for him.

'I asked you a question. Now answer me.' This time his voice was lower, and was accompanied by the most punishing slap so far.

'Fuck, yes ... yes! It's good,' I yelled, unable to hold back. Because it *was*.

Slap!

Slap!

I bit my lip, trying to stop the grunting sounds. Finally, his hand gentled, then stopped. I heard him drop to his knees as he calmed my reddened bottom with his lips. Kissing lower, he opened my damp lips, spreading them apart and inserting his tongue into the opening. He searched the wet folds while his fingers pinched my clit, pushing down and circling it, increasing the pressure, building it to a maddening throb. His hand still gripped my hip, controlling my movements, making me match his rhythm as he fucked me with his tongue. Lapping at my wetness, relentlessly working in and out, making me wriggle. Licking the full length of my slit before drawing my hot clit into his wet mouth and probing the swollen bead with his tongue. It slithered. It slid. It licked. It was exquisite torture. Oh, God, he was wicked. My face was flushed. I wanted so much to make this last. Until I couldn't bear it any longer.

'I – I – now. I want to feel you inside me – please, now'. Panting, I barely recognised my own voice. I thought I would scream with frustration.

'Beg me. Tell me how you want it,' he taunted.

There was no hesitation. He'd stripped away more than my clothes.

'Please fuck me, fuck me hard, fuck me deep. Just fuck me! Now! *Please!*' I moaned. It almost came out as a sob.

Through with waiting, I could hear as he unzipped his trousers. Then he was between my legs. He held me firmly, raising me slightly to meet his hard-on. With one powerful stroke he pushed his huge prick where his mouth had been only moments before, plunging deep into my waiting sex. I bucked and cried out as the full length of his cock filled me up. He felt massive inside me and I wanted it all, every inch.

Swivelling his hips, he deepened the penetration, burying his beautiful cock to the hilt. His shaft opened me wide, stretching my swollen lips, and as I arched back into him he began to thrust, again and again, slow to begin with, testing me. Then more forcefully, his hands maintaining their grip on my arse, guiding me as I ground against him. Oh, he felt so damn good!

I squeezed and gripped his prick with my muscles, clamping his shaft. He gasped and jerked forward. His front cleaved to my back as he pulled me by my hair, causing my neck to arch so that my head was closer to his, and whispered in my ear how wet I was, how tight I was, how he was going to fill my hot cunt with a load of his warm cream. Releasing me, he reared back, thrusting his cock even deeper.

Knowing I couldn't hold out much longer, he reached round and pushed his fingers between my legs, burying them in the hot wet cleft of my lips and prising them wide open; a single finger, gently pressing, tormenting my plump clit back and forth. Applying just a little more pressure with each stroke.

Lost in my sightless black world, I surrendered, *loving it*, loving this secret dark place he'd created for me, where the only thing that mattered was him and what he was making me feel.

Pressure was rising, blood was thundering, sweat was rolling down my thighs. My muscles were seizing, and I was unable to bear any more as my throat filled with a scream and I came. I'd never felt this with anyone else. Still shuddering from my own orgasm, I felt him jerk, ramming even deeper into me, forcing my hips still so that I couldn't pull away until he was finished squirting his load into me. Shaking from the intensity of my orgasm, my arms and knees too weak to support me any longer, I collapsed forward on to the bed, taking him with me.

He pulled free, the scent of our sex hanging heavy in the air, and turned me over on to my back to face him. He removed the blindfold. It took me a few moments to focus and when I did he was smiling sweetly down at me.

'You did good, baby,' he whispered.

As our breathing returned to normal, he used his thumbs to gently wipe away the spilled tears. Cupping my face in his hands, he kissed me for the first time with unbelievable tenderness.

How did I come to be naked in a hotel room with this stranger with the moss-green eyes? Purely by chance.

I'd gone out with friends. It was still early and we'd not long met up. I was having a laugh and a gossip when I felt the hairs on the back of my neck stand on end. I could feel someone staring at me. I tried to ignore it but they weren't giving up, so I turned. It was him. And if I'm honest I knew who it was even before I turned.

He smiled and nodded in my direction.

Not sure what I was about to get myself into, I looked him straight in the eye and smiled right back. He had my attention. It was obviously what he'd been waiting for. I sucked in my breath as he finished off his drink and walked towards me. He bent his head very close to mine and whispered in my ear.

What did he whisper? That he'd been admiring my tattoo and would I leave with him – now. Then the cocky bastard actually licked my ear.

I must have been mad or desperate or something, because that was exactly what I did. Right then. I left the pub, my drink barely touched, leaving my friends gobs-macked at what had just happened. We walked to his hotel. He asked me my name, then we went to his room. Maybe I should have been nervous but I wasn't. It was unlike anything I'd ever experienced.

Then it was morning. He had business. And I was alone. But not before he told me I should be ready for eight o'clock – we were going out.

At the restaurant, after the waiter had taken our order, he asked me to go into the ladies' and remove my bra and panties because he wanted to know I was naked beneath my clothes while we ate.

Surprised, but curious and feeling very naughty, I fixed him with a determined look as I excused myself from the table. I suspected it was some kind of test, and I wanted to please him.

On my return, feeling very liberated and brave, I flourished them in front of his smiling eyes before dropping the tiny black wisps before him, the smile extending to his lips as the couple at the next table tutted loudly. He left them there for a moment, but, as my new-found confidence deserted me, I started to squirm a little uncomfortably, a blush staining my cheeks, so he scooped up the lacy scraps and bunched them into his jacket pocket like some absurd hankie. He smiled wickedly at me.

I couldn't help dwelling on my nakedness. I was acutely aware of my body and how my hard nipples were sensitised further by the brush of material. Although if he suffered any of the same distractions he didn't show it. Was this his idea of some kind of weird foreplay? I could only assume that it was. After last night he knew my body intimately. He knew how to turn me on and make me beg for him, yet he didn't know me at all. It was bizarre. But I was ready to play his game.

He wanted to know everything about me. So I told him. The first thing I told him was my surname. The next thing I told him was that I was twenty-two years old, a photographer, and had lived in this small town all my life. I then told him why I had left the bar with him last night. I admitted I'd been overwhelmingly attracted to him and afraid not to act on it – what if I never experienced those instant overwhelming emotions ever again?

'What if . . . ?' I'd spent a huge part of my life that way. It was easier that way, safer that way, in my cocoon, surrounded by people I knew, in a place I knew. But I was changing. I wanted more. To feel more. To see more. Experience more. I wanted to be me. Yet the thing holding me back was me.

What surprised me most was that he listened. Really listened. As our food was served and we ate he was happy to let me talk. And I talked. His unwavering attention and my near-nakedness was a heady combination building on the raw attraction I already felt for him. I didn't know what this was, or what it might become. It might not become anything and that was good, too. But it felt right and for now I was happy to follow him on this merry dance.

Once we were outside, he led me round the back of the restaurant. Why had we gone this way? We shouldn't have been here. It was cold and narrow and it was smelly. I walked close beside him, following his lead, my nose wrinkling at the smell of urine and rotting food. We stopped part of the way down and he turned me towards him, his fingers brushing my thigh, gathering my skirt, brushing it higher and higher until my thighs were exposed. I put my hand over his, nervously looking to see if anyone was around. I could hear voices from the street but couldn't see anyone. Satisfied no one would see, I turned my attention to what he was doing. I'd sat through dinner in near-nakedness, anticipating the sex. I just hadn't expected it to be here. By now he had my skirt up over my hips. His hand trailed over my belly, lower, to cup me between my legs. It was so intimate, even after everything else we had shared last night.

'Why so scared, Emma? Isn't this what you want? Isn't this what you've been thinking about all through dinner?' he taunted. This was *exactly* what I wanted – I just hadn't known it.

My thighs parted. My breathing changed, grew more rapid. The fingers framing my pussy were already wet as I pushed my hips to meet him, as he slid one inside me.

'Tell me. Is that what you've been waiting for? Have you been thinking about this, wanting this?'

I told him I had, my 'yes' drawn out in one long breath.

'How about another? Are you ready for more?'

He never waited for my answer. It was accompanied by a fierce thrust as he added another finger. I was moaning loudly, no longer caring if I could be heard. This was all that mattered. Here. Now. His fingers dipping in and out as my cunt slurped at them.

I needed to touch him. His rigid cock was already uncovered and waiting for me. My fingers clamped around his straining prick, my thumb brushing the head, sliding against the juices that leaked there, and I began to work my hand up and down, up and down, as another finger slid in and out of my cunt. His eyes never left my face. He was always watching me. His chest was rising and falling, his eyelids growing heavier as my hand pumped up and down.

'Suck my cock.' As with everything, it wasn't a request. From hip to high-heeled foot I was bare and exposed, kneeling in this filthy alley sucking his thick, hard prick, deep inside. I couldn't help a small smile of satisfaction as he groaned loudly.

Reaching down, he cupped my shivering breasts. My breasts as well as my bush were now uncovered, displayed. By now uncaring of the surroundings, lost in my own pleasure, I surrendered to the mounting tensions, closing my eyes, focusing on the cock nudging back and forth within my mouth.

'Don't stop, but there's a someone watching us,' he whispered in panting bursts. 'Does that excite you as much as it excites me?' Fear and lust coursed through my veins. It could be someone I knew. They might recognise me. Although, most likely, it was someone dumping rubbish from one of the restaurants. *But did it excite me?*

Yes it did. I felt safe. I trusted him. I knew he wouldn't let anyone harm me. I looked up at him so he could see the excitement in my eyes. I could feel the stranger's eyes upon us. Spurring me on. I licked his cock more fiercely than before, looking him straight in the eye. My lips exerted pressure as my tongue moved up the shaft in tiny lapping licks before returning to the head and licking heartily.

'That's it. Just like that, baby.'

One his hands was pressed against the wall, the other clasped behind my head, bunched in my hair, guiding my movements. His thighs steeled beneath my touch as I increased the tempo.

Then, without warning, he withdrew from my mouth. I felt cheated. But my efforts were rewarded with a flood of come flowing from my throat to my breasts, creamy white and fragrant.

'Turn so he can see you. Let him see you rub my come all over your tits.' Debauched, I wanted only what he wanted, so I bent my head to lick a drop from my nipple, then lovingly massaged the rest in before he dragged me up off my knees and on to my feet, pushing me against the cold wall and cupping my face between his hands, kissing me very hard. His mouth devoured mine. Our kissing was noisy as our tongues and teeth collided.

He was brutal. I loved it.

'You drive me crazy, you know that? How do you know you haven't done yourself out of a good fuck?' he growled against my lips.

I didn't, but there was something very satisfying about having a big dick in your mouth. It was an even bigger thrill when it was in this dirty back alley while some stranger watched.

I felt naughty. Euphoric. Wanted.

Before I could catch my breath to answer, he kissed me again. His body pressed against mine, pinning me against the wall, the brick rough on my back. It was one of those hard wet kisses that you just can't get enough of. I almost forgot to breathe. I clutched his shoulders as he wrapped his arms around me and hoisted me up to wrap my legs around his waist. His hands held my bare bottom, supporting me. He dipped his head and flicked his tongue over my nipple, sucking it into his mouth, tugging gently. I groaned. He sucked harder, then released it with a popping sound. The chill atmosphere clinging to the shiny residue of saliva and the steady stream of warm air as he blew against it combined to turn my nipple pebble-hard. It felt utterly amazing. He licked up the slope of my breast and the length of my throat with the flat of his tongue, leaving a moist trail, before finally plunging deep into my hungry mouth. At the same time, without ceremony, he forced himself into me, driving his swollen prick home. My legs tightened around him, welcoming him in, the heels of my shoes scoring his buttocks, forcing him even deeper. I desperately wanted this violent fuck. The throb from my cunt was almost more than I could bare and my heavy lids began to close.

'Open them. I want to see your eyes, to watch your face as I fuck you. I want to see you come,' he demanded. I dragged them open, my insides giving a little flutter as his green eyes locked with mine, holding steady. I know it wasn't his intention but what I saw there was beautiful.

We fucked each other, finding the perfect rhythm. Hips joining and parting, we slammed together, hard up against the wall, as he pinioned me there with his thrusts.

'Oh man ... Oh, Jesus ... I'm gonna come ...' He slapped the wall.

There was no way he was going over without me – not this time. I gripped him tighter. I worked my hand down between our bellies, squeezing it down those cru- cial few inches until I reached my goal, stroking rhyth- mically. Fast. It needed to be fast. I worked faster, harder. My clit felt massive. Oh. Yes. Faster – *now*! Tightening, spasms vibrated through me. I screamed out my own noisy orgasm, letting them hear I didn't care any more. Almost sobbing, I felt his passion spurt into me. Shudder- ing convulsively, he bit hard into my neck, stifling his yell.

I had no idea at what point our watcher vanished, but I'd like to think he enjoyed witnessing the crude exhi- bition that was us in that seedy alley.

I was a mess. Bruised. Dirty. Overwhelmed. Truly fucked and yet strangely free.

He's facing me from the other end of the bath. My foot rests on his shoulder as he soaps my calves; his fingers creep dangerously higher. He's giving me that look. And I'm getting to know that look very well. He turns his head and kisses the tattoo on the inside of my ankle.

I lay my head back and close my eyes, a smile playing across my lips. Unconsciously, I touch a finger to them, tracing the swollen outline. It isn't only my mouth: my whole body aches; but it's a good ache, one I can live with. I feel a twinge everywhere he's been, everywhere he's touched. Images replay in my head. He's had me in every hole in just about every way; there's not a part of he hasn't known.

I have to ask, 'How did you know?'

He runs his thumb over my swollen lips and I can sense him watching me. My tongue snakes out and draws it into my warm, wet mouth. I don't think he's going to answer me but eventually he does. 'It was all over you – that day we passed on the street. When I looked into your eyes, I knew.'

His name is Padraig. Padraig Doyle. He's thirty-four years old and he hails from Belfast. We met three days ago. I don't know why he's here. And I don't ask. I don't even know what he does for a living. And I don't care. And, despite his answer, I'm still not sure why he chose me.

All I do know is that he makes me feel free to be myself. Be the person I want to be and not the one I think I should be. I know he will be patient and not ask for anything I'm not willing to give. I know he will never judge me.

I also know he's leaving here in the morning and that I'll be leaving with him, and for now that will be enough. No promises. That's how we want to play it for now.

As he rinses the soap from me, I allow myself this indulgence and promise it will be the last time.

What if ... I'd said 'no'?

# Having His Cake
## Elizabeth Coldwell

So there I was, lying handcuffed to the bed with only a thin layer of cream and strawberry jam protecting my modesty, waiting to give Matt Henderson his thirtieth-birthday surprise. It hadn't seemed like such a stupid idea when my brother had first suggested it to me – though Robbie could probably persuade an Eskimo to buy a fridge-freezer – but now, as the wax from the party candles that topped my nipples threatened to spill down on to my tender breasts, I was starting to feel uncomfortable and just a little bit vulnerable.

I'd be lying if I said I hadn't gone into the whole crazy scheme without an ulterior motive. I can't think of any girl I know who wouldn't jump at the chance to get naked in the presence of Matt Henderson. He's the goalkeeper in the Sunday League football team Robbie plays for, and, as he never tires of telling anyone within earshot, he used to be a pro. He was on the books of Rotherham and Preston North End before a back injury finished his career prematurely, and now he works in insurance and relives his glory days once a week on the local council playing fields. But he's still fit – and I mean that in any sense of the word you care to choose. Six foot four, broad and muscular, with thick, glossy dark hair cut to look its best when he's running his fingers through it. He knows how attractive he is, but then he's hardly a shrinking violet. If you wanted to be polite, you'd say he was sure of himself; cocky is probably a better description. Whatever, he had left a trail of broken hearts and damp knickers in his wake since he'd first joined Robbie's team, and, though I wasn't sure whether or not I actually liked him, that isn't always a prerequisite for wanting to fuck someone, despite what all the agony columnists and your mother have always told you.

The plan was simple – Robbie arranged to throw a party for Matt, and I was to turn up an hour before the guest of honour, which would give me plenty of time to get into what was laughingly referred to as my costume. I think it all stemmed from some drunken conversation the lads had had on one of their Friday night pub sessions, when they were discussing Matt's impending birthday and the subject of celebrations involving a girl jumping out of a cake was brought up. That, Matt said, was old hat, and, anyway, they usually made those enormous gateaux out of cardboard, so you couldn't even enjoy a slice of the thing after the stripper had done her stuff. His idea of a good time, or at least the way it was relayed back to me, involved eating cake off the body of a naked woman – and that was where I came in. Quite why I was put forward as some kind of human dessert plate, I wasn't sure, although Robbie happened to be the only one of the group discussing the original idea who had a sister, and I suspect none of the rest of them would trust their girlfriend alone with Matt in any stage of undress. If you met him, you'd know why.

All it needed was someone to actually help me get ready, given that I didn't want Robbie involved in that stage of proceedings. I mean, there may be some places where it's considered quite normal to take your clothes off and fiddle around with your sibling, like the back-woods of Virginia and the Forest of Dean, but Robbie and

I didn't have that type of relationship, so Jamie volunteered to do it instead.

Jamie Brown and Robbie had been best buddies since the age of five, inseparable since Gresley Road Infants and now Greengate Rovers' deadly twin strike force, the pride of the Aughton Industries League Division Three – or so they always claimed. All I knew was that, if one of them was involved in some kind of scam, the other one wouldn't be far behind, and that was why it was Jamie who accompanied me into my brother's spare bedroom with all the accoutrements necessary to turn me into the sweetest of treats for Matt.

I glanced round the little room, my eyes drifting from the extensive rack of CDs and the computer-games console Robbie kept in what he regarded as his study-cum-den to the small single bed, which had already been spread with an old beach towel gaudily patterned with fat fish and skinny seahorses in all the colours of the rainbow. I knew I should start undressing, but my bravado, even fuelled as it was with a couple of glasses of sparkling wine, was fading rapidly and I was trying to delay the moment of my exposure as long as possible.

'Well, come on, then, Jules,' Jamie said, not unkindly, 'get your kit off, so we can get you ready before the birthday boy arrives.'

I kicked off my shoes and reached for the waistband of my jeans, suddenly feeling awkward. Looking back, I suppose I could have gone into the bathroom and changed there, but Robbie, reasonably enough, didn't want to run the risk that Matt would turn up early and accidentally bump into me, ruining the surprise. It just seemed so strange to be sliding my jeans down to my ankles under Jamie's watchful stare. Four years younger than I, I'd known him since he was a little kid, playing with Robbie's Action Man in the back garden and running around with scraped knees and a snotty nose; and, while I'd had the odd crush on a couple of Robbie's friends, I had never imagined myself taking my clothes off in front of Jamie. I simply didn't think of him that way. He was just Jamie, with his angular face dominated by a big nose, which had been broken by a stray cricket ball in his teens. Jamie, who carried his six foot of height gawkily, as though ashamed of being a head taller than his parents. Jamie, who wore his curly brown hair in no particular style and slobbed around in old jeans with his T-shirt permanently untucked at the back. Jamie, in short, who was as different from the handsome, confident, outrageously horny Matt as it was possible to get.

All of which should have made what was about to happen easier, but it didn't.

I hesitated before reaching for the hem of my top. My breasts are so small I never bother to wear a bra, and though Jamie must have known this from the way the points of my nipples sometimes poked through my clothes – usually, it has to be said, when we were all sitting together in the pub and Matt's thigh was resting against mine beneath the table – it had never seemed like an issue till now. Finally, aware that I was risking stretching his patience, I pulled it up and over my head in one swift movement, baring myself to him. He said nothing, but I saw his eyes drop to my tits, and, when his gaze finally returned to my face, there was a guilty flush on his cheeks.

'When I was thirteen,' he said, speaking through a sudden constriction in his throat, 'I would have given anything to see you do that. Ask Robbie about the time you were in the bathroom and – No, on second thoughts, forget I ever mentioned that.'

Pushing thoughts of committing fratricide to the back of my mind, I turned my attention to the process of removing my pink lacy knickers. Turning my back on Jamie, I pushed them down and stepped out of them, half expecting him to retrieve them from the floor and either sniff them or try wearing them on his head in an attempt to break the growing tension in the room. He did neither. Instead, when I turned back to face him, fighting the urge to use my hands to shield my pussy from his gaze, his next words dumbfounded me.

'You haven't shaved.' As I gaped at him blankly, he asked, 'Didn't Robbie tell you to?'

Now my thoughts were of torturing my brother slowly with a toasting fork before dispatching him. 'It must have slipped his mind,' I replied with the merest hint of sarcasm. 'After all, at what point in the conversation do you casually mention to your sister that you need her to whip her pubes off?'

'Well, we're going to have to do it now,' Jamie said. 'There's still time. Otherwise, Matt's going to be dining on hair pie tonight.'

'How tactfully put,' I murmured to his receding back as he disappeared from the room. Moments later, he was back with a razor and a can of shaving foam plundered from Robbie's bathroom, together with a bowl of hot water and a flannel.

'Right, I want you to lie on the bed, Jules.'

'I'm not sure about this,' I protested, feeling that things were starting to move to a level I hadn't expected when I had first agreed to this.

'Look, it'll be quicker if I do it. Trust me.'

Trust me. The fatal words. And yet what choice did I have? Following Jamie's instructions, I lay back on the spread beach towel, making myself comfortable against the propped-up pillows. And that was when he sprang his real surprise.

He took something from the little bag of tricks he and

Robbie had put together, and my mind just had time to register the shape of the shiny steel bracelets before he caught hold of my wrists and snapped the cuffs round them, securing me to the bedrail.

'Jamie? What the...?' I struggled, pulling at the short length of chain that joined the cuffs and had been looped around one of the slats in the bedhead, but it held firm.

'Matt happened to mention it,' Jamie said blithely, picking up the shaving foam. 'I think he's got a thing about tying his women up.'

This was starting to get seriously out of hand. No one had ever done this to me before. No one had the right to do this to me without my permission. And yet, if that was the case, why did I like the feeling so much? Why was my cunt starting to throb at the idea that I couldn't free myself and, if he chose to, Jamie could do whatever he liked to me?

'Just a moment, I don't want to mess this up.' Jamie quickly stripped off the faded khaki T-shirt he was wearing. Underneath it, he had an unexpectedly good body, lean and lightly tanned, his abdominal muscles gently defined. Though, with everything that had gone before, I suppose nothing about my brother's best mate should have surprised me by now.

In the living room, Robbie had turned on the stereo, the thudding of the bass seeming to keep time with the pulse beating between my legs. I fidgeted, conscious of a prickly burst of heat down there, heat that was almost cooled whom Jamie sprayed lemon-scented foam over my mound and down the length of my crease to my dimpled arsehole. Almost – but not quite.

There's obviously a detached, professional way to shave a pussy, otherwise nurses would get the sack on a regular basis. Jamie's manner, however, could not have been less detached. It wasn't that he was failing to remove the hair – far from it, as the mousy specks in the foam he was sweeping away with the razor had testified. No, it was the way he used his fingers to softly part my lips, opening me up so he could get into every nook and cranny. His touch was teasingly light, inflaming nerve endings that had woken up the moment the handcuffs had clicked into place; and when he brushed my clitoris, so lightly that it could almost have been an accident, I knew I was lost. He must have heard the needy whimper that escaped my lips, as a smile flickered across his face, but he ignored it.

Instead, he urged me to lean back and raise my knees to my chest, so he could get down to the hair around my anus. I couldn't remember the last time I had been made to display myself so brazenly to anyone, and, though I should have been humiliated by the willingness with which I was obeying Jamie's commands, the truth is I was enjoying it. I suppose it helped that it had been a while since I'd last slept with anyone, and I knew Jamie was on his own, too. For the first time, it occurred to me that he was preparing me for another man – a man who could get any woman he wanted simply by snapping his fingers. What was Jamie getting out of this? I wondered, and then his finger strayed over my clit once more, and I lost all coherent thought as I gave in to the sensation.

Abruptly, he pulled his finger away, and I felt the damp flannel being wiped over my sex. 'There we go,' he said, sounding pleased with his handiwork. 'All done.'

I squinted down my body, trying to see what Jamie had done to me, and caught a glimpse of soft pink flesh where I normally expected to see a tangle of brown hair. There was something unexpectedly kinky about being bare there, and the bulge that was all too obviously pressing against the zip of Jamie's jeans showed how much he, too, liked the sight.

I couldn't help myself. I wanted his fingers back where they had been moments ago, working into the depths of my pussy. 'Please, Jamie,' I murmured, 'touch me again.'

'Like this?' The flat of his palm strayed lightly over my mound, well away from my sex lips. 'Or like this?' Now, they traced their way along my slit, causing me to shiver and spread my thighs wider in response. I knew I was acting like a slut, offering myself so blatantly to Jamie, but I didn't care.

'God, you're really gagging for it, aren't you?' Jamie's finger pushed at the entrance to my cunt and slid inside to the second knuckle, finding no resistance. 'I bet you'd do anything for me right now.' A second finger slipped in beside the first, and his hand began to pump gently, rhythmically. 'Suck my cock. Let me spank you. Maybe even offer me your arse.' His thumb settled on my clit, rubbing it with just enough pressure to propel me on the road to what I just knew would be an incredible orgasm. The images his words had created in my mind were doing the rest: my lips, wrapped around Jamie's thick shaft; my bum cheeks, glowing and smarting with the imprint of his palm; my anal hole, opening up to take him into my virgin passage. I was close, so unbelievably close. My hips were thrusting up to meet his steadily wanking fingers, and my breath was coming fast and ragged. And then he stopped.

'Please, Jamie.' The forlorn catch in my voice made it all too obvious that I was begging. 'Please make me come.'

'But we shouldn't be doing this, should we, Jules? After all, I thought it was Matt you were interested in.'

His eyes met mine, demanding honesty. 'I am. But I could be persuaded to change my mind.'

'I know you could. But I'm still not going to let you

come. Apart from anything else, you look so cute when you're horny and frustrated.'

Before I could tell him exactly what I thought of him at that moment, he had pulled a can of dairy cream out of the kit he and Robbie had put together, and was shaking it vigorously. 'Come on, let's finish you off.'

That's what I've been begging you to do, I thought, as cold cream swooshed over my freshly shaved pussy, making me squirm. 'Won't be much longer, I promise,' Jamie said, turning away from the bed again, 'but I've got to make sure Matt gets the message.'

Now he was holding a tube of some sort, and I realised from the brightly coloured packaging that it was the sort of smooth strawberry jam designed for fussy little kids who don't like it with lumps of fruit in it. This was aimed in a cursive jet at my belly. There wasn't a great deal of room for Jamie to manoeuvre, but, as I squinted down my body, I realised he was spelling out 'HAPPY 30TH, MATT.

I thought that was the final flourish, but I was wrong. Jamie had discarded the jam and appeared to be rolling something between his fingers. A faint scent of almonds made me realise it was marzipan. Why the hell does he need marzipan? I wondered. 'Hold still,' he said, and smoothed a ball of the stuff over each of my nipples. I did a double-take when I saw what he produced next: candy-striped party candles, already stuck in those little flower-shaped holders.

'Oh, no,' I said, shaking my head. 'You can't be serious.'

Jamie said nothing, just pushed the candles firmly into the marzipan, then reached into his back pocket for a cigarette lighter. As I lay there, too stunned to protest, he lit the candles.

'Perfect,' he breathed. 'All I've got to do is go and get Matt. Don't run away now.'

'Very funny,' I said, as he disappeared out of the bedroom. I lay there, trembling with arousal and anticipation, and waited. And waited. I couldn't see a clock from where I was, but it seemed as though at least five minutes had passed, and there was no sign of Jamie. Was there a problem? Had Matt failed to show up? Or was this all just some elaborate prank Jamie and Robbie had cooked up between them, and were they about to come in with a camera and record my humiliation?

I shifted position slightly, my arms beginning to ache, and, as I did so, I caused a thin stream of wax to dribble down on to my breast. Pain blossomed where it touched, but somehow it served only to reignite the fire of my long-denied orgasm. I was still desperate for release, and furious with Jamie for having done this to me – and with myself for letting him do it so willingly.

And then the bedroom door swung open.

'Happy birthday, mate,' I heard Jamie say. I glanced at the two men silhouetted in the doorway, a grinning Matt looking immaculate in a black turtle-necked T-shirt and dark jeans, and Jamie still bare-chested and with a tuft of his hair sticking up at the back. As my anger gave way to relief, I knew it was no longer a question of choosing between them: I could – would – have them both. If only Jamie would release me from these wretched handcuffs.

'I can't believe it. This is brilliant,' Matt said, coming closer. He was about to reach out a finger and scoop up some of the gooey mess that covered my pussy – and then he stopped. 'Hang on. Is that fresh cream?'

'It's that squirty stuff out of a can,' Jamie explained, 'but it's as good as the real thing.'

Matt shook his head. 'But you know I'm allergic to dairy products. I can't go near that or I'll swell up like a bullfrog. Cheers, Jamie, some birthday present this is.'

'Sorry, mate, I completely forgot.' Jamie sounded sincere enough, but one look at his expression told me he'd been entirely aware of Matt's allergy when he had decorated my body. I was expecting Matt to turn on his heels and leave the room in crestfallen disappointment, but Jamie's next words sent renewed excitement pulsing through me. 'Why don't you let me deal with the cream? I'll get it out of the way for you while you blow the candles out.'

Matt's face broke into a grin, and he came to kneel beside the bed. He trailed his finger through the jammy writing on my stomach before bringing it to his mouth to lick it clean, and I swear my cunt muscles clenched with lust at the sight. I felt his breath huff across my chest, extinguishing the little flames, before he peeled away the candles, blobs of dried wax and scraps of marzipan and bent his head to take one of my nipples in his mouth. Jamie, meanwhile, had pulled down his jeans and boxer shorts to let his cock spring up erect, as solid and meaty as I'd hoped it would be. As his tongue made contact with my cream-covered clit, the orgasm I had been building towards for so long finally hit me. And as I shuddered, arching my body up involuntarily to let one man feast more greedily on my tits and the other on my pussy, I realised there was an old saying I would have to consign to the dustbin. Well, what was happening to me so clearly proved that you could, after all, have your cake and eat it.

# **To You, Watching** Gardenia Joy

I like to think of you watching me. When I'm dressing I turn demurely from the window, but I don't close the curtain, and I look back briefly so you can see my face, the way my neck curves. My movements are no longer impatient and unplanned: now I slip easily into my clothes and bend at the waist to buckle my shoes. Your vigil makes me graceful.

When I first realised you were watching, I felt almost shy, almost violated, almost like I wanted you to stop. But then I started to think about what you see, how I look when I walk, when I sip my drink, answer the phone, smile hello to someone else. I look in the mirror and turn my head to the side. Do you like the way my hair brushes in front of my eyes?

When you call me I am alone in my bed, but I have been thinking of you.

'Hello,' you say.

'Hello,' I answer. Then we are silent. Finally I ask, 'Where are you?' It is a stupid question.

'Never mind,' you say, and we are silent again. I am thinking of how to ask you what you see, why you watch me, who you are, a hundred questions. I am naked, and there is a small bruise on the outside of my right thigh, just below the curve of my hip. I wonder if you know it's there. I am surprised when you say, 'I notice everything.'

'You notice everything,' I repeat, and my voice is ambiguous.

'Do you want me to stop?' I don't answer and you repeat your question. Then you command, 'Answer me.'

You are being unfair. I do not want to say no.

'No.'

'Good.' You do not sound displeased or surprised.

I *don't* want you to stop watching, I want to know what you have seen. What did you see when I was with my last lover? Did you see his mouth on mine, his body on mine? Where were you then?

After a few moments listening to the sound of your breathing, I ask you, 'What do you see?'

'Right now?'

'Yes.' But suddenly I don't want to know any more. 'No, don't tell me.'

But you have started speaking quietly, and I must listen. 'I see you on your bed. Your hair is tied up and you have one hand resting between your legs.' I startle and move my hand away. 'Put it back,' you tell me, and I do; then I wait for what is next, but you are silent again.

I finally ask, 'How long have you been . . .?'

'Watching you.' It is not a question when you say it.

'Yes.'

'That doesn't matter.'

'OK.' We are silent for several more minutes. I am wondering if you saw me the first time I was with a man. Did you see the way I approached him, wearing my best friend's borrowed top? The way I tilted my head to one side and laughed when he looked at me, how I asked his name? Did you see me take him back to my room, filled with plans for losing my virginity, then change my mind, then change it again as he kissed and caressed me? Did you see the way he knelt between my nervous legs until I was shaking, but not from nerves? Did you see us sit on the floor and eat chocolate cake afterwards, exhausted? The simple kiss goodbye in the morning? 'How many of my lovers have you seen?' I didn't mean to say that out loud. You don't answer.

'I have a date tomorrow,' I tell you. I want you to say that I can't go, that only you can see me.

Instead you tell me, 'Bring him to your bedroom.'

This order makes me angry. 'Why, so you can get off on watching me have sex with someone? What is your deal anyway?' But I want you to watch me with him.

'I've already asked if you want me to stop. You said no. Was that a lie?'

'No.'

'I'll call you tomorrow,' you say, and hang up. You are gone.

As I dress for my date, I am worried. I am afraid that I have made you angry, afraid that you will not be watching tonight. I slide my stockings up my legs, each movement deliberate, and I am willing you to see. Wearing my bra and thong, stockings and shoes, I turn slowly in front of the window, holding my dress on its hanger and pretending to check it for wrinkles. Really I am making sure that you see that I am dressing for you, not for him. I peer through my reflection in the window, into the night, then slip my dress on and step into my shoes.

You have not called when I leave to meet my date, and so I impersonate myself, uneasy in my movements. If you are not watching, then I do not want to be here, in this restaurant, talking to this man, feeling his fingers paw my leg under the table. He speaks Spanish, and, if I knew you could see, I would say the one Spanish phrase I know: '*Por que no me metes el dedo debajo de la mesa.*' I gamble that you are watching, whisper the request, see the self-assured excitement on his face as he moves his hand between my legs and slides one finger, then two, inside my underwear. Can you see?

'I'll give you a ride home,' he says after dinner, 'unless you want to go for a drink.' He is playing the gentleman, hoping that will gain him points and a trip home with me. He is coming home with me, but it is only because you have told me to bring him. I'm still not sure if you're watching tonight, but I must act as though you are. This man I'm with would be deflated to know that I can't feel his touch unless I know you can see it.

'Shouldn't we close the curtains?' he asks when we are in my room and he is clumsily undressing me.

'It doesn't matter,' I say, turning for him to unzip my dress, and then moving away so that I can slip it slowly down, exposing my body inch by inch. He is enjoying the show that I am putting on for you. I am again in my stockings and bra, and I start to take his clothes off, my movements like gossamer. I want you to see how pretty I can look when I'm doing this; I want you to be jealous. I am mad at you for making me wonder where you are tonight.

The phone rings, and I tense. He is still wearing his trousers, and I move away from him casually. 'I'll just make sure that's turned off,' I say with a sexy smile, and force myself to walk slowly to the other room and the phone, leaving him believing that he's got me so turned on that I don't want any interruptions. But what I really want is to hear your voice. I pick up the phone and say nothing.

'Good girl,' you say.

'Can you see?' I ask in a whisper.

'Leave your bra and stockings on. Come by the window. Don't let him touch your breasts.' You hang up and I listen to the silence for a few moments, then put down the phone and return to the bedroom.

He has undressed and is lying back on the pillows. The sound of your voice has wakened my body, and my breasts are aching to be sucked. I remember your instructions, though, and leave my bra and stockings on as I shake my hair down and move close to the window, commanding him to follow. He comes up behind me, and as he reaches for my breasts, I push both his hands down between my legs and use my own hands to tug my nipples out from under the lacy edges of my bra. He is gentle between my legs, and when I am ready he slides me on to him from behind, holding me across my hips with one arm and stroking my neck lightly with his free hand.

I drop one of my own hands between my legs, and I love how cool my dancing fingers feel next to the heat of sex. With my other hand, I circle one nipple, then the other, back and forth in syncopated rhythm. As our tempo accelerates, I hear your voice in my head saying, 'Come by the window. Come.' As I come I turn my head and bite down on my own shoulder. He comes too, but his noises are drowned out in my head by the silence that I heard when you hung up the phone.

As he backs away from me and sits down on the bed, he grins. 'Shall I stay tonight?'

'No.' He looks a little disconcerted as I hand him his clothes and watch him dress. I am still wearing only my bra and stockings as I lead him to the door and allow him to kiss my cheek.

'I'll call you,' he says as he starts his car, but I have closed the door.

You call less frequently now, but I know that you still watch me, and I move all the time with the easy grace that your attention awakens in me. When you do call, we talk of my partners, or your special instructions for me, although you don't have many – you like what I like. When I haven't heard from you for a while, I can make you call by going to sit in the park till dusk. I have done it twice, and, when I return, the phone is always ringing.

In the park now, there is a quiet man sitting on the only bench. He is holding a white cane and a guide dog lies at his feet, resting, but alert. The dog lifts his head and the man turns, open eyes unseeing, to face me as I approach.

'Good evening,' I say, to verify my presence – he has sensed me but cannot see me, cannot know I am there until I tell him – and he nods his head. The dog settles back down and I sit on the bench next to the man, lost in my own thoughts, wondering where you are, when you will call, whether the phone will be ringing when I return. As darkness approaches, the man gets up to leave, his cane sweeping from left to right and his dog obediently by his side.

A few feet away from me, he stops, turns back, and your voice says, 'I'll call you tonight.' Then you turn, and I hear the tap-swish-tap of your cane as you walk away.

# La Déesse Terre Madeleine Oh

Why on earth was she doing this?

Other women, when their husbands walked out on them, got drunk with their best fiends or gorged on Swiss chocolate until they saw double. Dea Sullivant ran away from the US and fled to France.

It seemed a good idea at the time but, as she peered though the twilight and the driving rain, Dea began to realise why they offered cheap flights in March. Her decision to leave the autoroute because of blinding rain had been a mistake. As the country road stretched through the night, the dark seemed filled with echoes of Rob muttering about her uselessness, her stupidity, her abysmal map-reading skills, and her general inadequacy.

'Fuck you, Rob Sullivant!' she yelled. 'Your idea of a big trip is driving to Blacksburgh for a ball game. I'm in Europe!' And lost. But what the hell. No one here knew she'd been declared obsolete, and replaced by a skinny speech therapist with acrylic fingernails.

No one cared. She wouldn't either.

The road forked. Dea took the wider one into a deserted village square. A few chinks of light showed from shuttered windows, but the only other sign of life was a stray dog lurking by the darkened church. So much for her dream of a charming country inn with soft beds, quaint rooms and fabulous food.

As the windshield wipers dragged back and forth, the prospect of a soft bed grew from want to lust. Dea turned down a narrow lane between shuttered houses and a row of darkened shops. Surely, somewhere – yes! There was an inn, on the right, beyond the last cottage. Dea turned into the parking lot and almost crashed her rental car into an immense standing stone. After swerving around it, she parked and killed the engine. The rain had eased to a steady and miserable drizzle but the lights of the inn spread a welcoming warmth. On her way to the front door, Dea paused by the menhir. There was just enough light from the inn to see it was a rudely carved, female stone figure. She looked ancient and weather-worn, much the way Dea felt, but Dea had the advantage of not having to sit out in the rain. Hefting her bag on her shoulder, Dea glanced at the painted sign over the door and entered La Déesse Terre.

She stepped straight into a large room with a beamed ceiling and a wide stone fireplace with a crackling fire. Three men clustered round the warmth turned to stare. Across the room, a woman sorted knives and forks at a side table. She gave Dea a cautious nod.

Dea walked up to her. 'I'm looking for a room for the night.'

'Of course.' The woman put down the pile of gleaming forks and gestured Dea to follow. She led her up the side oak stairs to a large room with an immense, carved bed. The air smelled of lavender and old dust but the sheets looked crisp and clean. There was no bathroom adjoining but Dea decided not to get picky. She had antique furniture, a stone fireplace and shutters painted with the moon and stars. The room overlooked the parking lot and the stone woman, which seemed larger than ever in the moonlight.

'What is that statue?' Dea asked.

The woman crossed herself. '*La Déesse Terre.*' The Goddess Earth? No, Earth Goddess, the Earth Mother.

Made sense, given the name of the inn. Dea reached to open the window.

The woman stopped her, and swept into a long torrent of French. Dea caught something about the evening and some sort of presence outside.

A sudden squall threw rain hard against the glass, slashing into the window panes and drumming on the roof overhead. Thank heavens she was out of the weather. All Dea wanted now was a hot shower and something to eat, preferably with a couple of glasses of good wine. The woman apologized, saying that the restaurant was closed but offered ham and cheese and the possibility of soup.

The bathroom was across the landing. Dea gathered up towels and soap and took herself off. The water was hot, the towels large, and the soap deliciously scented with herbs. She stood under the warm water and washed away the worries of the last few weeks. Relaxed by the warm spray, she lathered up her hands, spread the soft bubbles over her breasts and belly and turned full face to the shower jet. Her breasts tingled under the fine points of water. She shifted to let it flow over her belly and her pussy and turned to let the soap run off her back and flow down her thighs to pool at her feet. The vast towels smelled of sunshine and fresh air and Dea slathered her body with scented lotion. This might be the back of beyond but they understood comforts for travellers.

Pulling on jeans and a sweatshirt over her still-damp skin, Dea made a turban of one of the smaller towels and padded barefoot back to her room. From downstairs came the sound of singing – not exactly singing, more a melding of plainsong and humming. Male voices blended together in a strange, almost sensual cadence. The sound enticed and fascinated. Dea was halfway decided to descend and listen closer, when she realised she was barely dressed.

No way was she bopping into that bunch of yokels barefoot and wet-headed. Better get back to her room, dry her hair and wait for Madame to bring the promised sandwich.

Dea's door was ajar and she'd darn well closed it. Squaring her shoulders, Dea pushed it open wide and stepped in. 'Hello!'

'Madame.' The woman was on her knees, laying a fire in the grate. As Dea watched, she arranged the last couple of logs from a stack in the hearth and struck three or four matches, dropping each one in the bed of pine cones and crumpled paper. Satisfied the fire had caught, she stood up and launched into fast French.

Dea understood about a tenth of it.

She did catch her apologies, that they were honoured to have her stop by, and her arrival had caught them by surprise. As she spoke, rain slashed against the panes. The woman looked over her shoulder at the open shutters and turned to cross the room and close them.

'No,' Dea said, 'leave them open.'

That seemed to bother her, but Dea wasn't budging. Rob had always insisted on sleeping with drapes tight shut. She'd celebrate her singleness by leaving the shutters open to the night and, OK, the torrential rain.

Accepting Dea's wish, the woman nodded and asked if there was anything Dea required.

'A bottle of good wine.'

Having assured her she'd pick one out herself, she closed the door, shutting off the chanting. The only sounds now were the logs crackling as the fire caught and the intermittent slash of rain against the window. She was utterly alone in a foreign land and she'd left all worries and heartache an ocean away.

Minutes later, Madame reappeared with a laden tray.

For a last-minute, unexpected, scratch supper, she hadn't done too shabbily. A small tureen held a thick meaty soup that wafted herbs and garlic as Dea lifted the lid. The promised ham came with thick slices of crusty bread, and, for good measure, Madame had added a dish of poached pears and a wedge of crumbly blue cheese. Best of all was the freshly opened bottle of wine, neatly wrapped in a linen napkin.

Dea had a crackling fire, hot soup and wine. She had no complaints, even if the chanting was getting louder. Or did she hear it more now the wind had dropped? No matter, it wasn't an unpleasant noise, just monotonous, and they could hardly keep it up all night.

Two glasses of wine and a good supper later, Dea stretched out by the fire, wineglass in hand, and watched the flames play over the sweet-smelling logs. Were they fruit trees of some sort that they gave of such an aroma? Magical, mythical trees that scented the air and her dreams? Slowly Dea sipped on her wine and contemplated her flight.

She'd run away. Plain and simple, she'd retreated. Why not? She'd been supplanted by a younger woman with skinny hips and a flat chest. Dea glanced down at her ample breasts. OK, they weren't up to the endowment of *la Déesse* outside in the parking lot, but boyish she'd never be. Seemed Rob wanted young and androgynous these days. 'Tough shit, Rob,' Dea muttered to the twisting flames. 'See if I care.' Surprisingly, she didn't any more. Was it distance easing the rejection and the hurt? Or plain common sense coming to the fore? Common sense hadn't sent her buying the first cheap ticket to Europe. More like craziness or primal urge. Here, in the warmth of the fire. She did did feel primal. Why not? Hadn't she found her way to the abode of the Earth Goddess?

Dea watched until the fire died down. Then she pulled on flannel pyjamas, fished her book out of her bag and took herself and the rest of the wine to bed. She'd just drained the last glass when the storm strengthened with renewed force, smashing rain hard against the windows as great gusts of wind tore at the outside walls. A clap of thunder vibrated off the windows, followed fast by a flash of lightning, and the lights went out.

Great! She'd hold her breath and her wineglass and count to ten for the lights to come on again. They didn't. Not even for fifty. There was just enough light from the fire to see and she had a flashlight. Damn, it was in the car. That wasn't stopping her. The house had gone quiet. With no one about, she'd slip out and back with out any trouble. Dea stepped into her shoes, and pulled on her raincoat over her pyjamas.

She made it almost to the bottom of the stairs when Madame stepped forward carrying a lamp. Over the woman's shoulder, Dea saw the group still seated round the fire. So much for slipping out unobserved. Dea jabbered about looking for something, pulled open the heavy door and stepped out.

Big mistake. Water bucketed down from the sky. The path from the inn resembled a small stream and she could barely see her car. Dea splashed down the path and squelched over the gravel. As she opened the passenger door, the rain came down even heavier, beating a wild tattoo on the roof.

She shoved the flashlight in her pocket and stepped back out. The rain come horizontally now, slashing into her face, running down her neck and stinging her legs. She should have stayed dry and warm and lumped the dark. She pulled her raincoat over her head and ran. Losing a shoe, she turned back trying, to find it, but gave up and raced the rest of the way, half blinded and totally drenched. A misstep on loose gravel pitched her forward. Reaching out to save herself, Dea fell slap into the granite bulk of *La Déesse*.

Wrong direction entirely.

Or was it?

The bulk of the Goddess protected Dea from the wind and the worst of the rain. Nice to find a woman broader and even better endowed than she was. Dea raised her hands to cup the splendid stone breasts, the weather-worn stone smooth and cool under her fingers. Another loud clap of thunder and almost simultaneous lightning had Dea pressing closer for the shelter the Goddess offered. Dea stayed, breasts flattened against the Goddess's granite torso, unwilling to step away and face the relentless storm.

She had no idea how long she clung to the Goddess. Dea's hands began to tingle as if drawing power from stone – rekindling life and passion not yet dead. Dea moved her hands. Her fingers itched. Her body throbbed with the cadence of the storm. She cupped her own breasts. Her nipples were hard with cold and her flesh was soaking with desire. Desire to feel the power once again. She closed her eyes, reached out her arms and stepped into the Goddess's embrace.

Dea's entire body shot with sweet darts of fire, meeting the cold and damp with an inner warmth that swelled like a spring tide. A small, far part of Dea's mind insisted she was nuts, plastering her body to a standing stone in the middle of a parking lot in rural France. That part was soon silenced by the peace and warmth that flowed though every pore and pulsed with each heartbeat.

The rain stopped. The wind calmed. Dea looked up at the weather-worn face of *La Déesse Terre* and smiled. In the moonlight the Goddess smiled back.

Gathering her useless raincoat around her, Dea paddled back to the inn. She was minus both shoes now but scarcely noticed. The life force of the goddess afforded more warmth than a pair of sneakers. A wild heat flowed in Dea's veins, her hands still tingled, her nipples throbbed hard under the damp flannel, and wetness ran between her legs. She looked back at the Goddess, half expecting the stone to turn and nod encouragingly. The Goddess never moved. She couldn't. She'd handed over her power to Dea.

The door stood half open. The inn waited. Dea slipped inside and let her clothes drip for a few seconds. A row of small lamps and night lights lit a path up the wide staircase. She'd better sneak back up to her room and take her aroused body with her.

'Ah, *Madame Déesse*!' The woman stepped forward, clasped Dea's hand and led her towards the fireplace.

The men waiting stood and bowed, the firelight casting shadows on the ceiling and their faces. The same sweet wood burned in this fireplace, and an ancient oil lamp glowed on the low table.

Dea was doubly, triply, aware of the wet flannel plastered against her breasts and legs and the sodden raincoat flapping round her ankles. They didn't notice, or rather they saw but regarded her with admiration.

'*Déesse*,' the oldest man began. As if unsure of her response, he spoke slowly. She followed each word, understanding without needing to translate. He was asking her to choose. One of them.

Her body rippled in reply.

The dim light flattered them all but the flickering illumination showed beyond their exteriors. In the old man, Dea saw wisdom, a mind shaped by long years fighting the elements but never conceding failure. The youth possessed a vigour and an energy Dea envied, but he lacked the substance and depth of the older man. It was the third she looked at longest, the one nearest her own age. He stood tall and broad-shouldered. His dark eyes glimmered in the firelight, and in their depths burned a raging desire – for her.

Without a word, Dea smiled and held out her hand.

The other two stepped back, as if ceding the field to the victor, as he took her hand and knelt at her feet. His dark hair fell forward, exposing the tanned nape of his neck.

'*Madame, la Déesse,*' he said, his voice thick with promise, 'Lucien Valpert, à votre service.'

Was it the close warmth of the room, or the heat from his bowed body that spiked her own need? 'OK, Lucien,' Dea said, squeezing his hand and raising him to standing. He was so close, a half-step would bring their bodies into close contact. 'Let's go.'

Dea turned and climbed the candlelit staircase, Lucien's footsteps heavy on the broad steps behind her. Her bedroom door stood open. Someone had built the fire up to a roaring blaze. A row of candles burned on the mantelpiece and four more flickered, one on each post of the bed. And Lucien waited just inside her open doorway.

'Come in, shut the door.' Had she spoken English? French? It hardly mattered as he closed the door with a soft thud and crossed the floor and prepared to kneel. 'No.' She stopped him with her hand. His eyes met hers, questioning. 'I want you upright for now. You can get on your knees later.' She rested the flat of her hand on his chest. Feeling warm muscle under the soft-washed shirt, Dea looked him in the eye and parted her lips.

He lowered his mouth.

Slowly.

His lips were warm and male and opened hers with a promise of sweet fire. Wet heat roared between her legs as his tongue swept hers. His arms closed round her shoulders in a fierce grasp. Her breasts flattened against his chest, his thigh eased between hers, his erection pressing against her belly. He was more than ready. She wasn't. Not yet.

'Wait,' she said, pulling back. He obeyed. The twitch in his jaw showed his effort to serve no matter how she willed. 'Soon,' Dea promised, relishing the wild light in his eyes as she slowly opened his shirt. Each button gave at her touch until she parted the faded cotton and ran her hands over warm flesh and soft hair, his heart racing under her hand. His breath caught as her fingers rubbed his nipples to stiff points. She ran her tongue over his left nipple, sensing his need and relishing her power. She moved back as he gave a little gasp.

He was watching her with glinting eyes, his broad chest rising and falling with each slow breath. 'Strip,' Dea said. He stared, not understanding. She brushed his shirt off his shoulders and watched it settle on the floor by his feet. 'You take off the rest.'

Lucien got her meaning. With controlled but efficient movements, he unbuckled his belt and stepped out of his pants and underwear. Dea walked behind him as he bent to undo his shoes. Nice butt. Nice back. Splendid body. Firm muscles shaped by years of physical labour, not workouts on chrome-plated gym machines. She walked back in front as he stood up, and she smiled. Lucien might have been surprised at being chosen, but he was more than ready for the office. His cock was magnificent, jutting at her from its nest of dark hair and hers for the having.

She skimmed her fingertips over the erect flesh and circled him with her hand. He gasped as she moved up and down, easing back his foreskin to reveal the dark head of his cock. She squeezed.

'Madame!' Lucien gasped. A glistening bead of moisture gathered on his cock. He'd have stepped back, she was certain, but she had him hard in her hand. She stroked the head of his cock with her thumb, spreading his moisture, fascinated by the tender end of his erect cock and how his foreskin moved at her touch.

'OK,' she said, letting go of him. 'Now you undress me.'

He stepped behind her and removed her raincoat, crossing the room to hang it on the wall. Her pyjama top he unbuttoned and tossed on the chair. His eyes widened with admiration at her breasts. He reached out but paused, looking at her for consent. Unable to hold back a smile, Dea nodded. 'You may.'

His fingers were rough but gentle and certainly not untutored. He caressed the full undersides of her breasts with cupped hands, slowly eased his thumbs over the swell of her breasts until he caught her nipples between thumbs and index fingers and tugged. He rubbed her areolae until little nubs around them stiffened and she shuddered with desire.

His hands eased down her belly and he paused, waiting for her approval. She smiled. Heck, she grinned, and with a nod of understanding Lucien eased his hands into the elastic at her waist and lowered the last of her clothes. He knelt at her feet as she stepped away from the damp cotton. Dea looked down at his dark head and tanned shoulders and the hand around her ankle, his eyes gazing at her pussy as if she were the wonder of creation. He looked up, his eyes dark with need. 'Madame, *vous permettez?*'

Aware of her awesome power, Dea watched him for a few seconds. 'Oh, yes.'

Warm air brushed across her pussy, ruffling her curls like a quickening breeze. His fingers opened her. Wide.

His breath came closer as the flat of his tongue lapped her. She whimpered as his arms closed around her thighs and a gust of rain hit the windowpanes. If the glass had caved in, she'd never have noticed. Lucien was devouring her with slow perfection. He covered her with his lips as his tongue narrowed and played her clit, flicking and teasing until she moaned with need. He paused and she grabbed his head to hold it to her. He could not stop. Not now. She would not permit it.

But he'd paused only to slide one hand from her thigh. The other held her as firmly as ever. His mouth continued its slow caress as he pressed one finger, then two, inside her cunt. He played her, his fingers pulsing a beat that matched the thrust of his tongue.

She was lost. She was found. She was all and everything she'd ever longed for as a lover knelt in homage at her pussy. His fingers, slick with her arousal, smoothed her ass as his tongue drew her towards climax. Need blazed deep in her belly. She cried aloud as his fingers curved deep and his mouth worked her faster. He was merciless. He was magnificent. He was all. She clutched his head, thrusting her hips into his face, reaching for her coming climax. Her shouts increased as her need climbed. Until she came in a wild crescendo of joy and release that had her screaming aloud as her legs buckled.

Lucien held her firm. Steadying her as his mouth fluttered little kisses up her belly. It was almost too much. She would never have enough.

He gathered her up in his arms as easily as if she were a lightweight. His mouth, wet and warm with her juices, met hers. A slow kiss, gentle as a whisper, that sent her body wild. Nothing could satisfy her but his magnificent cock deep inside. He grinned with knowing pride and male arrogance as he sat her on the bed and turned her on to all fours.

He stroked her ass, smoothing up her back as he dropped soft kisses up her spine to her neck. The mattress shifted under his weight as the power of his erection pushed between her legs. He grasped her shoulders. He was hard against her, pressing to meet her need. His hips rocked. His cock slid though her wetness. Dea cried out as he thrust. She was tighter than she'd expected and Lucien filled her, stretched her, and possessed her. Driving with grunts and animal need, pressing into her soul with his male heat. Pumping her, taking her, possessing her, giving all a man could. He was Primal Man, potent and firm. She was Goddess, power and life. They melded in one life rhythm that took them both higher and harder through his grunts and her cries until, with a relentless thrust, he drove deep as she screamed aloud her triumph and he poured his jism into her heat.

She collapsed, his weight pressing her into the mattress, his cock embedded in her cunt, her mind drunk with joy and life, and her heart racing at one with the storm outside.

Through a haze of grogginess, Dea felt his weight ease off her. Lucien shifted her so her head rested on the pillow. Lips pressed on her forehead, arms held her close and she passed from frenzy to satiated rest.

She woke to electric light blazing overhead. Damn! The power outage. She'd left the lights on. Padding across the room to flick out the switch, she realised she was naked. Her night clothes lay in a crumpled heap in front of the last dying embers and she was wet halfway down her thighs.

She had just fucked a total stranger!

So what? It had been stupendous and her body still vibrated with the memory of Lucien's tongue on her skin and his cock planted deep.

But fucking a completely unknown man! She made herself stop. No longer was she thinking like Rob Sullivant's wife. She was Dea. Goddess. She curled up between sheets that smelled of sex and life.

Bright morning sunshine woke her later. Time to be on her way. She may have to face Lucien over coffee, but so what? He'd fucked a total stranger too. Her shoes waited, cleaned and polished outside her door, and breakfast was set at a lone table by a window.

As Dea sat down, Madame appeared with croissants and fresh bread, and a slab of firm cheese and little curls of butter. 'Did you sleep well?'

Was she being facetious? A look at the woman's face and Dea decided it was a routine enquiry asked of any guest. 'Yes, very well. Apart from the storm.' No need to specify which storm.

Madame nodded. Fierce storms were to be expected. It was the time of year, the *point vernal*.

The vernal equinox: the season of wild tides and gales that marked the beginning of spring. A time of new life and renewal. Of course. Dea was alive, well satisfied, and drinking aromatic coffee several thousand miles from her humiliation. She cut off a corner of cheese, chewed it slowly and decided to stop and pay homage to the Goddess in the parking lot, on her way forward.

# Double Take Jacqueline Silk

His tongue licked around her nipple, teasing it until it was hard. She stroked the soft hair at the back of his neck, wanting him to take the whole of her breast in his mouth. She couldn't explain it, but she just wanted more. Lately she had felt as if she needed an alien entity to take him over and start eating her up, starting at her breasts, then moving right down over her body. The phone rang. Addie slipped her bra back on and leaned across to answer it. Robert groaned as he rolled off her,

'Christie?' she almost shouted into the phone. 'My God, how are you?' It was her sister calling from the States. 'Did you get my message?'

The line was bad and Addie had to strain to hear her sister's voice. She half noticed Robert getting dressed out of the corner of her eye and she felt a moment's disappointment that their pleasure would remain unfinished for that day. He had to be back in the office in half an hour. Then he had to go south for a business meeting, so she probably wouldn't be seeing him for a few days.

Christie's voice picked up volume every other word so that Addie received a garbled version which she had to decode. 'Back ... Wednesday ... pick up'.

Addie noticed Robert putting on his wristwatch and checking the time. 'I can't make you out,' she said. 'I'm going to have to call you back.'

'No ... time. Wednesday ... five o' ... clock,' came the garbled reply. Addie just had time to write it down on the notepad beside her bed before the phone went dead.

She looked across to Robert, then got up and put her arms around his neck, twining her fingers in the silky curls at the back of his head.

'I'm sorry, my love,' she said. 'It was Christie. I've been waiting for her to ring.'

'Why she can't just send you an email I don't know,' Robert said petulantly.

'Christie doesn't know anything about computers,' replied Addie. 'Don't be cross. We'll catch up when you get back.' She cupped her hand over the front of his trousers, where his penis was still hard for her, and reached up to kiss him. She was pleased to discover that he smelled of her. He would be smelling of her all day.

'So will I get to meet your mysterious sister this time?' Robert asked. 'Is she as beautiful as you?'

'More so, apparently,' smiled Addie. 'But you'll have to judge for yourself. She's arriving on Wednesday.'

'Well I'll be back on Thursday.' Robert reached out for the door handle, taking a last check of his appearance in the mirror on the wall. 'Keep the bed warm for me,' he said. Then he left.

Addie and Christie were twins. Most people couldn't tell them apart, though they themselves knew that Addie had a small birthmark on the inside of her left thigh, just as wide as her thumb. They had taken rather different routes in life. Christie had left home at seventeen and gone to London, where she had been signed up by a small modelling agency. She complained about the lack of pay, yet, as Addie often commented, she was never out of work and was often flown all over the world – all expenses paid. Addie herself had stayed at school, gone to university and now made her living from writing. It wasn't what she would call serious writing, but there was a definite market for her romantic fiction, aimed mostly at the over-thirties. She had bought a flat in Manchester, the city in which she was born. It looked out across Piccadilly and the bright lights of China Town beyond. She loved her flat and wouldn't give it up – even for Robert, who had repeatedly asked her to move in with him since they had met two years ago. He had been her agent back then, in the early days when she had first been offered a book deal. She had changed to a different agent once their relationship had become a sexual one.

That Wednesday she arrived at the airport early and picked up a magazine from one of the stalls. She sat down on a seat near the gate through which Christie would be emerging and began to flick through it. It was the usual collection of dull articles, most of them aimed at women who wanted to be reassured that life wasn't passing them by. Of course it probably was, Addie mused to herself, if they found it necessary to read such trash. One of the pages caught her eye. It contained a picture of a rather demure-looking girl of about eighteen, standing between her parents for a graduation ceremony. The picture next to it was very different. The girl was again standing between two people, but they looked like bouncers – at least they were dressed in formal black suits and were heavily muscled. The caption said, 'Sarah Sutton, two years later, in the club where she first started out before she became *Playboy*'s Centre Spread of the Year.'

Addie looked carefully at the girl in the picture. She wasn't particularly beautiful but there was a certain sensuality about her that couldn't help but communicate itself. She was dressed in a high-cut white leotard, just transparent enough to reveal the pinkness of her nipples and a darker 'v' between her legs. She had one leg raised on to a platform and she was leaning across with a tray of drinks as if serving one to an invisible customer. Her dark hair was piled elegantly on her head and her eyes and lips were heavily made up. What really arrested Addie's attention, however, was the hand placed on her backside by the man the other side of her. With her back turned to him he had rested it just where the bare flesh of her inner thighs met the slightly exposed buttocks. Addie could tell that one of his fingers had slipped down between her legs, possibly inside her leotard. It was such a small detail, she could have missed it. But sitting there, in a busy airport, looking at this scene, she felt herself grow wet. Her clitoris grew hard and began to ache. Almost unconsciously she uncrossed her legs, just to feel the heavy denim of her jeans rubbing against her crotch.

She began to read the article. The girl had 'slipped', as the journalist put it, into a life of pornography, shocking her elderly parents, family and friends, who had all imagined her set up for a career as a lawyer. She had obtained a degree from Nottingham, then moved to London. But it was here, the article suggested, that she got into bad company.

Addie had heard it all before. It was a regular theme – college girl gives up promising career for seedy life in the city. It purported to be a social-comment article, but really, Addie knew, it was included for titillation purposes. How many women in supposedly respectable careers had dreamed of swapping their job for one such as this girl's? Who hadn't seen Catherine Deneuve in *Belle de Jour*? She looked across again at the picture. It was that placing of the hand, she told herself. Their apparent obliviousness to it. The man's face betrayed no emotion, no lust. Yet his dirty secret sat on him like a crime. He was probably hard beneath his wide-cut trousers. The girl's eyes were heavy-lidded. She smiled up at the other man as she offered him the drink. Could she feel the finger slipping inside her, reaching up slowly, carefully, so as not to make her spill the drink?

Addie was so aroused now that even the feel of her wet knickers was delicious. She slowly moved her buttocks against the hard seat. She was desperate to slip a hand down the front of her jeans, imagining how her cunt would feel – so juicy, so slippery. She looked up at the large airport clock. Ten minutes until her sister's flight arrived. But where could she go? Not the ladies' toilet. It was such a cold place, so clinical. She scanned the open space in front of her. It was getting busy. People walked by with briefcases and papers tucked under their arms, cups of steaming coffee in one hand, which they drank on the go. Most of them were commuters or people coming home from business trips. Addie stood up. Over to the left of all the gates was an exit sign. She headed straight for it, her jeans nudging against her clitoris as she walked.

Outside the fresh air came up to meet her like a caress. She wanted to feel it on her bare flesh, between her legs, spread them wide so it could cool her swollen labia. She walked past a series of corrugated-iron huts. She was probably not supposed to be there – it looked like somewhere that the aircraft mechanics might work – but she didn't care. She tried a door that said *private*. It was locked. Then she noticed a small covered passageway leading between two of the huts. It seemed to end at a stone wall, though it had doors opening off from it. Addie turned down it. When she got to the end, she leaned against the wall, felt the hardness of it against her buttocks. Keeping an eye pinned on the other end of the passage, she reached down and undid her jeans, sliding open the zip. Her other hand reached up and slipped under her shirt, undoing just enough buttons to feel the breeze caressing the swell of her breast above her bra. She ran shaky fingers along the fragile line of her knicker elastic. Then she deftly slipped her right hand inside. The stone on her ring twisted round so that she felt its coldness travel across her pubic bone to the cleft where her lips began. Her eyes were half open.

She could make out the passage in front of her, still empty. She nudged the ring to her clitoris and began to rub at it gently. Her breath came in small gasps. She groaned and twisted, pinching her nipple harder, arching her back so that her breast was suddenly fully exposed to the cool air. She felt as if there were a million eyes upon her. Perhaps it was being outside that made her feel so naked. She felt desperate. If someone came along she would let them take her. Man or woman, old or young, she didn't care. The sensation between her legs was so tight, so focused, it was beautiful. She stretched out her index finger and rested it at the entrance to her cunt. The wetness trickled around it. She opened her legs wider and closed her eyes completely.

In an office to the side of the passageway, Jake Hood clicked back to security camera 4. Staring into his monitor, he reached up and stroked the dark stubble that lined the underside of his chin. A slight smile began to play across his lips. He pressed zoom and the picture on the screen magnified. He leaned closer. She was definitely touching herself.

The woman's body was pressed up against the brick wall and she had her head flung back, one hand pushed down into her opened jeans. Her other hand was playing with her exposed breast. It was a beautiful breast, Jake thought, high and firm, the nipple large as a flower.

He had come across her by accident. The mechanics

had to have cameras everywhere for security purposes, but they rarely looked at the monitors. He had been taking a quick coffee break while the others went to lunch and happened to glance across.

She's certainly sexy, he thought, and wondered what she would look like completely naked. She seemed so brazen. It excited him. He saw her move her head to one side, then slowly back again, her hand moving more quickly beneath her jeans. He felt himself grow hard beneath his overalls just watching her. But Jake was not a mere spectator. He stood up and finished his coffee, hastily wiping at his lips with the back of his hand. Then he opened the door that led into the passageway.

Addie could feel her clitoris hardening beneath her fingers. Her pleasure seemed connected, as if on a string between her nipple and her cunt.

'Fuck,' she moaned, 'fuck'. She was close to coming.

'I'd be happy to oblige.'

Addie opened her eyes in shock. She hadn't heard anyone approach, but a man stood before her, a look of amusement on his face. She started to slip her hand from her jeans.

'No, no,' he said, moving closer. He grabbed her hand and began to stroke her glistening fingers with his own. 'Now it really would be a shame to stop there.'

Addie noticed that he was very tall, well over six foot. His face was unshaven, his hair shoulder-length, dull, brown-streaked with occasional threads of grey. It fell over his eyes, giving him a boyish look, though Addie guessed he must be well into his thirties.

'I . . . I . . .' she began, but he put his finger over her lips. She noticed that it had already taken on the smell of her sex, a sweet, musky scent that mixed deliciously with the faint trace of oil he gave off. Perhaps it came from the blue overalls he was wearing; perhaps it was emanating still from his fingers.

'I've been watching you,' he said, stroking a finger along the curve of her chin. 'Watching you fuck yourself.'

He was very close now; Addie could feel the warmth of his breath against the side of her cheek. She looked beyond him to the empty expanse of the alley. There were no windows, no hidden balconies. How could he have been watching? He seemed to read her thoughts and turned her head gently with his hand to the guttering on the left-hand wall. Just below it, camouflaged against the black paint, was a small security camera. A red light flickered somewhere near the base. Its one, black, telescopic eye was pointing directly at her. Addie shivered with excitement.

'Who are you?' she whispered.

He leaned down, putting his mouth close to her ear. 'Jake.' Then, uncurling his body to its full height, sinuous as a snake, he commanded, 'Come with me'.

The look in his brown eyes struck Addie as so deeply sexy, so dirty, that she couldn't sustain eye contact. She focused instead on his mouth. But it also was so sensual, curving sardonically above the strong chin, that she felt her legs begin to give way. Mutely, she let him take her hand and lead her down the passageway to a door, which hung slightly open.

Inside, the smell of oil was stronger. It was a dimly lit room but fluorescent lighting leaped in to brighten it as he hit a switch by the door. There was a large Formica table in the middle, a few tools scattered on top of it and lots more around the edge in boxes. Addie noticed a small CCTV screen in the corner, which played images of the alley, including where she had been standing a moment before. There was also another camera in the room, focused on the table. He went over to a control box by the TV screen and flicked a switch. A red light appeared underneath the camera and, turning her head, Addie saw her own face reflected on the monitor. The camera was recording.

Jake walked slowly towards her and calmly backed her against the edge of the table.

'I think you like to be watched,' he said. 'I think it turns you on.'

He watched her lick her lips.

'And what about you?' she said. 'Does it turn you on?'

'*You* turn me on. And thinking of the things I'm going to do to you.'

Her jeans were still open and he had no trouble in slipping them over her hips and down to the floor. Addie found herself stepping out of them as if this were an everyday occurrence, as if the whole charged scenario had been minutely rehearsed. His large hands slipped over her belly, circling it, with his two thumbs pressed gently across her hip bones. He knelt down and looked up at her, his face level with her cunt. His eyes had that same intensity, a slight humour lurking at the back of them.

He wants to eat me, she thought. *So fuck, eat me!*

Jake lowered his nose until it rested between Addie's thighs, only the thin silk of her knickers separating him from her. He could smell her, feel her juices where they soaked through. He nudged her legs further apart with his elbows. His penis was straining against the rough material of his overalls, demanding to be let out. But he ignored it. Instead he fixed her again with his gaze, then, with a sudden movement, he reached up and pushed her shirt up towards her head. Her arms went with it, trying to help him remove it. But he didn't want to remove it. He pushed it up so that it trapped her, her face hidden, her arms stuck above her head, her breasts completely exposed.

Addie let out a strangled cry, her own breathing suddenly louder, magnified by the imprisoning material of her shirt. She felt Jake stand and lean in close to her.

'Just relax,' he said. 'I promise not to hurt you. You asked me what turned me on. It's this. You not being able to see, not stopping me.'

He began to undo her bra, one arm around her back. Then she felt him bend down and take a nipple into his mouth. He sucked noisily, no other pressure applied, just his tongue occasionally flicking at it, his teeth grazing against it as if they might bite. Addie moaned. The thin material of her shirt was like a gag and blindfold in one. She loved not being able to move. She could just make out the shape of his dark head, his strong arms gripping the table either side of her. Then she felt herself lifted on to the table and laid down.

'You have beautiful breasts,' he said. 'Now let me see the rest of you.'

Jake hooked his thumbs around her knickers and pulled them slowly down. Addie raised her hips up to help him and felt the silken material brush over her ankles. She gasped as she felt Jake's hands, one on each thigh, pushing her legs apart, so wide that they met the edge of the table. Then she heard his sharp intake of breath, a slight groan.

'God, let me look at you.'

His voice was slightly muffled, but she felt his breath against her opened cunt. Her face was still covered by the shirt, her arms pinned above her head. She turned her head to one side and closed her eyes. There was no touch, no movement, but the wonderful agony of the air circulating between her open legs.

Jake wanted to sink his tongue into her, but he held

himself back. She was so deliciously exposed, so wide open, her cunt unbelievably wet and pink. Her blonde pubic hair curled like tiny question marks around her swollen lips. Her suntanned thighs, spread so wide, emphasised the succulent flesh between. She was like an opened shell.

'Please,' Jake heard her whisper, and he saw again that movement of her hips, the thrusting of her buttocks, which spread her even wider. He moved his head down.

Addie jerked at the sudden dart of his tongue. Just a quick flick, then nothing for a few seconds, then another, stronger lick. She felt his head against the inside of her left thigh and an exploratory finger probing the entrance to her cunt. She ached for him to push his finger inside. He pushed her lips gently apart and she felt his hot breath again, closer.

'God,' she moaned, 'please!'

His large tongue flicked again and his lips pushed up against her clitoris. This time his tongue poked down, circling at the entrance to her vagina, dipping slightly inside, then reaching up again to flick and flick, again and again. Addie felt the juices streaming out of her, trickling down the crack in her buttocks on to the table. She wanted to grab his head, to pull it closer, but her arms were trapped. She began to twist her body slightly, to arch her back.

'That's it,' she heard him say, 'wider.'

She bent both knees to make herself wider and she heard his licking become more furious, the saliva on his tongue mixing with her wetness to make a wonderfully dirty smacking sound, all the juices gathering around his mouth. She wondered how much longer she could last without coming.

Then she felt him draw away momentarily, the sound of him reaching for something. It sounded metallic.

'Do you trust me?' he asked her. His voice was husky, low. Addie moaned and arched her hips by way of an answer. She felt his hand rhythmically stroking her inside thigh.

'Turn over,' he said.

Jake helped her to roll over on the table, taking care to shield the side of her face, cradling her under the stomach with one arm. Then he pulled up her hips so that she was kneeling. For a moment she was completely open to both his and the camera's gaze. Her buttocks shone golden in the florescent light. They gleamed where her juices had leaked on to them. He reached up a hand and smoothed the wetness with his fingers, feeling the tautness of her skin, the slippery cleft that dipped to her anus. Then he slipped a finger inside her cunt, marvelling at the way she seemed to grip it. As he pushed it in and out, Addie swung her buttocks towards him, trying to take more in. He pulled his finger out slowly, teasingly, and, holding her open even wider between his first finger and his thumb, slid in something thick and metallic.

Addie gasped. The object seemed larger than a penis, rounded and very cold. The thrill of it pushing inside her made her want to cry out. Jake reached forward with his free hand and began stroking her clitoris, gently moving the object further in, watching as her swollen lips closed around it. Addie opened her knees wider and pushed against it. She heard herself moaning, heard her own voice echoing in the room.

'Fuck,' she moaned, 'fuck me.'

The sensation was unbearable. She knew she was going to come. His hand moved slowly in and out with the strange implement he had found for her. Gently, he built up speed. Addie had no idea what it was: she didn't care. Everything inside her clung to it. She came furiously, deliriously, arching her back and thrusting her buttocks to the camera.

'You're late,' Christie muttered as Addie took her suitcase apologetically and bundled it on to a nearby trolley.

'I know,' Addie groaned. 'I'm sorry.'

'What happened? Did that man of yours demand one last blow job before he would let you leave?' Christie lowered her sunglasses from where they had been resting on top of her head as the airport doors opened and they walked into the glare of the sun outside.

'Something like that,' Addie muttered.

'How are things, anyway?' asked Christie. 'Still in *lurve*?' She often adopted a fake American accent for Addie's benefit, though in fact she still retained her northern English one.

Addie felt herself redden, an occurrence that she was sure would not escape the notice of her sister. In fact she had not thought of Robert at all during the proceedings of that afternoon. It was strange. She had never been unfaithful to him before. She had thought she loved him.

'Oh dear,' said Christie, eyeing her sister's rosy cheeks, 'looks like we need a good sisterly heart-to-heart. You certainly work quickly. I haven't even met him yet and it looks like he's already on the way out.'

Back at the flat Addie told her sister all about the events of that afternoon – well, most of them: some of the more salacious details she kept to herself.

'I can't believe you sometimes!' her sister said, leaning back in her chair and rolling her beautiful blue eyes. 'I thought I was the one who had adventures. You really are a dark horse.'

Addie sighed. 'I don't understand it myself. I just felt so horny. Anyway, you're one to talk. You're the darkest horse out of the two of us. The way you've been flying back and forwards to America these last few weeks, not showing your work to any of us, well, it's been raising a lot of suspicion lately, I can tell you.'

Christie laughed, flicking her straight blonde hair over her shoulder. 'I've been really busy,' she said. She reached one hand behind her neck and began coiling a strand of her hair between her fingers. Addie recognised it as something her sister often did when she was wondering whether to confide something important. Addie took a sip of her wine and waited.

'Well,' Christie began, 'I suppose I have been a bit secretive.' She smiled, looking up at her sister coyly from between her lashes. 'You've got to promise not to tell Mum,' she said. Addie saluted. 'No, seriously, Addie. It'd give her a heart attack.'

Addie put her hand on her heart. 'I promise,' she said. 'Now come on, Christie, spit it out.'

Saying nothing, Christie reached into a leather bag at her feet and pulled out a small, black portfolio. She handed it over to Addie. 'Well, go on,' she laughed, 'look!'

Addie opened the book. She turned the pages silently, the ticking of her carriage clock becoming suddenly louder in the room. It had been a gift from her favourite aunt.

'Well?' prompted Christie, leaning forward so that her hair brushed the glossy photographs that lay in Addie's hands. 'Aren't you going to say anything?'

'You're naked,' Addie remarked.

'Yes,' agreed Christie.

'And you're not alone.' Then the two girls looked at each other and burst into laughter. 'I hope they paid you well,' Addie commented once she could catch her breath.

'Loads,' replied Christie.

Addie leaned forward again to pore over one of the

photographs, which showed Christie kneeling between two men. 'Did you enjoy it?' she asked.

Christie tilted her chin to the ceiling and stared into the corner. A look of thoughtfulness crossed her usually untroubled face. 'I think I did to begin with,' she said. 'I liked the idea of being looked at – you know, all of me. But after a while I found the cameras a bit offputting. After all, *you* were always the one who liked cameras, not me.'

Addie knew exactly what her sister was referring to. When they were young and still living at home – about sixteen or seventeen – their father had let them use his video camera. He had been most upset one day to find a film accidentally left in it that showed one of them having sex with her boyfriend of the time. From the angles they had been taken at, he certainly couldn't recognise which of them it was, and he hadn't wanted to study it too closely. He tried to get the guilty party to own up by punishing them both, but they were stubborn and kept the extrovert's identity hidden. Their parents never did find out which of them it was, though they probably suspected Christie.

'Anyway,' said Christie, breaking into her sister's momentary reverie, 'that's the end of it, I think. It got a bit boring to be honest. When I go back this time I'm going to tell them that's it. No more porn. Only stuff I can show my mother.'

'And not the stuff I might show my dad,' retorted Addie, and they both broke into laughter again.

'Well,' said Christie, 'that's enough about me. What's going on in your life? How about showing me a picture of this latest man of yours?' She coughed stagily. 'Well,' she continued, 'I mean latest man but one!'

'You'll see him tomorrow,' Addie said. 'He's coming back.'

'Even so,' pouted Christie, 'I still want to recognise him when he comes.'

Addie reached across to a drawer and pulled out a photograph from inside. It was one of Robert on the beach when they had spent a weekend in Cornwall last summer.

'Wow,' gasped Christie, 'he's gorgeous!'

Addie watched her sister scrutinising the photo for all the clues it could offer. She was practically slavering at the mouth.

'I do like blond men,' she said. 'You didn't tell me he was blond.' Addie nodded her head. 'And those curls and baby-blue eyes. He's just my type.'

Addie thought it strange but she didn't feel she'd ever really noticed Robert's eyes.

'Well, if you don't want him, give him to me,' Christie said, placing the photo down on the coffee table and turning it towards her so that she could continue to look at it. 'I must say I wouldn't miss meeting this one for the world.'

When Addie went to bed that night she couldn't sleep for thinking of the day's events, particularly the mysterious stranger who had fucked with her body so completely. She thought of Robert's lovemaking, which was always generous, but somehow lacking. She wondered what it was that he couldn't do for her. Perhaps he's *too* generous, she thought; perhaps I like my men greedy. She thought of Jake's eyes looking up at her as if they would eat her up. When she had left him, after he had pulled her shirt down and courteously handed over her clothes, she had risked one last glance back into the room, only to see him standing on a chair, taking down the camera that hung in the corner. She must have looked concerned because he immediately moved back across to her, laying a hand on her arm. 'I hope you don't mind,' he had said, 'but I would like to watch you again.' And, when she had said nothing, he had pulled a small tape out of the camera and held it out to her. 'Take it if you want,' he said. But she had left it. She had got up and walked out, leaving him with that memento of their time together. He didn't try to stop her.

Now, lying in her bed, she felt excited at the idea that he might be putting the tape on somewhere and watching her. Perhaps he would leave the tape in there for some of the other men to watch – after all, it was meant to be there for security reasons. Perhaps he couldn't take it away.

Addie smiled to herself as her fantasy became more elaborate. 'I like to be watched,' she muttered to herself, slipping a hand down between her legs and gently stroking herself where his mouth had been. She imagined a camera in the room now. A room filled with men. How strange, she thought, as she drifted off to sleep, that picture in the magazine this afternoon, Christie's photos, all of it something I keep imagining happening to me. How would it change my life? She went to sleep with her hand still nestled between her thighs.

The next morning the two sisters stood side by side regarding themselves in Addie's full-length bedroom mirror.

'We still look the same,' said Christie. 'Neither of us has put on weight. I bet even Mum and Dad wouldn't be able to tell us apart now that you've grown your hair long again.'

Addie laughed. 'I expect they would,' she said, 'but I reckon we could fool most people.'

Christie looked across at her sister's reflection, trapping her eyes in the mirror. 'I bet Robert wouldn't be able to tell the difference,' she said. 'Or my people at the porn agency, either.'

Addie couldn't take her eyes away from the intensity of her sister's glance, the clarity of her meaning. 'You really are wicked,' she whispered.

'Oh no,' replied Christie, 'you're the wicked one.'

When Robert arrived back from his business trip he was slightly surprised but not disappointed to find the lights out, curtains drawn and Addie waiting for him in bed. Her sister was nowhere to be seen.

'I'm sorry,' she whispered breathlessly as he caught her in his arms to say hello, 'she just couldn't stay. It's a shame because she did want to meet you.'

'Oh well,' said Robert, tracing a line down the side of her face with his finger, 'who cares about your sister when I've got you? Now, I hope you've been keeping that bed warm. She nodded, gazing up at him, the lust building in her eyes.

Robert stood up and reached over to turn on the bedside light as he pulled off his clothes. She quickly grabbed his arm.

'No, Robert, let's have the lights off.'

He raised an eyebrow. 'That's not like you, Addie.'

But he complied, switching the light back off so that they were in semidarkness. He lay down on the bed, letting her kneel over him to take his penis in her mouth.

'See how I've missed you, Addie,' he said, tangling his hand in her hair, then letting it drop to caress the side of her neck, the lobes of her ears, pulling at her earrings. With his other hand he reached up to caress the smooth skin of her inner thigh. For once he didn't hold back as she took him deep into her throat. He came immediately, delighting at the whiteness of his spunk as it slipped out of her opened lips to decorate her chin, her neck, the ends of her hair.

Then he rolled her on to her back, pinning both arms above her head by the wrists.

'Did you get my emails, Addie?' he asked softly.

She wriggled uncomfortably and shook her head. 'Emails? What emails?'

'The ones I sent you. The ones I always send you, my love.'

Again she shook her head and he watched as she bit her lip. 'I guess I forgot to check,' she murmured.

'And when did you get your ears pierced?' Robert continued, flicking at the golden hoops that hung from both ears. 'I thought you were dead against it.'

He felt the heat from her body, sensed she was blushing even if he couldn't see it.

'Honey,' she stuttered, 'I guess I changed my mind.'

Robert nodded solemnly, transferring her wrists into his left hand and using his other hand to push her legs fully apart. Then, with a sudden movement, he reached over to turn on the bedside lamp.

'Well, *honey*,' he drawled, deliberately adopting a thick American accent to emphasise the sarcasm behind his words, 'forgetting to check your emails I *guess* I can take. Having a sudden reversal as to your beliefs about body piercing – well, maybe. But removing that birthmark from the inside of your thigh? Really, do you take me for a fool?'

# It's Good to Stalk
## Joanna Davies

The four-poster bed shook wildly as the couple made love with unashamed abandon on the white muslin sheets. He was dark, curly-haired, with a trademark sensuous mouth, Malteser eyes and brown, muscled torso. She was blonde, curvaceous, spoiled and a very lucky bitch. They were about to orgasm when – flash! The picture disappeared as a very pissed-off Paul stood in front of the TV set.

'Paul! Switch it back on! We're coming to my favourite part, when he shoots her after orgasm!' Cassie looked at Paul with annoyance in her green eyes.

'For God's sake. Cassie. You've seen the bloody film five million times already. It's Gawain bloody Hughes this, Gawain bloody Hughes that. And what sort of name is "Gawain" anyway?' Paul ran his fingers through his hair and looked at her in despair.

'Actually,' Cassie explained coolly, 'It's an Arthurian knight's name. He's Welsh, you know.'

'I know! Now, are we going to go out to the pub or what?'

Paul didn't wait to hear her reply. Grabbing his denim jacket and cigarettes, he was obviously champing at the bit to get down to some serious drinking. Cassie agreed to keep the peace. After all, the video would be there for her to watch when Paul had gone to bed that night.

She didn't remember how her fascination with the

film and TV star Gawain Hughes had started. Still only twenty-eight, he'd appeared in a popular TV series as a swashbuckling eighteenth-century naval hero and had captured the hearts of girls everywhere, including Cassie's. That was soon followed by other high-profile TV work before a role in a Brit gangster flick had catapulted him to worldwide fame. She didn't know what it was about him. Sure, he was a pretty boy, but there were plenty of them around. But it was it that X factor – that thing that had made Paul Newman so irresistible, Steve McQueen so damn cool and James Dean so unobtainable.

Cassie loved poring over her cuttings and pictures of Gawain: Gawain at home with his mother and father; Gawain at the BAFTAs; Gawain celebrating St David's Day; Gawain with his, thankfully, now *ex*-girlfriend.

As Paul snored gently beside her that evening, Cassie closed her eyes and dreamed of a four-poster bed with Gawain and herself making it sing. Cassie was thirty-two. Not a stunner, but certainly not a minger. Short, blonde and very intense, she took a lot of getting used to. A TV magazine journalist, she loved the entertainment world, worshipped at the altar of *Heat*, *OK* and *Hello!*, and had to be the first with the media news.

On her way to work on the bus that day she had thought about Paul. Could she really be arsed to keep seeing him, particularly as he seemed to be getting in the way of her and Gawain?

And there was Gawain – in the Virgin Megastore window, dressed in jodhpurs and period frilly shirt, possessively clutching a young, big-bosomed milkmaid. It was the release of his movie *Cornfield of Desire* on DVD. Cassie closed her eyes and she was instantly there – in an open cornfield fighting off the unwelcome attentions of Hubert De Clare (weren't all nineteenth-century blackguards called De Clare?), until, suddenly, he appeared, hell-bent on her rescue.

'De Clare! You filthy swine! Take your hands off her instantly.' After a hard battle that involved near misses with scythes and other farmyard implements of yesteryear, De Clare was vanquished by brave Gawain.

'Cassandra,' Gawain breathed in her ear, 'did he – did he harm you?'

'No, darling.' And just as they were about to kiss a baby's yell broke her fantasy as the bus jolted to a halt. Damn! It was her stop.

Twenty minutes later Cassie was sitting at her desk in the offices of *Now In Wales* with an industrial-strength coffee at her side. She logged on on to her favourite website, Astronet, to check her daily forecast. Astronet was the best website ever, where romantic compatability charts were concerned. She and Gawain as a Gemini and Libra were perfectly suited astrologically. Ah, yes, here she was: 'Psychic Sue, what today holds for you'.

Suddenly her reverie was broken by Fat Fiona, who spitefully threw a note on to her desk. With the swift movements of the guilty, Cassie got rid of Astronet and opened a work file. Fiona beamed at her cattily. 'Note from the boss, Jones. What have you cocked up now?' Cassie ignored her and the note until Fiona got the hint and waddled back to her desk. Then Cassie opened it to read, 'My Office. 11.30 a.m. Ellis.' Shit!

At 11.29 a.m. Cassie huffed her way to Mr Ellis's office. He was a strange fish – looked like a cross between Homer from *The Simpsons* and JD Hogg from *The Dukes of Hazzard*, and had a Tubbs lookalike secretary who did everything for him, bar what she'd really like to do *to* him.

'Ah, yes ... erm ... Cassie, come in and sit down.'
Cassie obeyed him, wondering again about the magnifi-
cence of his ugliness. 'I have an interesting job for you,
my dear.' Cassie didn't hold her breath. Ellis's definition
of 'interesting job' usually involved VHS copies of the
latest DIY borefest for her to review. 'Gawain Hughes ...
I'd like you to interview him. Usually I'd ask Lois, but
she's away so I thought you could do it.' Cassie, for once
ignoring the implication that Lois was her superior,
almost fell off her chair with excitement. 'G-G-G...'

'Yes, you know, that new Taff who's flavour of the
month for some reason. You've heard of him?'

Oh, the ignorance of the man! 'Yes, absolutely.'

'Well, he's coming to town to promote his latest TV
movie.' Some shuffling of papers as Ellis looked for the
title. 'Ah, yes, *Magic Box*. Apparently, more risqué than
his usual offerings. He's doing a press conference at the
Hilton on Wednesday and will be available for a five-
minute interview with you. So don't fuck it up!'

Cassie looked at his noble visage with a determined
passion in her eyes and marvelled how she could have
thought of him as ugly. 'You can count on me.'

She danced out of the office like a Moulin Rouge minx
on acid and smiled beatifically at his PA, Annette. Astronet had been right. Her planetary conjunctions were on
a par with Gawain's. It was fate! It was destiny!

On her way back to her desk, still not quite believing
what had just happened, she ran into Fiona, who'd been
lying in wait, fangs exposed. 'So, what did you do wrong
now, then? Or was he really impressed with your article
on Merthyr Tydfil's carnival?'

Without skipping a beat, Cassie responded, 'Actually,
it will be you as a *junior* reporter who'll be covering
events like that from now on. I've actually been given a
very important assignment. Going to London to inter-

view *Gawain Hughes*. Ellis said that he needed somebody who could mix with celebs and I was the best person for the job.'

'Bollocks!' said Dennis, Fiona's greasy-haired minger of a sidekick. 'He only wants you 'cause Lois Lane's away.' (Lois Evans, a.k.a. 'Lois Lane', was Ellis's right-hand woman, and had the brain of Germaine Greer and the beauty of Cameron Diaz. She was the usual whipping boy among the envious *Now in Wales* hacks.) Fiona joined in. 'Yes, we all know that she's the star reporter. Anyway, I've heard that Gawain Hughes is gay. Haven't you, Dennis?'

Dennis, being gay himself, was a self-appointed authority on who was and who wasn't, and joined in with gusto. 'Oh, yes, definitely a member of the Lavender Hill Mob. You can forget him being boyfriend material for you, Cassie.'

'Yes', added Fiona. 'Different league, different team.'

'No *Pretty Woman* scenarios here,' Dennis chortled.

'Well. there might be a chance if you looked like Julia Roberts.' cackled Fiona.

'At least I don't look like *Alf* Roberts!' Cassie snapped.

As she returned to her desk, Cassie consoled herself with the fact that those two saddos were jealous. It was fate that meant Lois bloody brainbox Lane was covering the Celtic Film Festival in Brittany. This was Cassie's opportunity, her big chance to shine journalistically and grab the man of her dreams. But as she passed the office mirror she came face to face with a catastrophe – her own image. She would have to have a complete makeover.

The next two days resembled a high-level military exercise. Never in the field of human endeavour had such effort been put into glamorising a girl's physical appearance. Cassie got stripey blonde streaks, blew £200 on an aquamarine trouser suit and £100 on a pair of black fuck-me shoes from Faith. A new briefcase, dictaphone and upgraded Samsung mobile completed the executive look as she surveyed herself in the mirror on D-Day.

'Ah, yes, Cassie, nice to meet you.' An excessively pretty blonde and bouncy PR girl, Keli Kirby, greeted her with a handshake that wouldn't have been out of place on *The Rock*. 'Gawain is in here.' And, with that, Cassie was ushered into the executive suite of the Hilton Hotel where *he* stood waiting to greet her.

*Oh my fucking good God!* He was even better in the flesh. He was dressed in a black gangster-esque pinstripe suit, purple shirt and matching tie, and she could see that the curls at the back of his neck were still slightly damp from the shower. And the side of his neck – that brown, 'eat me' neck – was even more gorgeous than on the screen. Shit! He was looking at her in a puzzled way and she realised he was holding out a tanned, large hand. Fuck! Get a grip! Snap out of it! And act professional.

She would remember the next five minutes for the rest of her life. The questions rolled out of her with ease. She was charming, witty, she was a female Groucho Marx but sexier! She could see that Gawain appreciated her easy wit; he was very candid with his replies to her questions and obviously impressed by her knowledge of his work. There was only one moment of awkwardness when she asked him about his love life. 'Nobody special at the moment. I'm too busy with work to commit to anybody seriously.'

'But what if "the one" came along?'

'Well, that would be different, wouldn't it?' He smiled

at her with his dark eyes penetrating her very core. Gawain and Cassie, they would be like Olivier and Leigh, Bogart and Bacall, Tracy and Hep –

'Thank you, Cassie. Did you get what you wanted?'

For a moment her dictaphone transformed itself into a machine gun as she blasted a hole through kookie Keli's Colgate smile.

'Just about.' Cassie smiled at Gawain, who returned her smile with, if she wasn't mistaken, a hidden suggestion. Damn! If that bitch hadn't come in he might have asked me for her number, she thought. Balls! She'd do it anyway.

'Erm ... here's my card, anyway.' She handed it to Gawain, who smiled warmly at her before she left the room. (It was lucky that she didn't hear his next comment to Keli as he fondled her breasts possessively. 'What a weirdo!' They giggled and kissed passionately.)

Hi, Cassie, it's me, Paul, your boyfriend, if you remember who I am. I don't know if you're busy tonight – ironing your Gawain clippings. If you're not, give me a call.'

Well, he could sod off for a start. Paul was nice enough in a boring, solid kind of way but how could a mere stockbroker compete with what she now had? That night she couldn't think of anyone but Gawain. But how could she see him again? She would *have* to see him again. She couldn't have mistaken the vibe between them: it was pure electricity, she was sure of it. The next few weeks at work were pure tedium. Her article was received grudgingly by Ellis, who did acknowledge that it was a very 'intimate' piece. It was a double spread, the first she'd ever had in the mag, and featured a half-naked Gawain with a strapline she was proud of: 'The Magic in your Box is Welsh rarebit Gawain Hughes'. Not until Fat

Fiona sniggered at her unintended double entendre did she realise that Gawain might think her an extremely dirty bitch!

Ah, well. He would, hopefully, view her as 'sexually liberated' and confident enough to take on the threats of numerous starlets and harlots. She would adjust his dickie bow and straighten his tuxedo while dressed in a Liz Hurley frock, and together they would wow the paparazzi. Actually, she'd have a sneaky peek at his fan site again, just in case there were any new entries.

Being so engrossed, Cassie hadn't noticed that Fiona and Dennis had been watching her like two excited weasels eyeing a baby bird. 'Den, honey bunch?' Den, looking up, faking nonchalance responded, 'Yes, sweetkins?'

'Did you see that article in the *Guardian* yesterday? About stalkers?'

'Stalkers? No, what did it say?'

'Well, a special police contingent held a conference about it in London yesterday. Fastest-growing crime in Britain, according to some quarters. Especially the stalking of celebs.'

'Well, I know. You wouldn't want to be too famous these days,' Dennis added.

'Exactly,' said Fiona taking a peek at Cassie, who was by now half listening to the conversation.

'Yes,' said Dennis, 'and you have to be extra vigilant if you're a blonde celeb. Stalkers do tend to go for blondes, curiously.'

'What is it about these saddos, Dennis? The report said they were usually isolated individuals, lonely, in their thirties, desperate for attention.' Fiona carried on ruthlessly, her mouth moving in exaggerated movements, like Les Dawson. 'Compulsive obsessive.'

Dennis, moving in for the kill, addressed Cassie outright. 'What do you think, Cassie? You're quite obsessed with that Gawain Hughes, aren't you?'

Cassie, bridling, responded angrily. 'If you want to know, cretins, Gawain and I got on famously, and he said he'd love to have a drink with me next time he's in town. He insisted on getting my business card and everything so he could have my mobile number.'

Dennis puffed with laughter. 'So he could screen his calls, love!'

'Well,' said Fiona, 'if that's the case, then you should know that he's filming a new version of *How Green Was My Valley* in Dinas Powys next week.' She tossed a copy of the *Western Mail* on to Cassie's desk.

'Yeah, and before you blag that gig, I've already okayed it with Ellis and I'm doing a set visit and spending a whole day with Gawain.' Fiona looked as if she'd discovered a vat full of chocolate sauce. 'Funny that Gawain didn't mention this to you, and you both such pals!'

In Cassie's head, Fiona now lay spread-eagled on a butcher's slab, naked, fat, begging for mercy. 'The chops first,' Cassie's murderous alter ego commanded the jolly apple-checked butcher as his sharp cleaver descended . . .

Fiona smirked at Cassie and chomped happily on her third Mars bar. No way would Flubber get her job. Suddenly, Cassie had an idea . . .

The next day Dennis was desolate as he told everybody that Fiona was in hospital, suffering from acute food poisoning and would be out of work for a few weeks. Cassie hot-footed it to Ellis's office and asked to do the Gawain Hughes interview. He looked up with uninterest and told her that Lois was back in town earlier than expected and she would do the interview with Gawain herself as their chief reporter. Ugly bastard! Just because he wanted to sleep with his star reporter. If Lois fucking Lane looked like the back of a bus, she'd be schlepping it down to Pontypridd writing shit about non-events in the Valleys like the rest of them.

Cassie stomped her way out of the office. Lois . . . Fiona had been easy, but Lois – how could she get rid of her? Another case of food poisoning would be too risky. Then she remembered that Lois drove everywhere on her Vespa as part of her Audrey Hepburn image. These scooters were notoriously unsafe, particularly on oily surfaces . . .

It was with regret that the next day Ellis announced that Lois had suffered an accident on her scooter the previous evening and was hospitalised with a broken leg and shoulder.

'You will have to do her assignments, Cassie.' He nodded abruptly at her before returning to his office, followed by a fawning Annette.

What a day it had been! Better than she'd ever imagined. She'd read up on *How Green Was My Valley* and knew the author's shoe size by the end of her research. She could tell that Gawain was not only intrigued by her quirky good looks but also by her intensive knowledge. She shadowed him for the day, admiring his broad back in the Welsh tweed waistcoat and tight breeches. The only buzzing bluebottle in the soup was Keli, the annoying PR woman who also insisted on being Gawain's shadow for the day. Everywhere Cassie went, Keli stayed by her side like a leggy limpet. She was hoping to give her the slip during lunch and have a close tête-à-tête with Gawain, but Keli insisted that she and Gawain were having a private meeting in his trailer and Cassie was demoted to lunching with the camera crew.

But after the final take of the day, Cassie finally had an opportunity to speak to Gawain privately. She had picked up signals that he was keen to do so too and, as they stood together in the middle of a field in Dinas Powys, surrounded by crew, props and various locals dressed as Welsh women and coalminers, she felt an immediate connection with him. He kissed her lightly on the cheek, leaving a sooty stain. He brushed it off and Cassie just looked at him adoringly.

'I hope you got what you wanted, Cassie. I look forward to seeing the article.'

'Y-yes ... thank you, Gawain.'

'Hope it wasn't too boring for you.'

'Not at all.' Oh, he was modest too – the gods had indeed been lavish with this wondrous creature.

That evening Cassie waited for six hours in her little Nissan Micra for Gawain to leave the charity do, hopefully unattended. Finally, there he was, ushered to his moonlight blue Audi TT by a valet. Cassie couldn't believe it! She could finally get to see his pad! Tentatively, she followed him. Obeying the rules learned from *Magnum P.I.*, *The Professionals* and the ever-dependable *Starsky and Hutch*, she made sure she left a car or two between them at all times. Finally, he stopped outside a town house in trendy Cardiff Bay. It was a basement flat with a side entrance and a back garden. Perfect! It would be easy access.

Cassie waited for him to slip into something more comfortable before making her move. It wouldn't be long now. Tentatively she tiptoed around to the back garden and spotted an open window. It was a sign! He'd left it open for her on purpose! She clambered through as silent as the Milk Tray man and looked at her surroundings with pleasure. It was minimalist and tasteful, just what she would have expected. A quick nose in the bathroom cabinet revealed his exquisite taste in cologne – she had a quick sniff of aftershave before venturing to the bedroom. But horrors! What was that noise? That awful, mind-numbing, earth-shattering, animalistic grunting, shouting, moaning! It couldn't be! No, he would only be masturbating ... But no ...

As if sleepwalking, she and approached the bedroom. Gawain was on top. Underneath him, moaning with pleasure, was the most beautiful blond youth that Cassie had ever seen. Not more than twenty years old, he had the face of an angel, and the dark features of Gawain were a perfect complement to his fairness. Cassie had never understood why some women found the idea of two men making love so erotic – until now. As she watched Gawain thrusting triumphantly and heard the soft moans of the young man, she felt a rush of arousal that was stronger than anything she'd experienced before. Tentatively, she caressed her nipples until they grew harder to her touch, and then her hand moved lower (thank God she'd worn her best underwear!) as she masturbated slowly and then with more urgency.

Without realising, a moan escaped from her lips. Suddenly, she realised that the lovemaking had stopped and that both men were looking at her in surprise. Gawain's eyes narrowed as he looked at her before a flash of recognition came to his face.

'I'm sorry ... I ... I only wanted to see you.' She turned to leave, mortified that he'd caught her in such a compromising position. Gawain looked at her before saying gently, 'Why go anywhere, Cassie? Come here.' Slowly, like a shy kitten, Cassie moved towards the bed. Now that her fantasy was coming true, she didn't know what to do with herself. Shivering from head to toe, she was experiencing the most intense arousal of her life. The blond boy smiled at her sweetly before holding out his hand and pulling her on to the bed. What followed was the most memorable experience she had ever had. While Gawain kissed her gently all over, the blond boy gave her expert cunnilingus.

Holding her thighs open, she could feel them quiver like butterfly wings as his tongue probed deep inside her. Gawain carried on kissing her more intensely, fondling her breasts as he did so before she started to suck his cock, first with awe and then with passion. It was better than she'd dreamed of, and so good that in her head she was pleading for them never to stop. Slowly, she reached a plateau of intense pleasure and she realised that tears were running down her face as her world exploded in a hot, blood-red orgasm.

But, just as she reached heaven, Gawain abruptly pulled himself off her and gave a yell of fury. In a daze, Cassie looked up and saw two strange figures in the bedroom. One of them held a camera that flashed relentlessly at the sweaty threesome in the bed.

The next few months were horrific. Cassie was notorious. She couldn't leave her flat without the paparazzi attempting to snap her and the headlines were relentless.

GAWAIN HUGHES, EXPERT SWORDSMAN,
CAUGHT IN THE ACT
THREE'S NOT A CROWD FOR SEX-MAD GAWAIN
CASSIE'S MAGIC BOX

However, the tabloids paid well and Cassie decided to sell her story. After all, she might as well set the record straight. And so began a string of money-spinning ventures: a weekly slot on *Morning Coffee* and a sexpert column in the *Daily News*. And Gawain? She never saw him again. Following the scandal, his fan base changed gender somewhat, but as for the blond angel, whose name she discovered was James, she found out that they had a lot in common. To begin with, they found refuge together against the onslaught of the press, compared notes and got drunk as they relived that unreal night. But, slowly and surely, Cassie began to rely on his company, his advice and most of all the warmth of his muscular body next to hers.

And gradually Gawain Hughes disappeared from her thoughts as she realised that reality was better than any fantasy.

# LOOK OUT FOR THE ALL-NEW BLACK LACE BOOKS – AVAILABLE NOW!

*All books priced £6.99 in the UK. Please note publication dates apply to the UK only. For other territories, please contact your retailer.*

## BEDDING THE BURGLAR
### *Gabrielle Marcola*
ISBN 0 352 33911 X

Maggie Quinton is a savvy, sexy architect involved in a building project on a remote island off the Florida panhandle. One day, a gorgeous hunk breaks into the house she's staying in and ties her up. The buff burglar is in search of an item he claims the apartment's owner stole from him. And he keeps coming back. Flustered and aroused, Maggie calls her jet-setting sister in for moral support, but flirty, dark-haired Diane is much more interested in the island's ruggedly handsome police chief, 'Griff' Grifford. And then there's his deputy, Cosgrove, with his bulging biceps and creative uses for handcuffs. There must be something in the water that makes this island's men so good-looking and its women so anxious to get their hooks into them – and Maggie is determined to find out what it is by doing as much research as possible!

**MIXED DOUBLES**
*Zoe le Verdier*
ISBN 0 352 33312 X

When Natalie Crawford is offered the job as manager of a tennis club in a wealthy English suburb, she jumps at the chance. There's an extra perk, too: Paul, the club's coach, is handsome and charming, and she wastes no time in making him her lover. Then she hires Chris, a coach from a rival club, whose confidence and sexual prowess swiftly puts Paul in the shade. When Chris embroils Natalie into kinky sex games, will she be able to keep control of her business aims, or will her lust for the arrogant sportsman get out of control?

## Published in November 2004

**WILD BY NATURE**
*Monica Belle*
ISBN 0 352 33915 2

Talented chef Juliet Eden imagines she has the perfect marraige to Toby – a titled aristocrat – and no need to stray from her vows of fidelity. Yet when temptation comes in the form of rough sex with the barely civilised gamekeeper, Ian Marsh, she finds it surprisingly easy to give in. Naughty Juliet persuades her husband to accept an invitation to a boating holiday, only to discover that the hosts are also offering the lure of saucy delights. Neither Juliet nor Toby is able to resist. But once on board, there's a clash of sexual personalities. There's a foxy minx called Annabelle in the crew and she's got her eye on Toby. However, eveyrone is determined to get to grips with the notorious rogue who calls himself the spanking Major. **Full steam ahead for an orgasm-packed excursion!**

**UP TO NO GOOD**
*Karen S. Smith*
ISBN 0 352 33589 0

When Emma attends her sister's wedding she expects the usual polite conversation and bad dancing. Instead, it is the scene of a horny encounter that encourages her to behave more scandalously than usual. It is lust at first sight for motorbike fanatic, Kit, and the pair waste no time getting off with each other behind the marquee. When they get separated without the chance to say goodbye, Emma despairs that she will never see her lover again. But a chance encounter at another wedding reunites Kit and Emma – and so begins a year of outrageous sex, wild behaviour and lots of getting up to no good. *Like Four Weddings and a Funeral* – but with more sex and without the funeral.

## Also available

**THE BLACK LACE SEXY QUIZ BOOK**
*Maddie Saxon*
ISBN O 352 33884 9
£6.99

- What sexual personality type are you?
- Have you ever faked it because that was easier than explaining what you wanted?
- What kind of fantasy figures turn you on – and does your partner know?
- What sexual signals are you giving out right now?

Today's image-conscious dating scene is a tough call. Our sexual expectations are cranked up to the max, and the sexes seem to have become highly critical of each other in terms of appearance and performance in the bedroom. But even though guys have ditched their nasty Y-fronts and girls are more babe-licious than ever, a huge number of us are still being let down sexually. Sex therapist Maddie Saxon thinks this is because we are finding it harder to relax and let our true sexual selves shine through.

*The Black Lace Sexy Quiz Book* will help you negotiate the minefield of modern relationships. Through a series of fun, revealing quizzes, you will be able to rate your sexual needs honestly and get what you really want from your partner. The quizzes will get you thinking about and discussing your desires in ways you haven't previously considered. Unlock the mysteries of your sexual psyche in this fun, revealing quiz book designed with today's sex-savvy girl in mind.

# Black Lace Booklist

Information is correct at time of printing. To avoid disappointment check availability before ordering. Go to www.blacklace-books.co.uk. All books are priced £6.99 unless another price is given.

## BLACK LACE BOOKS WITH A CONTEMPORARY SETTING

| | | |
|---|---|---|
| ☐ SHAMELESS Stella Black | ISBN 0 352 33485 1 | £5.99 |
| ☐ INTENSE BLUE Lyn Wood | ISBN 0 352 33496 7 | £5.99 |
| ☐ A SPORTING CHANCE Susie Raymond | ISBN 0 352 33501 7 | £5.99 |
| ☐ TAKING LIBERTIES Susie Raymond | ISBN 0 352 33357 X | £5.99 |
| ☐ A SCANDALOUS AFFAIR Holly Graham | ISBN 0 352 33523 8 | £5.99 |
| ☐ THE NAKED FLAME Crystalle Valentino | ISBN 0 352 33528 9 | £5.99 |
| ☐ ON THE EDGE Laura Hamilton | ISBN 0 352 33534 3 | £5.99 |
| ☐ LURED BY LUST Tania Picarda | ISBN 0 352 33533 5 | £5.99 |
| ☐ THE HOTTEST PLACE Tabitha Flyte | ISBN 0 352 33536 X | £5.99 |
| ☐ THE NINETY DAYS OF GENEVIEVE Lucinda Carrington | ISBN 0 352 33070 8 | £5.99 |
| ☐ DREAMING SPIRES Juliet Hastings | ISBN 0 352 33584 X | |
| ☐ THE TRANSFORMATION Natasha Rostova | ISBN 0 352 33311 1 | |
| ☐ SIN.NET Helena Ravenscroft | ISBN 0 352 33598 X | |
| ☐ TWO WEEKS IN TANGIER Annabel Lee | ISBN 0 352 33599 8 | |
| ☐ HIGHLAND FLING Jane Justine | ISBN 0 352 33616 1 | |
| ☐ PLAYING HARD Tina Troy | ISBN 0 352 33617 X | |
| ☐ SYMPHONY X Jasmine Stone | ISBN 0 352 33629 3 | |
| ☐ SUMMER FEVER Anna Ricci | ISBN 0 352 33625 0 | |
| ☐ CONTINUUM Portia Da Costa | ISBN 0 352 33120 8 | |
| ☐ OPENING ACTS Suki Cunningham | ISBN 0 352 33630 7 | |
| ☐ FULL STEAM AHEAD Tabitha Flyte | ISBN 0 352 33637 4 | |
| ☐ A SECRET PLACE Ella Broussard | ISBN 0 352 33307 3 | |
| ☐ GAME FOR ANYTHING Lyn Wood | ISBN 0 352 33639 0 | |
| ☐ CHEAP TRICK Astrid Fox | ISBN 0 352 33640 4 | |
| ☐ THE GIFT OF SHAME Sara Hope-Walker | ISBN 0 352 29935 1 | |
| ☐ COMING UP ROSES Crystalle Valentino | ISBN 0 352 33658 7 | |
| ☐ GOING TOO FAR Laura Hamilton | ISBN 0 352 33657 9 | |

| ☐ HOP GOSSIP Savannah Smythe | ISBN O 352 33880 6 |
| ☐ GOING DEEP Kimberly Dean | ISBN O 352 33876 8 |
| ☐ PACKING HEAT Karina Moore | ISBN O 352 33356 1 |
| ☐ SWITCHING HANDS Alaine Hood | ISBN O 352 33896 2 |
| ☐ CLUB CRÈME Primula Bond | ISBN O 352 33907 1 |
| ☐ BEDDING THE BURGLAR Gabrielle Marcole | ISBN O 352 33911 X |

## BLACK LACE BOOKS WITH AN HISTORICAL SETTING

| ☐ PRIMAL SKIN Leona Benkt Rhys | ISBN O 352 33500 9 £5.99 |
| ☐ DEVIL'S FIRE Melissa MacNeal | ISBN O 352 33527 O £5.99 |
| ☐ DARKER THAN LOVE Kristina Lloyd | ISBN O 352 33279 4 |
| ☐ THE CAPTIVATION Natasha Rostova | ISBN O 352 33234 4 |
| ☐ MINX Megan Blythe | ISBN O 352 33638 2 |
| ☐ DEMON'S DARE Melissa MacNeal | ISBN O 352 33683 8 |
| ☐ DIVINE TORMENT Janine Ashbless | ISBN O 352 33719 2 |
| ☐ SATAN'S ANGEL Melissa MacNeal | ISBN O 352 33726 5 |
| ☐ THE INTIMATE EYE Georgia Angelis | ISBN O 352 33004 X |
| ☐ OPAL DARKNESS Cleo Cordell | ISBN O 352 33033 3 |
| ☐ SILKEN CHAINS Jodi Nicol | ISBN O 352 33143 7 |
| ☐ ACE OF HEARTS Lisette Allen | ISBN O 352 33059 7 |
| ☐ THE LION LOVER Mercedes Kelly | ISBN O 352 33162 3 |
| ☐ THE AMULET Lisette Allen | ISBN O 352 33019 8 |
| ☐ WHITE ROSE ENSNARED Juliet Hastings | ISBN O 352 33052 X |
| ☐ UNHALLOWED RITES Martine Marquand | ISBN O 352 33222 O |
| ☐ LA BASQUAISE Angel Strand | ISBN O 352 32988 2 |
| ☐ THE HAND OF AMUN Juliet Hastings | ISBN O 352 33144 5 |
| ☐ THE SENSES BEJEWELLED Cleo Cordell | ISBN O 352 32904 1 |

## BLACK LACE ANTHOLOGIES

| ☐ WICKED WORDS Various | ISBN O 352 33363 4 |
| ☐ MORE WICKED WORDS Various | ISBN O 352 33487 8 |
| ☐ WICKED WORDS 3 Various | ISBN O 352 33522 X |
| ☐ WICKED WORDS 4 Various | ISBN O 352 33603 X |
| ☐ WICKED WORDS 5 Various | ISBN O 352 33642 O |
| ☐ WICKED WORDS 6 Various | ISBN O 352 33690 O |
| ☐ WICKED WORDS 9 Various | ISBN O 352 33860 1 |

To find out the latest information about Black Lace titles, check out the website: www.blacklace-books.co.uk or send for a booklist with complete synopses by writing to:

> Black Lace Booklist, Virgin Books Ltd
> Thames Wharf Studios
> Rainville Road
> London W6 9HA

Please include an SAE of decent size. Please note only British stamps are valid.


Our privacy policy
We will not disclose information you supply us to any other parties. We will not disclose any information which identifies you personally to any person without your express consent.

From time to time we may send out information about Black Lace books and special offers. Please tick here if you do <u>not</u> wish to receive Black Lace information.      ☐

Please send me the books I have ticked above.

Name ...................................................................

Address ................................................................

..........................................................................

..........................................................................

..........................................................................

Post Code ............................................................

**Send to:** Virgin Books Cash Sales, Thames Wharf Studios, Rainville Road, London W6 9HA.

**US customers:** for prices and details of how to order books for delivery by mail, call 1-800-343-4499.

Please enclose a cheque or postal order, made payable to Virgin Books Ltd, to the value of the books you have ordered plus postage and packing costs as follows:

UK and BFPO – £1.00 for the first book, 50p for each subsequent book.

Overseas (including Republic of Ireland) – £2.00 for the first book, £1.00 for each subsequent book.

If you would prefer to pay by VISA, ACCESS/MASTERCARD, DINERS CLUB, AMEX or SWITCH, please write your card number and expiry date here:

..........................................................................

Signature ............................................................

Please allow up to 28 days for delivery.